The Generations of *Hope*

By

Frank G. Davis

Copyright © 2021
Frank G. Davis

ISBN # 978-1-954253-97-1
VVP-Authors Wild Imprint
10 9 8 7 6 5 4 3 2 1

Editing, Cover, & Layout by: solfire@phoenix-farm.com

Dedications

The dedication for this book is divided into four groups of close friends. Each group is precious to me in very different ways. I have used their real names for the characters they represent with their permission. I have tried to model their characters with some of their personal traits I find endearing. They are listed in the order they appear in this novel.

Gary and Malinda Dagan - Commodore Gary Dagan, was the first commander of the generation starship *Hope* and his wife, Malinda Dagan, *Hope's* first executive officer (XO). I met Gary in 1965 at Arizona State University where we both began graduate programs in mechanical engineering. We were both registered in several of the same classes and became study partners. I was married at the time to my first wife and Gary was blissfully single. We became close friends during that year and both earned our Master of Science degrees and went to work for the same company as engineers. The company at that time was AiResearch Manufacturing Company of Arizona which is now part of Honeywell. They designed, developed and manufactured small gas turbine engines for military and commercial aircraft.

While at Arizona State University, we both joined the ASU karate club and transitioned to the Phoenix dojo after we started working. Shortly after beginning work, (when we could finally afford it) we both took flying lessons and earned our private pilot licenses. Gary was so enamored with flying, that after two and a half years working as an engineer and flying light planes, he wanted to fly jets, so he joined the Air Force, went through Officer Training School and pilot training and became a flight instructor and functional check pilot flying T-38s. While in the Air Force, he met Malinda, his future wife.

After leaving the Air Force he worked for a number of aerospace companies, Cessna in Wichita, Bell Aerospace in New Orleans, ending up at Boeing in Seattle. While he was in New Orleans, he joined the Air Force Reserve weather reconnaissance unit and flew C-130s as a hurricane hunter. He then joined Boeing, first as a ground instructor on the 747-200, ending as the manager overseeing their flight training program for the 747-400 introduction and later, the 777 introduction. He retired in 2007 after thirty years at Boeing and he and Malinda and their daughter Tiffany still live in the Seattle area. He no longer flies actively. His hobbies include restoring vintage Mustangs.

Gary has always been an inspiration to me. He got me the interview with AiResearch, where I worked for 36 years before retiring, he was my training partner during karate, he introduced me to Mike Archer, our first flight instructor who trained us for free. We only had to pay $10 an hour for the airplane rental. I ended up paying a total of $500.00 to get my private pilot's license. We flew in old Cessna 150s at Falcon Field in Mesa, Arizona. Gary is an energetic person, outgoing and fun to be around and exceptionally intelligent. I feel fortunate having him as my friend.

Björn and Britt-Marie Sjöblom - Captain Björn Sjöblom, was the third commander of *Hope*, and his wife Governor Britt-Marie Sjöblom, *Hope's* third governor. They were in charge of *Hope* when they reached Proxima-b, an Earth like planet orbiting Proxima Centauri, approximately 4 light-years from Earth. They were responsible for establishing the first interstellar human colony.

I met Björn and his wife in the late 1970s when he was working for Volvo's aircraft and spacecraft propulsion division. He and several other Volvo engineers spent one to two years living in the Phoenix area integrated into our engineering design and development teams, learning our processes. I was working in the Combustion Systems Group at the time and he was assigned to my group. He had a PhD in engineering and was very open to the interchange of ideas and procedures between us and Volvo.

He and his family moved close to me and my wife and we became very close friends. And that friendship continues to this day. Once they moved back to Sweden after his two-year tour, he would visit us when he returned to the U.S. for meetings. We took our family to Sweden and visited his family there. They are among the friendliest people I have ever known.

We are hoping to have another trip to Sweden this year if everything works out.

David and Kathi Davis and their son John - Captain David Davis, was the fourth commander of *Hope* when they left Proxima-b and began their journey back to Earth. Lt. Commander Kathi Davis, David's wife, was a senior shuttle pilot and squadron commander. Their son, John Davis, was the landscape specialist. First of all, I want to make one thing perfectly clear: we aren't related. We live in the same subdivision. Kathi is the president of our HOA and I'm the vice president However we aren't related.

When I began writing my science fiction novels, I happened to mention in passing that I was about to publish my first book. It was called "Future Histories." It consisted of three short stories and one novella. David said he would like to read it, so I gave him a complimentary signed copy. He in turn wrote my first review. It was a really good review and from then on, he has transitioned to becoming my beta reader, reviewing all of my books prior to them becoming published.

His efforts are truly appreciated. I believe his comments have improved the content of my books and made awkward sentences flow much better. Thanks for all your suggestions David.

Alicia Davis - This one is related. She's my wife. She is also the one that proofreads my manuscripts and makes numerous suggestions on how to improve my grammar and punctuations. Without her initial help I would be embarrassed to send it to an editor. My only excuse is that "I are an engineer," not an English major. Not only does she assist me in the writing process she is also very encouraging; an inspiration for me to continue writing. She puts up with me being late to almost everything when the words are flowing. God bless her for so many things. As I write this, it's July 4, 2021. It also happens to be our 46th wedding anniversary.

"I just finished, dear. Let's go out for dinner. Happy Anniversary!"

Introduction

There was a buzz of conversations among the attendees at the Alliance of World Nations (AWN) conference, all waiting with great anticipation to hear the secretary general's comments. After a few more minutes of verbal speculations on what she would recommend, a series of soft chimes was heard signaling the delegates to take their seats. A few minutes after everyone was seated and all conversations had subsided, the introduction was made.

"Ladies and Gentlemen," said a deep resonating voice, "all rise for the Secretary General of the Alliance of World Nations."

As one, the delegates stood and remained standing as the secretary general strode confidently to the rostrum. She was dressed in a dark blue business suit with a white blouse and a string of pearls around her neck as her only adornment. Her mixed Polynesian ancestry was obvious. She was a beautiful woman and today she was all business.

"Please take your seats," she said in a clear voice. Once everyone was seated, she began her presentation.

"Everyone here is aware, acutely aware, of the tragic rise of natural disasters that have befallen our world during the last century. The increase in these tragic events has grown exponentially. Most would agree, it began with the Covid-19 pandemic which occurred at the beginning of the 21st Century. Now, as we approach the middle of the millennium, the number of near extinction events has grown beyond belief. Too many, it seems Mother Nature is rebelling against us. Others believe the All Mighty is punishing us for our abuse of His creation. Whatever the cause, it has resulted in the deaths of tens of millions of men, women, and in my opinion, the most tragic of all, our children. These tragic deaths aren't limited to specific countries or regions. The devastation is world-wide and growing in intensity. If this trend continues, our scientists project before the end of this millennium the human race will cease to exist. We have experienced a plethora of natural disasters, from earthquakes, to floods, to erupting volcanoes and tsunamis; to fires, diseases and plagues, tornadoes and hurricanes. The list is endless. The only positive thing that has come from these disasters is that we aren't killing ourselves in wars any longer. We're too busy attempting to survive. We need to discover a way to save the human race.

"I'm sure none of what I just said is news to anyone here. During the last two decades, limited attempts have been made to escape these natural disasters. The lunar colony and the colony on Mars are two examples of our initial attempts. These two colonies were originally established as scientific missions of exploration. Both were very successful in gathering vast amounts of data on their respective worlds. However, it turns out neither were good candidates as Earth substitutes. Neither body has an acceptable atmosphere and the technology required for producing breathable air in comfortable quantities on either world is non-existent. The alternative would be to create underground habitats. However there are other reasons neither would be acceptable. One that comes to mind is the difference in gravity. The gravity on our moon is only one-sixth that of Earth; on Mars it is one-third. Our scientists believe these differences in gravity will certainly cause mutations in human development within the very first generation.

"Our goal has always been to find an alternate place for mankind to not only survive but to flourish. The orbiting habitats were once considered to meet those requirements. The living spaces were provided with artificial Earth gravity by rotating the habitat at the necessary speed to generate a 1-G environment. However, the tragic demise of 10,000 people two years after the construction of the Sky One Habitat has led us to rethink this as a viable substitute. As I'm sure most of you know, Sky One was struck by orbiting debris and lost its atmosphere in less than a few minutes resulting in the loss of everyone aboard. Adding to that tragedy, the habitat was knocked out of its orbit and ended up killing even more people on the ground when it reentered.

"Until recently, there weren't many viable suggestions on how to protect the human race from extinction. Now new data has been discovered that looks promising, very promising. During the last several years, advances in technology have permitted us to evaluate planets orbiting other stars to determine if they could support human life with little or no terraforming required. I'm happy to announce we have discovered what appears to be exactly what we were looking for. It is the first planet discovered that is very similar to our Earth with a breathable atmosphere, similar in mass to Earth and has a similar period of rotation, a little over 22 hours. Temperatures on the planet's surface range from a little below freezing during the winter months and in the high eighties in the summer. The latter is in Fahrenheit, which is the high twenties in Celsius. In addition, the most recent discovery has determined there is surface water on the planet; water in abundance from springs, lakes and rivers.

"Perhaps the best news is this planet orbits the closest star to our own sun. It is part of the Alpha Centauri cluster. The star is Proxima Centauri and the planet is called Proxima-b. The distance from our sun is a little over four light years. Our scientists and engineers believe the technology needed to build vehicles to reach Proxima-b exists today. I have approved requests for proposals be sent to worldwide government agencies, national corporations and multinational corporations which have been determined to have the ability to design and construct these vehicles. They have four months to respond with their proposals.

"We approach this effort with guarded enthusiasm. More detailed examination of the planet is required and will be conducted while the vehicle proposals are being prepared. I believe this may be our best shot at ensuring the survival of the human race. Of course, we will continue in our attempts to prevent, or at least control, these pervasive natural disasters on Earth.

"That concludes my comments. Thank you all for your attendance. Questions and comments may be submitted to my office and all will be answered in due course."

Part 1
The Preliminaries

<u>The Proposals--Secretary General Samoa</u>

I was sitting in my office reviewing the com messages my clerical assistant deemed worthy of my attention. I had almost reached the end of the list when I heard my chief of staff let out with a whoop. He was sitting in the lounge area watching a rugby match and the Polynesian Islands Province just scored. It was the team from Tonga, the birthplace of my Chief of Staff and he had played on that team during his twenties for three seasons.

"Who's winning, Tongo?" I asked.

"We're up by a lot," he answered.

"Are you sorry you gave up the pitch?"

"Not at all. I would never have met you if I stayed in the game. Besides, I'm too old to play now. Fortunately for you, I still have the body of a twenty-year old." He got up from his chair and turned toward me …, with a huge grin on his face, whipped off his shirt and gave me a double front bicep pose.

I laughed at his antics yet he really did have a fantastic build. "Perhaps you should consider body building instead of government life. I mean, you were the youngest Secretary General of AWN. You've reached as high a level in government as you can go. It's all going to be down-hill from now on."

He had left the lime light of rugby and pursued a career in government. We met in college and were eventually married. His career sky rocketed to a seat in the Congress of the United Provinces of North America, representing the Polynesian Islands Province for one term. He was elected to the senate, served as the first Polynesian to become a cabinet member, chosen by the president to become our representative to the AWN. When the ruling Secretary General was killed in a tsunami three years later, he became the acting Secretary General, then elected to continue to serve the following term. Under normal circumstances, I'm sure he could have been elected for another term however his two years of filling in as the acting Secretary General counted as one term and the AWN bylaws didn't permit more than two consecutive terms.

During Tongo's rise to fame and fortune, well maybe not fortune, certainly fame, I followed along on his coattails. When he became a senator, I took his seat in congress. When he served as a cabinet member, I became a senator. When he was appointed to be member of the AWN, I became a mother. During those three years before the Secretary General died, I had two children, a boy and a girl. When Tongo was elected to be the Secretary General, he asked me to be his Chief of Staff.

I was shocked at his request. I was happy being a mom taking care of the children but he was insistent. He actually brought in a cabinet member friend and the current senator for the Polynesian Islands Province. They were both very familiar with my political accolades and recommended I consider Tongo's request. I was overwhelmed by what they said. I made up my mind and said to him, "If I can have my mother come live with us to help with the children, I will accept your ridiculous offer." He agreed and we became the first husband and wife team in the AWN.

When his term was up, he encouraged me to run for Secretary General. My first reaction was to scream, "Are you nuts?!! No way. Absolutely not. I'm not qualified. I was never a representative."

He countered with, "You are the most qualified person for the position. You know all the ins and outs of the job because you were right there with me. You even made presentations to the assembly when I had to be away for emergency business. You took over the job for a week when I was down with the flu. Best of all you are the most intelligent person I know."

I thought for about a minute then nodded my head. "On one condition," I said. "You have to be my Chief of Staff."

He let out a cheer, then got all serious. "Does this mean I have to sleep on the other side of the bed?"

The rest is history.

Back to the real world. The chime on my com unit went off. "Yes?" I said to my assistant.

"The proposals have arrived. We received ten technical and financial proposals, each one with a general summary. They are now on our server being decrypted. I will let you know when they are ready to be reviewed."

When the proposals had been decrypted, we joined the review team in the conference room adjacent to my office. For security reasons, each reviewer had their own data pad that was never to leave the room. Each reviewer had specific proposal areas to examine. For instance, one area was the EM Propulsion System. Three of the reviewers would independently review only the proposal section covering the propulsion system. They would do that for all ten proposals. Three others would evaluate the Power System, another three would review the Environmental System and so on.

Beside the technical sections of each proposal, our financial experts reviewed the itemize estimated costs to design, fabricate, test and assemble each part of the ship. A minimum cost share of 20% was expected.

Tongo and I, along with other reviewers, concentrated on the summary document. Both of us had double PhDs, Tongo in engineering and political science and me in human resources and management however we weren't experts. We wanted to see if the overall program made sense to us, was it believable? I have to say we did this more out of curiosity than anything else, we didn't have any vote. We just wanted to be informed.

We read all ten of the proposal summaries in a cursory manner and then decided which ones we liked the best. We didn't reveal our choices to each other until all the reviewers had finished up their assignments.

The programs were divided into three phases:

- Phase 1-Analysis and Preliminary Design
- Phase 2-Detail Design, Fabrication, and Prototype Testing
- Phase 3-Devopment Testing, Subsystem Assembly, Ship Assembly, Flight Testing and Launch

Each phase was progressively more expensive and time consuming. Six of the ten proposals were selected and funded for Phase 1. Each contractor team had six months to present their results. Phase 2 was scheduled for three years. There would be four teams selected for Phase 2. Phase 3 was tentatively scheduled to run for six years and a minimum of two teams would be selected. It was possible that all four of the Phase 2 teams could be awarded Phase 3 contracts.

Hope Team Phase 1–Chief of Staff Tongo

I traveled with the review team to observe the debriefing of *Hope's* Phase 1 activities. The debriefing was scheduled to take at least three days. It could possibly last as long as a week. I stayed for the first three days and then returned to address other AWN issues while the review team stayed for an additional two days, then departed to conduct briefings by the other starship teams.

I was introduced to the woman who was Program Manager for the Oak Ridge National Lab (ORNL) team, her name was Doctor Judy Van Der Geist. She was a tall woman, almost as tall as I am, with an athlete's physique. She had bright blue eyes and naturally blonde hair. I found out later she had attended university on a volleyball scholarship and had played for the Dutch team during a previous Olympics. She greeted me with a bone crushing grip, which I returned in kind as we exchanged smiles. After the introductions were over, we sat down at the large conference table as Dr. Bone Crusher went to the rostrum to begin the briefing.

"On behalf of the team from Oak Ridge National Labs I want to welcome you all to our Phase 1 briefing. We are very excited to show you our preliminary design for the generation starship *Hope* and to present our assumptions and the analyses that led to the design. I will give you a high-level view of our program to be followed by breakout groups who will go into more detail. Feel free to interrupt with any questions you may have."

A view screen that took up most of the wall behind her lit up with a picture of the starship that looked so real I would have sworn it was a real picture and not computer generated. Against the black of space, amply sprinkled with stars, you could see the white-hot ions from the EM Propulsion system streaming out from the exhaust. You could even hear the roar of the engines as the ship moved slowly across the view screen (even though there wouldn't be any sound in space, it was a nice touch) and you could also see the large, cylindrical habitat rotating slowly generating a 1-G artificial gravity for the passengers and crew. The view panned in to a close up shot of the starship's bow showing the ship's name in bright white cursive letters, *Hope*. *It was breathtaking!*

The starship slowly faded from sight as she continued. "Our starship design will take about a hundred years traveling to the Alpha Centauri cluster. We plan to cruise at a sustained speed of five percent of the speed of light. When *Hope* leaves orbit it will contain four thousand passengers, one thousand Navy crew and three thousand civilians. It is expected the overall number of passengers when the ship arrives at Proxima Centauri will be five thousand; two thousand five hundred will leave the ship to begin the Proxima-b colony. The remaining twenty-five hundred civilians and crew will return to Earth."

One of the review team raised a hand and asked, "Why limit yourselves to five percent c? Why not cruise at ten percent? I'm aware drones routinely cruise at fifty. Don't we have drones now traveling that fast to gather more data on the Proxima-b planet?"

She smiled then answered, "Yes, we do have ten drones flying at fifty percent c to gather more detailed data on our target planet. They were launched several years ago and should arrive at Proxima-b in another three years. They are autonomous drones, requiring no interaction with Earth to complete their mission. To date, we are aware of four that went off line so far. We hope at least three make it to the planet. We really need the data for our mission planning. Flying at high percent of c is very dangerous. Not much is known however it is believed by many experts as the percent of c increases so does the danger. We have a lot of data on five percent c that says it is much safer than even ten percent c. Our chances of surviving the trip to Proxima-b at five percent and returning is a realistic goal. Any other questions?"

Another hand went up. "Dr. Van Der Geist, will your EM propulsion system survive a two-hundred-year roundtrip?"

"Absolutely not," she answered emphatically, then smiled at the shocked expression on the man who asked the question. "We don't have any data which would allow us to project the maximum life of the engine. None of our engineers believe they will last that long. Let me tell you how we'll handle that concern. First of all, we're going to design the engines to cruise at ten percent c however they will operate at only half that level. Secondly, after *Hope* has accelerated to five percent, we'll be essentially ballistic. Due to the drag caused by space particles, the EM engines will be used to produce a small amount of thrust to maintain that cruise speed; not nearly as much as when we are accelerating. Thirdly, there will be at least two spare engine sets which can be changed out if they run into any problems. The crew will be trained for space walks to replace the engines as needed. Lastly, we are looking at the feasibility of using booster rockets to assist us in accelerating from orbit to our cruise speed. These boosters will be nuclear thermal rockets heating the working fluid, which is water, to superheated steam. The water would be stored in external tanks. They will be filled upon arrival at Proxima-b for accelerating for the return trip to Earth, then will be ejected when they are empty."

Another hand went up, and she gestured for the woman to ask her question. "Dr. Van Der Geist, why are you planning on using EM ion engines instead of MHD or plasma engines? The specific impulse of those engines would be over many times greater than what the EM engines can produce."

Dr. Van Der Geist paused for a few seconds considering her answer, then said, "An excellent question. I think a detailed discussion of our EM ion engine choice should be addressed in one of our breakout sessions, however, I can give you a high-level answer in the time we have here. For those of you who aren't rocket scientists or propulsion engineers, which includes myself, I will attempt to give you a few simple answers.

"First of all, a definition: specific impulse is a measure of how much thrust you get for every pound of exhaust you produce. Since we will have a limited amount of working fluid you would want the highest specific impulse you can safely generate, which would seem to favor the MHD or plasma engines. However, there is another law of spaceship mechanics which says you can't go faster than the velocity of your exhaust. Since *Hope* will be operating at five percent c, our exhaust velocity must be at least five percent. Are you with me so far?"

Several heads nodded so she moved on, "All ion engines work by ionizing the working fluid into electrons, protons and neutrons. Individual electrons have very small mass compared to protons and neutrons which have a mass almost two thousand times the mass of an electron. Once the ionization is accomplished, the EM engines use a magnetic field to accelerate the electrons to the desired speed, five percent. MHD ion engines work fine at much lower speeds. Their magnetic fields accelerate both the negatively charged electrons and positively charged protons to the desired velocity however they have never demonstrated operation above two percent c. To accelerate the protons to five percent c would require a power source of prohibitive size. Such a power source has never been built and our design mandate was to use only existing technologies. That's the first reason we chose our design.

"The second reason is, after several engine failures, some catastrophic failures, MHD powered crafts are limited to drone vehicles and must remain within our solar system. Those regulations aren't applied to all the AWN members. I am told *Blue Streak* is considering MHD engines. I have no information on what the Asian countries are planning to use on *Golden Dragon*."

The overview by Dr. Van Der Geist continued on for the rest of the morning. There was a short break before the breakout groups met. I was sitting at a table having a cup of coffee when Dr. Judy asked to join me. "Of course," I answered. "I was very impressed by your presentation. The way you responded to the questions made me think you were fibbing about not being a rocket scientist."

I thought I detected a hint of color in her cheeks. She said, "Maybe a little. I just wanted to put the people asking questions at ease. I have a question for *you*, Chief of Staff."

"Please," I responded. "Call me Tongo."

She smiled and said, "Then you call me Judy." She paused and I detected a brief hesitation before she said, "Tongo, I want to make you an unofficial offer."

I smiled back at her and said, "Sorry, Judy. I'm a happily married man."

She looked shocked. "No! Not that kind of offer." Her cheeks were blushed a deep red and she took a moment to compose herself.

I reached forward and took her hand and said in a low voice, "I'm sorry. I didn't mean to embarrass you. I'm kind of a smart ass."

She didn't pull her hand away and the red in her cheeks faded quickly. "I'll have to remember that," she said. A very small smile appeared on her face as she said, "Would you and your family, including your gorgeous wife, Samoa, like to be passengers on *Hope*?"

Now it was my turn to be stunned. "Is this payback for messing with you?" I asked in a very low voice.

"Not at all. *Hope* won't be ready to launch for almost ten years. In olden days, sailing ships had what was called owner's quarters. Who better than you and your wife would be considered owners of *Hope*? Without the both of you this program would never have gotten funded. Ten years from now you will be done with politics. Think of *Hope* as your cruise ship for the rest of your life. It would be such an adventure, not to mention being free from all the disastrous events occurring on Earth."

I sat quietly staring at her. It was a preposterous request. I was intrigued. "How about you?" I asked. "Will you be going?"

She smiled again and answered, "Would it make a difference in your decision if I was?"

"Maybe," I countered. "Let me discuss it with Samoa. We'll get back to you within the week."

An aide came up to Judy handing over paperwork. "It's time for the breakout sessions to begin, doctor."

We stood and went our separate ways.

I attended several sessions during my remaining time at ORNL. Much of it became a blur of technical information way above my knowledge. One thing caught my attention. It had to do with the overall propulsion system. One of our reviewers asked how *Hope* was going to store enough propulsion fluid for a hundred-year voyage. The answer surprised me.

One of ORNL engineers said, "It will be impossible to store all the propulsion fluid needed to attain and maintain a speed of five percent c for a hundred-year trip. We will be acquiring the needed propulsion fluid as we make our journey. The universe is not a void of empty space. It is full of random gas atoms and various molecules as well as microscopic particles. Granted they are far apart however when you are traveling at five percent c the density of material will seem to increase. In fact, *Hope* will need to be shielded from erosion of the ship's exterior surfaces, and it will actually have a substantial drag factor on the ship.

"An analogy might be driving a car in the rain. When the car is stopped it will seem like a drizzle, hardly enough to need wipers to keep the windshield clean. However, as the car accelerates, the rain will appear to increase and the wipers will have to be turned up higher to maintain visibility. At high speed, the wipers need to be turned up to maximum to see through the windshield.

"*Hope* will have three ram scoops that penetrate forward beyond the ship's protective shield to capture space material and use it to replenish the propulsion fluid supply."

As I returned home, I was thinking what an incredible group of scientists and engineers made up the *Hope* team. While I couldn't appreciate their talents as much as our review team, I came away with a feeling of confidence they were really going to make this happen.

I was also thinking about what Judy offered us. I couldn't wait to tell Samoa. Ten years from now we could be on a spaceship bound for the stars!

* * *

"Are you kidding me?!!!" Samoa sat behind her desk and stared at me intently, attempting to determine if I was joking.

"No, dearest," I replied in my most sincere voice. "We wouldn't have to make any decision now. The launch is almost ten years away still maybe it would be worth our while to check out the status of the program. I recommend we do it at the end of Phase 2, which would be three years from now, just about the time we will finish with our term of service with AWN. You've always mentioned you'd love to travel after we retired. This could be the ultimate get away trip."

Samoa sat quietly for a few moments. I could imagine the wheels in her brain turning, considering the options. Then she smiled and said, "You're right, my darling husband. We should consider it and the end of Phase 2 would be the perfect time to decide. Why don't you com your new girlfriend and let her know we are very interested?"

I gave her my "you've wounded me deeply" expression and answered, "Honey, how can you say things like that? You know you're the only girl for me."

She just stared at me with a blank expression, then slightly shook her head and said, "How long have we been married?"

"It seems like forever... I mean that in a good way," I finished quickly.

She began to laugh. "I know it's not your fault, you are just so handsome and have a personality women love, they can't help throwing themselves at you."

"I never catch any of them, only you," I responded in my best pouty voice.

Her stern look melted into a smile. "Yes, my love. I know. Seeing you has made my day complete. Now leave and let me get some work done."

I left quickly blowing her a kiss on the way out. I comm'd Judy and told her we'd see her at the end of Phase 2.

The Phase 2 Teams—AWN Secretary General Samoa

Each of the four contractor teams had chosen names for their generation starships. Two were based in The United Provinces of North America. Their ships were named *Faith* and *Hope*. One was based in the European Commonwealth called *Blue Streak*. The last one was based in the United Asian Countries called *Golden Dragon*.

There was no way we were going to be able to follow the activities on all four ships. There were too many demands on our time for that. Instead, we chose one, the generation starship called *Hope*.

The coordinating contractor for *Hope* was Oak Ridge National Lab (ORNL), a government facility in the province of Tenntucky. It was under the Department of Advanced Energy Laboratories. ORNL and all of the major sub-contractors were based in the provinces of Mid America. All the major suppliers, and there were hundreds of them, were based in the Americas (north, mid and south).

In addition to acting as the coordinator for the entire program, ORNL was also a sub-contractor developing the cold-fusion reactors that would be used to power the propulsion and environmental systems aboard *Hope*.

Hope Team Phase 2—Dr. Judy Van Der Geist

Three years and six months later, the *Hope* team was ready to present their Phase 2 results. I believe we have an outstanding product and based on the information I have on the other three starship programs, we should be one of the top two contractors. It took us a little longer than expected and forced us to make some unforeseen changes to our Phase 1 plan, which, by the way, forced us to offer more cost share funds. Unfortunately that's the way most huge contracts go. And there has never been a program as big and complicated as the generation starship program.

As I walked up to the podium to present my opening remarks, I noticed there were a lot more reviewers present than for Phase 1. I also saw Tongo and Samoa sitting front-row center. We had chatted briefly several times during Phase 2 and I got the impression they were very interested in joining us on *Hope*. In the back of the briefing room were vid cams from several of the media and a sprinkling of media reporters who, I was sure, would be asking silly questions. I reminded myself I wasn't going to give away any technical details during the overview. That level of detail was reserved for breakout sessions. The media wasn't permitted access to the breakout sessions.

As I stepped up to the podium, the side conversations died down as the ceiling lights began to dim. A single spotlight shown down on me as I began. "Ladies and gentlemen, my name is Dr. Judy Van Der Geist, I'm the Program Manager for Oak Ridge National Labs generation starship program. I want to welcome you here today and for the duration of the evaluation of our Phase 2 accomplishments. Let me introduce you to our starship. It's called *Hope.*" The spot light above me began to dim until the room was in total darkness.

Behind me the enormous vid screen began to come alive. It began with a picture of a star-filled universe. In the distance a small dot, perhaps a star, seemed to be getting larger. It grew steadily as the background music changed from a soft melody to include what might be voices from a distant choir. As the dot continued to grow, so did the volume of the choir. Within a few moments the dot became recognizable as a ship, a starship … *Hope.* The sound of the choir continued. There were no lyrics, only their voices performing as if they were musical instruments. The image of *Hope* grew until it dominated the vid screen. Suddenly the choir stopped and the point-of-view of the vid cam moved along with the ship. It was a much more detailed image of the exterior of *Hope* than was shown in the Phase 1 debriefing. The vid cam began at the forward end of *Hope* as a baritone voice replaced the music and the narration began.

"This is the starship *Hope* en route to the Alpha Centauri cluster," the voice began. "This generation ship is crossing the void of interstellar space. It is the first manned interstellar mission to ensure the continuance of the human race. It is scheduled to leave orbit seven years from now to begin its hundred-year journey to the planet Proxima-b. *Hope* will be populated by three generations of passengers and crew during its voyage to Proxima-b. Upon arrival, twenty-five hundred of the third generation will leave the ship and form the nucleus of our colony on their new home planet."

The vid cam moved aft and focused on the huge barrel-like object which was rotating. The narration continued, "This long cylindrical object is the habitat for three generations of passengers and crew for the outbound leg of their journey and the additional three generations of inhabitants for *Hope's* return to Earth. The habitat is rotating to generate the equivalent of Earth's gravity on the inner wall of the habitat. This inner surface will be turned into a small town with housing for all the people as well as farm land to grow all the food required to sustain life for multiple generations. This includes all breeds of livestock. Manufacturing sites will also be incorporated as well as raw material storage."

The vid cam seemed to penetrate the wall of the habitat and showed the fully developed interior. There were apartment buildings, schools, medical centers, places of worship, farmland and pastures, recreational areas, everything one could think of for a small town. There were lakes and trees and rolling hills and streams of water, even a waterfall. At the center of the barrel was a large tube that ran the full length of the habitat from forward to aft on which the habitat rotated. The central tube also housed three mini-suns that provided daylight conditions. At ship's night, the mini-suns transformed into mini-moons accompanied by twinkling stars.

At the forward end of the habitat was the crew quarters, the majority of the information systems and the flight control center. These were to be operated by Navy personnel with the ship's captain as the leader. Forward were also the offices of the ship's governor and the regional managers and department heads who would be responsible for the civilian population.

The vid faded to background and the lights came up and I faced the audience and was greeted with applause for the vid.

"I hope the vid you just watched answered some of the questions you might have," I said to the audience. "It probably also generated even more questions. If you have questions, please raise your hand and be recognized. I will do my best to answer them. Remember, this is an overview, detailed questions will be addressed in the breakout groups that follow."

A young woman with media credentials hanging around her neck was the first to raise her hand. I pointed at her and the drone with the vid cam and microphone quickly moved to her location and her image was sent to the vid screen so everyone could see and hear her question. "Dr. Van Der Geist, how soon after *Hope* leaves LEO will you begin to spin up the barrel? Second question: How long will it take to spin at full speed?"

"Interesting question," I said. "Actually, we need to bring the habitat up to speed to generate 1-G approximately a year before we leave orbit. We need to have a 1-G environment at the surface before we can build everything we need to build; all the apartments, the businesses, shops, recreation centers, worship centers and everything else. In addition, we need to put in all the dirt, irrigation systems, lakes, streams and waterfalls and plant crops well before we bring the crew and civilians aboard. When we leave orbit, everything needs to be in place. To answer your second question, once the support frame for the habitat has finished construction and the skin of the habitat has been installed and successfully pressure checked for leaks, we will begin a very slow buildup in the rotation of the habitat assembly. It is estimated it will take at least a month with periodic pressure checks made at specific intervals as the G level slowly ramps up to 1-G."

Another hand went up and the drone quickly repositioned itself. This time a man, also with media credentials hanging around his neck, asked, "How will the ship handle the linear G load when the ship's ion drives kick in to leave orbit and accelerate to five percent c? Won't there be some tremendous Coriolis effect which, when combined with 1-G of the spinning habitat, would make it almost impossible for people to move around?"

"Another good question," I answered. "If we were accelerating at 1-G to leave orbit while the barrel was rotating, the Coriolis effect would make it impossible to even stand up let alone to be able to walk around. That's why we will be leaving orbit with a one-tenth G thrust. That's less than the one-sixth G of gravitational pull of our moon and shouldn't cause much discomfort while we accelerate to five percent c. It will take us approximately six months accelerating at one-tenth G to reach five percent c. At which point we only need to operate at a fraction of one-tenth G to maintain speed."

Another hand was raised. Again, it was another woman from the media. I've found that media people are more outspoken at the open session. I guess the reviewers figure they will bring up their questions during the breakout sessions where media people can't quote them to the world audience. "Dr. Van Der Geist, could you tell us if the people on board *Hope* will age at the same rate as the people on Earth. I have heard that when a ship is traveling at close to light speed, the passengers on the ship age more slowly. How will the people on *Hope* age compared to the people on Earth?"

I paused for a moment before responding, then said, "What you are referring to is called relativistic time dilation. The passengers on a ship traveling at a speed that is very close to the speed of light will in fact age more slowly than their counterparts on Earth. There is a simple equation that can determine the time difference between the ship and the Earth. For example," I picked up my vid com and input data as I spoke to the audience, "a ship traveling at ninety-five percent of the speed of light for a hundred years Earth time," I paused and looked at my vid com, then looked up at the audience and said, "those aboard the ship will only age thirty-one years." There was a collective gasp by some of the audience, mostly the media types. "However, if your ship is traveling at five percent of the speed of light for a hundred Earth years," I looked down at my vid com again, then up at the audience and said, "those aboard the ship will age. . . 99.85 years." That caused some laughter in the audience, mostly the reviewers.

After a few more questions and answers, I said, "I'm afraid that's all the time we have for questions. We will recess for thirty minutes before we go to our breakout groups. Please feel free to enjoy the refreshments provided by ORNL."

<u>A Side Meeting—Judy Van Der Geist, Samoa & Tongo</u>

Samoa and I stood as Dr. Van Der Geist stepped down off the podium and walked towards us with a huge smile on her face. "Judy," I said as I gestured toward my wife, "let me introduce you to my wife. Judy, this Samoa. Samoa, Judy."

Judy took Samoa's hand in a warm handshake (no bones were broken) "It is such a pleasure to meet you at last madam Secretary General," she said as she shook her hand.

"Please, just call me Samoa."

"Thank you, Samoa," Judy replied and turned towards me, took my hand and shook it firmly with minimum damage. "Good to see you again, Tongo. Please, both of you join me in the VIP lounge. It's a little less crowded and has better refreshments."

We went past two large security guards into the VIP lounge which was decorated with a collection of pictures and paintings of projects ORNL had been involved with. The largest painting was of the starship *Hope* which dominated the far wall in front of a line of tables laden with every type of *hors d'oeuvres* I had ever seen and drinks of all kinds to help wash them down. We filled our plates, grabbed some drinks and sat at a reserved table.

Samoa took a bite and rolled her eyes. "This taste's marvelous and this juice tastes freshly squeezed."

"It is," replied Judy. "I hope you enjoy it. We are so honored to have you attend this meeting. I wish I had more time to meet with you two alone. Unfortunately, I have other duties I must attend to soon. I have two questions to ask you before I leave. I know Tongo spoke with you about joining us on *Hope*. Have you had time to discuss it? I'm not asking for a commitment now. I just want to know what your thoughts are regarding this offer."

Samoa looked at me and I nodded. "You have the floor madam Secretary General." I wanted her to have the final official say.

Samoa smiled at me and turned back to Judy, finished her appetizer and took another drink of juice before answering. She wiped her mouth with a napkin then said, "We are seriously considering your offer. My term as secretary general will be up in a couple of years and neither one of us wants to continue in politics. Assuming your team is chosen to continue Phase 3, I think there is a very good chance we will be joining you. However, you must understand, none of this must ever appear in any media ever, even after our term of office expires. It would look too much like favoritism. I can tell you we are very favorably impressed with your program. However, remember we have no vote in selecting which contractors will be chosen for Phase 3."

A huge smile formed on Judy's face. "Thank you so much. I'm very encouraged by your comments."

A young man approached our table and whispered something into Judy's ear. She nodded and stood up, then abruptly sat down. "Let them wait. I need to ask you one more question before I leave: are Samoa and Tongo your real names?" I let out a loud laugh and Samoa started to laugh also and covered her mouth when everyone in the room turned to look at us. I said, "They are now our legal names. They're not our given names. Polynesian names usually contain many syllables and are very hard for most people to pronounce. I was born on the island of Tonga and my wife was born on the island of Samoa so we adopted variations on the names of our birth islands that were easy to say and understand."

Judy stood up abruptly and said over her shoulder as she hurried from the room, "Keep in touch." Then she was out the door to her next important appointment.

We sat quietly finishing our food and drink as most of the rest of the VIPs made their exit to the various breakout sessions. When we were done, Samoa reached across the table, took my hand and said to me with a serious expression, "Do you think the chef who made these fantastic appetizers will be on the starship? Because if he or she is, you can count me in."

<u>Retirement—Samoa and Tongo</u>

The applause for Tongo and me was deafening as the AWN assembly all stood and praised us for our terms as secretary generals. Many requested I stay on for a second five-year term however one was enough for me. Tongo had served a term and a half and I saw the toll it took on him. In spite of our best efforts the natural disasters continued to increase. We were ready for a vacation. We hadn't seen our children and grandchildren for over a year except by vid com. Talking with their avatars was fun, still, it's hard to hug an avatar and I missed the smell of the babies.

It seemed there was no end to these tragedies. Just as the retirement ceremony was ending, we were contacted by my former information officer. She said there was a totally unexpected eruption of several previously dormant volcanoes on Fiji and Cook Islands. She said that the eruptions were immediately preceded by a series of earthquakes which also resulted in tsunamis throughout the Polynesian Islands Province where our children live.

Technically, we were still in office for the next week and the entire assembly insisted we take an AWN shuttle to evaluate the damage and as an aside to check on our children and their families. God bless the assembly for their gift. We were in the air within an hour.

We tried over and over to com our children as soon as we were airborne but the com system in the Polynesia area was offline. We watched the satellite news feeds and our hearts sank in despair. The damage was horrendous. The destruction caused by the earthquake and the accompanying tsunami was devastating throughout all of Polynesia. The erupting volcanoes on Fiji and the Cook Islands compounded the problem for the whole region. One report showed the top of one volcanic mountain on Fiji blew completely off spraying liquid lava all over the remaining mountain side. *How can anyone survive this violence?*

Our children live on what used to be called American Samoa until a hundred years ago when the Polynesian Islands Province was formed. We hadn't been in the air for more than an hour when the pilot informed us Pago Pago International Airport was no longer operational. All landing areas were currently underwater, swamped from the tsunami. The airport was closed to all traffic until further notice. Both of our children live in the foothills of Olotele Mountain, about three miles west of Pago Pago airport and a thousand feet above sea level. They should be safe from the tsunami as well as being secure from any damage from the earthquakes and volcanoes hundreds of miles south.

We gave the pilot coordinates for our children's homes and asked if he could set down somewhere near there. Ten minutes later he informed us he could and our ETA was a little over an hour. God bless hypersonic flight. I don't think I could have waited much longer to find out the welfare of our children and grandchildren.

True to his word, we descended into a park located within walking distance of our son's house. The coms were still out and you can't imagine the shocked look on our son's face when he opened the front door. He stepped back and closed his mouth before letting out a scream and lunged at Tongo lifting him off the ground in a bear hug I thought would break a normal man's spine. "Papa!!!" he shouted, "I can't believe you are here. How…"

He was interrupted by the sound of little feet running and a baby boy's squeal of delight to see his grandpa. When he saw me, he began jumping up and down and squealing again. I picked him up and swung him around, kissing his chubby cheeks.

In a few seconds, we were joined by my daughter-in-law and my granddaughter, a beautiful girl name Leila. A few seconds afterwards we were all crying tears of joy, hugging and kissing. Even the children's two puppies were excited to see us, barking and dancing on their hind legs.

When things finally calmed down, our daughter and her family walked in and it was chaos all over again. I said a silent prayer thanking God for everyone's survival and good health and asked for mercy for the Polynesians that weren't as fortunate as we. *Amen.*

After a few hours and a meal for everyone, including our flight crew, we had to leave. We needed to visit as much of the rest of Polynesia as we could in a few days and get an estimate of the damage. The shuttle's vid coms gave us close up views of the damage. It was heartbreaking. So many people died or were maimed. It was beyond the capacity of the local hospitals to treat all those in need. The beaches were littered with bodies. It reminded me of an ancient vid, I think they called it a documentary movie, of the beaches in a place called Normandy during a long-ago war. This was worse, much worse.

Large transport shuttles with medical supplies and doctors and nurses were arriving continuously everywhere we went. They saved those they could and buried the remains of those they couldn't save.

I couldn't eat. I couldn't sleep. I kept dreaming of all the bodies on the beach and those who died in the earthquakes and erupting volcanoes. I kept feeling their fear, their pain and their anguish as their lives were snuffed out. It took us almost a week before we returned to work for a final briefing and goodbye.

I stood before the assembly for the last time. I began to give my report with Tongo at my side. I felt strangely calm, detached from my feelings. About half way through my briefing, everything changed. I began to feel nauseous, my legs gave out and I fell to the floor. Tongo grabbed me around the waist to steady me; I vomited and passed out in his arms.

I woke up in a hospital with Tongo in a chair beside my bed. It was night and he was fast asleep. He hadn't shaved for several days and a beard had begun to grow. I couldn't remember much of what happened from the time we got into the shuttle to return home until I just woke up. It was all a disjointed series of memories, terrifying memories.

I laid there in the darkness with only the dim light of the monitors on my bed. I felt ashamed of myself for putting my darling husband through all this. I should have been stronger. Samoan women aren't supposed to be crybabies. I signaled for the nurse. He arrived a few seconds later. I told him to take all the monitors off of me. I wanted to get up and use the bathroom, take a shower and leave this place. I had work to do!

The young man looked perplexed as he removed all the leads to the monitoring equipment and assisted me from my bed. I felt weak. I willed myself to stand up. The nurse still had a hold of my arm, planning to help me walk into the bathroom. I would have none of that. I glared at him and said, "Thank you, young man. I can walk on my own from here."

He released me and I took several steps toward the bathroom when I heard Tongo's voice, "Samoa, are you aware your gown is open in the back and you aren't wearing panties?"

I continued on, not missing a step and replied to him, "I'm sure the young man has seen a naked butt before. It's no big deal."

In a sheepish voice I heard the nurse say, "I didn't look, I swear I didn't look...I'm leaving now."

I was feeling much better.

Tongo and I spent the next few days recovering. We did almost nothing except eat, take walks, talk a lot about future plans and rest. I wasn't yet totally committed to taking Judy up on her offer, so we certainly had a lot to work out. Before we left Samoa and our children, we talked with them about it. We asked them if they would like to join us on *Hope* and escape from this madness that was becoming the norm. It only took a few minutes for them to decide. They would stay on Samoa. It was their home. Whatever God had in store for them, they would face it on Samoa. They encouraged us to go. We deserved a long vacation after all the pain and suffering we had gone through, they said.

After a few weeks of rest and relaxation, I was getting bored. So was Tongo. We started looking around for something to keep us busy when we got an offer.

Hope Program Manager— Judy Van Der Geist

I vid comm'd Samoa and Tango to see how retirement was treating them and to make them an offer. "Hello, you two," I said to their images on my vid screen. "How's your retirement going? Are you living the life of leisure?"

Tongo chuckled and said, "We're both going a little stir-crazy right now. We need more diversity than just walking the same path around the park every day. How is your project going?"

"On schedule and on budget. However a new task is coming up very soon and I was wondering if you two might be interested."

"You mean going to work for ORNL?" asked Samoa.

"Would that be a problem for you?" I replied.

Tongo interrupted, "Do you see how she always answers a question with a question?"

Samoa ignored him and said, "No it wouldn't be a problem for either of us. We were never asked to sign any documents forbidding us from working for a government agency. In fact, most of our life has been working for the government in one capacity or another."

I smiled at the screen. That was the answer I was looking for. "In the not too distant future we are going to begin crew and passenger selection but before we do, we have to establish selection criteria. Samoa, I know one of your PhDs is in human resources so I thought something like this would be right up your alley."

Again, Tongo interrupted. "What about me?" he asked in a fake whiny voice. "Besides my two doctorate degrees, I also have a master's degree in thumb twiddling. So, I'm qualified for almost anything."

"I'm sure I can find something for you to do, Tongo. Better yet, why don't you figure out what type of job your skills would prepare you for. Why don't you guys think about the offer and get back to me in a week?"

They agreed and we signed off. I hoped Tongo came up with something. I didn't have a clue where he could help us.

A week later they comm'd me. Tongo was very excited, "Ombudsman," he gushed. "I can be your ombudsman reporting directly to you."

I considered his offer but I wanted to make sure we had the same understanding of what an ombudsman does, "Could you tell me what you think your responsibilities would be for the *Hope* program?

"Sure," he replied enthusiastically. "I'd be your trouble shooter, the person who resolves conflicts between all the vast components of the program. That would include technical conflicts as well as personal or departmental conflicts. I believe the *Hope* program is one of the most complex undertakings ever attempted. There are bound to be conflicts as you begin integrating all the various facets of the program."

He paused and I waited to see if he had more to say. Apparently, he had finished his pitch. I quickly considered what he proposed. He was right; we needed someone outside the program to resolve integration issues. Up till now, most of the program activities were compartmentalized. Recently, as we moved into Phase 3, I noticed occasional conflicts occurring as we began to integrate the thousands of details into a coherent package. It would only get worse as time went on. Tongo certainly had the skills and experience necessary to quickly resolve such conflicts.

"Okay," I said. "You're hired. When can you start working for me?"

In the background I heard Samoa's voice, "What about me? Am I hired too?"

"Of course," I answered. "It's a package deal. Do you think you could relocate to Oak Ridge within two weeks?"

"Absolutely," Tongo said. "Our bags are already packed and we have one foot outside the door. See you tomorrow, boss."

<u>Phase 3, Construction—Judy Van Der Geist</u>

As soon as we were awarded the Phase 3 contract, we began construction. *Hope* was to be built in a low Earth orbit (LEO) approximately 225 miles above Earth's surface making one orbit every 90 minutes. Before we could begin the assembly on the starship, we needed to build a structure to assist the construction crew in building the ship. This structure was called the fabrication and assembly hanger, better known as the hanger. Adjacent to the hanger would be the construction crew facilities.

The material needed to build the hanger was prefabricated on the ground and launched into LEO by a conventional transport vehicle along with five assembly workers. Everything was modularized. They assembled the hanger and the assembly crew quarters in three days. I know you might be thinking, *That's impossible. It should be more like three weeks.* I assure you, it took three days. The crew also had assembly bots which really cut down on the build time. They returned to Earth in the transport.

At that point we were ready to build the exterior shell of the habitat or, as it was sometimes called, the barrel. Let me supply some critical background information. Our first rule in building *Hope* was we would use at least 90% existing technology. We borrowed (some may say, stole) some technology developed for the Sky One Habitat. Actually, we paid handsomely for the same company that built Sky One to act as subcontractor for the *Hope* design and build. Whatever could be modularized was built on the ground and transported to space. In less than a year the exterior shell was completed. I heard one of the construction workers comment, "We really don't build it. It's more like assembling Tinker Toys, only they're much bigger."

Once the shell was completed, it was sealed and pressure checked and any and all leaks discovered were repaired. The next step was to begin the construction on the inside of the barrel. This included apartments, dormitories, offices, restaurants, recreation centers, medical clinics, worship facilities (multipurpose buildings which served as churches, mosques, synagogues and so on) and a host of other things were all completed in zero-G conditions. That step was completed when every structure was anchored to the inner wall of the barrel.

Once the inside of the barrel was completed, maneuvering rocket motors were placed on the exterior framework of the barrel and it slowly began to rotate. It took several days of low, careful acceleration to reach a 1-G condition on the inside surface of the habitat wall. Numerous inspections of structural integrity were made during the run up to 1-G.

Once the barrel was certified operational, the real work began. It took almost a year to outfit the interior of the habitat, turning it from a dark, gray plastisteel metal alloy barrel to a finished product that for all intents resembled a small town in mid-northern America, complete with farms and pastures for livestock, parks and a small-town look with businesses, manufacturing sites, and residences. It took almost another year to install the ship's information systems, flight control, environmental systems, power plants and everything else required to operate the ship. All that was missing were the people. Bots and drones maintained *Hope's* habitat until it was time to bring the crew and civilians aboard.

While this construction was going on, Samoa was overseeing passenger selection as well as training them for their new life and Tongo was making sure the integration ran smoothly. I don't know what I would have done without them. Having them in those positions gave me the time I needed to ensure we were on schedule and on budget. Well, almost on budget. But what's a few trillion credits between friends?

<u>Passenger Selection—Assistant Director Samoa</u>

It had been a long time since I had developed an employment plan. Fortunately, Judy gave me a staff of people who were very familiar with positions we would need to fill and there were literately hundreds of different categories. They were divided into two main groups: military and civilian. The military, Space Navy in our case, would have responsibility for the operation of the ship. Navy personnel would make up one thousand of the ship's passengers. The civilian side would be responsible for the survival of the people aboard the ship. At the time *Hope* was scheduled to leave LEO, there would be three thousand civilian personnel on board. That number would grow to four thousand by the time the ship reached Alpha Centauri.

We began our selection process a year before *Hope* was due to begin her journey. We advertised on vid networks and established websites with detailed descriptions of requirements for each position. We were looking for highly trained individuals with at least ten years of relevant experience. Each applicant filled out a very detailed application which then had to be extensively fact checked.

By the end of the first week, we had over 20,000 applications. A computer program reviewed each application and selected the best 10,000 for further review. Each of these individuals had to pass a very comprehensive physical and psychological evaluation before even beginning the interview process. A total of three interviews were conducted, the first being done by vid com. After the first interviews we were left with 8,000 applicants invited to visit our facility for face-to-face interviews. By the end of the third interview, we selected 6,000 applicants to begin training for their selected positions. The last month of the selection process we finalized our passenger list to the 4,000 who would be the first generation of voyagers aboard *Hope*. We also maintained a list of 1,000 alternates just in case of any unforeseen eliminations or withdraws of the selected passengers.

For the military positions, we expected to recruit heavily for personnel currently in the Space Navy or recently retired. Our plan was to start with selecting the captain who would have total command of the ship's operations. Once he or she had been chosen, the captain would assist in the selection of the executive officer (XO) and operations leaders. There would be a total of ten ops leaders:

1. Flight Control
2. Power Systems
3. Propulsion Systems
4. Environmental Systems
5. Astrogation
6. Information Systems
7. Transport Beam System
8. Security Detail
9. Chaplain
10. Medical/Dental Clinic

Each ops leader would also participate in the selection of the crew who would work under their leadership. The number of personnel assigned to each group would vary significantly, from a few dozen to several hundred. The first four groups on the above list were in this latter category. These groups needed to be fully staffed for three shifts every day. Most of the others needed less coverage.

The captain of a ship, any ship, is a title. Their actual rank can vary from commander to rear admiral. The XO rank can be lieutenant commander to captain. Ops leaders ranks can vary from lieutenant to commander.

In addition to the officers, approximately half the military would include warrant officers and enlisted personnel, the lowest rank being petty officer third class. We would only consider candidates with considerable relevant experience.

I was part of the selection committee for the ship's captain. There were two candidates vying for the position, both very well qualified.

The committee was made up of five members: two civilians and three Navy officers. Judy and I were the civilians; the Navy was represented by a commodore, a rear admiral, and a vice admiral. The vice admiral was the chairman of the committee.

Our first candidate was Captain Gary Dagan. His current assignment was as the commander of a 300,000-ton transport ship operating between Ceres, a large asteroid in the belt between Mars and Jupiter and the Lunar Colony. The ship was named the *UPNA Andromeda*. Rock miners would deliver the raw ore they had mined in the belt to Ceres where it would undergo preliminary processing and be stored until *Andromeda* or one of her sister ships arrived. They would take on the cargo and deliver it to Lunar Colony for final processing and delivery to Earth by the commercial shuttle fleet. *Andromeda* made six round trips per Earth year. It sounds routine however attacks by pirates were common and required a great deal of skill by the ship's captain.

Captain Dagan was led into the interview room by a yeoman. He stood by the conference table surveying the room. His dress uniform had been tailored to fit perfectly, his hat under his left arm, his salt and pepper hair cut short, his face cleanly shaven. He was a man of average height with an athletic build. He scanned the room, taking in everything with stern blue-gray eyes. He missed nothing, including the five chairs across the table from his own chair. A moment later, a door at the side of the room opened and our group entered and stood behind our chairs. Captain Dagan came to attention and saluted the Naval officers with a precise salute. The officers returned his salute. Vice Admiral Amanda Jackson said, "Everyone please be seated."

The captain took his hat from under his arm and laid it on the table then took his seat. I noticed he looked very calm, self-assured, as he sat with his hands resting on the table top. The vice admiral introduced the committee to the captain and asked the first question. "Captain, why did you apply for the position of ship's captain?"

A large smile formed on the captain's face. "Is that a trick question, Admiral? I'll bet every ship's commander in the fleet applied."

"You'd be surprised," she answered. "Less than half of the commanding officers applied. Please answer the question."

"You're right, I am surprised," he replied. He paused for a moment then said, "I applied for two reasons. The first is that being the first commander of a generation ship is the logical next step for me. It is what I've aspired to be ever since I heard the rumors there would be generation ships. The overall mission of the ships is a noble cause that I want to be part of."

He paused as if to let that information be considered by the committee members. Then he resumed, "My second reason for applying was that I'm the best candidate for the job. No one else in the fleet comes close to my credentials. I am your best choice for a successful mission."

I was momentarily taken aback by his brashness but when I studied his face, I was sure he wasn't bragging. He was confident there was no one better qualified than he was.

The vice admiral's expression revealed nothing. In a neutral tone of voice, she said, "What would you say if I told you we have another candidate just as well qualified as you?"

Captain Dagan's expression was also neutral as he answered, "With all due respect, Admiral, I think you need to recheck my record and compare it to the other captain's accomplishments."

"Already done, Captain," the admiral said in that same emotionless voice. "The other candidate is not a ship's captain, she's an XO."

The captain's mouth dropped open and he sat back in surprise as the admiral continued, "She had been the commander of the *UPNA Orion* who decided to step down and accepted the position of XO in order to spend more time with her husband and family."

The captain snapped forward in his chair and slammed his hand down on the table with a resounding boom. "My wife! You're talking about my wife!" Then he began laughing as he shook his head. "So,

Malinda applied? That sneak. She never told me. And yes, she *is* just as qualified as I am."

He looked at the shocked expression on all of the faces of the committee except the Vice Admiral. She smiled at the captain and said, "I'm the one who requested she apply."

She turned to the rest of the committee and said, "I apologize for all the theatrics. I believe both of our candidates are equally well qualified however we can have only one ship's captain. I recommend we accept both candidates as skilled enough to be captains. However, Malinda has graciously decided to accept the role as XO as far as the chain of command is concerned." She turned back to Captain Dagan and said, "Do you agree to these terms, Commodore?"

"Absolutely, Admiral." A small frown appeared momentarily on Dagan's face. "Did you make a mistake about my rank, sir?" he asked.

"I'm a Vice Admiral, I don't make mistakes, Commodore. Report for training with your XO Monday morning."

<u>Selection of Civilian Personnel—Ombudsman Tango</u>

I served on the panel that made the final selection of the civilian passengers. There were five of us in all, the other four much better qualified than I was. As Ombudsman, I only had a vote when there was a tie between the four smart people voting. Thankfully, that didn't happen very often.

Similar to what Samoa reported regarding the military personnel, we began with the selection of the overall leaders and worked our way down in order of responsibilities. The leader of the civilians would be the governor. He or she would have an assistant, much like the Captain's XO for the military. Reporting to them would be the leaders of various disciplines. Those disciplines are listed below:

- Agriculture (Farms, Husbandry)
- Medical (Doctors, Dentists, Vets, Counselors, EMTs, Clinics, Hospital, Nurses)
- Habitat Maintenance (Carpenters, Masons, Electricians, Plumbers, etc)
- Manufacturing (3D Printer Operators, Machinists, Wood Working)
- Food Preparation (Cooks, Servers, Restaurants, Fast Food)
- Recreation (Spa Operators, Gyms, Trainers, Coaches, Pools)
- Civilian Worship Centers (Jointly with Military Chaplain)
- Recycling Centers (Air, Water, Waste)
- Police (Officers, Detectives, Courts, Judges, Jails) Jointly with Military Security
- Administration
- Schools (Day Care, K -12, College, Graduate School, Teachers and Professors)
- Information Systems (eBooks, Audio Books, Books, Vids of every type imaginable)
- Miscellaneous

The goal was to duplicate everything a normal small town on Earth would have. What wasn't covered on our discipline list would be added as we went along.

We began our selection process with the position of Governor. I suggested that a town of three to four thousand people didn't warrant a Governor; perhaps Mayor would be a better title. That suggestion was met with a glare and stony silence by the other four members of the Selection Panel. After a short pause, the senior member of our group stated the guidelines of our selection process. He added the title of Governor was justified by *Hope's* unique mission. The people the Governor would be leading weren't just ordinary people, they were, he said, "The cream of the crop. Not just a group of unrelated individuals who could come and go as they pleased."

Three candidates were being considered for Governor: two women and one man. All three had spent a considerable time both as city mayors and governors of UPNA provinces. Their ages ranged from mid-forties to early fifties. Two were currently severing as governors, the third had recently completed his term of office and declined to run for another term.

The panel met for half a day with each of the candidates. It was a difficult decision; each of them was exceptionally well qualified and had the kind of charismatic charm I was used to seeing of high-ranking politicians; senators or perhaps cabinet members.

Once the interviews were completed, the panel met to make their decision. After several rounds of discussions, we chose Ms. Anita Ataksak, the former Governor of North Western Canlaska Province. She was of mixed ancestry, a descendant of an Inuit leader.

The position was hers until she decided to step down. The other two candidates were offered positions reporting to Governor Ataksak. One accepted, the other declined. I found out later the Inuit name Ataksak meant goddess of the sky. I hoped it turns out to be prophetic for *Hope's* voyage.

The Governor immediately began the selection process for choosing the leaders of the various disciplines. I was available to assist whenever needed, however, I began spending most of my time taking part in a variety of training opportunities.

<u>Crew Training—Commodore Gary Dagan and Captain Malinda Dagan.</u>

We began training of the Navy crew in our ground mockup of the entire Navy facilities they would be living and working in aboard *Hope*. We spent six months working in the mockups before going aboard *Hope* for onboard training. We restricted the crews to living in the mockups for the entire six months. As far as Malinda and I were considered, we were now on active duty. Outside contact with family and friends was limited to 30 minutes per day of vid coms, just as it would be once we were on *Hope*.

Malinda and I divided up leading the various Ops Teams training; I had Flight Control, Propulsion Systems and Astrogation. Malinda covered Power Systems, Environmental Systems and Information Systems. The other Ops Systems were monitored by specialists in those areas.

We can't give enough praise to the contractors who were part of the crew. These were the scientists and engineers from ORNL and subcontractors who had designed and fabricated everything in the ship. They wrote the training manuals and led the teaching activities. It would have taken much, much longer to complete our training without their contributions.

For the first three months we worked on understanding each person's responsibilities, writing up full job descriptions. Then we learned how to operate their equipment under normal circumstances. Then we swapped jobs to make sure we could operate everyone else's job within the disciplines in case of emergencies.

The next three months were dedicated to emergency drills. Every conceivable thing that could go wrong was looked at, analyzed and solutions determined. We practiced them all until we could recognize every potential problem and more importantly, could resolve it before it became a catastrophe. When our time was up for mockup training, we moved to the ship and started over again with the real systems.

Assembly of the ship was quickly approaching completion. The habitat had been spun up to speed and began operating with full gravity. All the systems had been successfully installed and checked out before we moved into the ship. The fusion reactors and the EM propulsion drives were the last to be installed. Static tests were successfully accomplished and any fine-tuning completed. All that remained was to bring all the passengers on board and begin flight tests.

One particular piece of training I found fascinating was checking out our new transport beaming system. This was one of the few new technologies that had been recently developed. ORNL had been working on the concept for decades. Fortunately for us, they were able to build and test a prototype during Phase 2 of our program and had managed to construct an operational system during Phase 3. The system had been installed on *Hope* just as we began our training aboard the ship.

I had no idea how it worked however I was amazed at what it could do. Using a combination of advanced laser technology and mag-grav field generators (a precursor to artificial gravity? Who knows?) as well as very specialized computers, the contractor team demonstrated how we could lock on to an object on the ground, capture it and bring it up to the ship, all while we were moving in orbit. Similarly, we could take an object on the ship and transfer it to a desired spot on the ground.

It had the capacity to transport objects weighing several tons or as little as a pound. During our training, we brought aboard a twenty-ton piece of equipment into our cargo bay. And just for fun, we transported a carton of eggs from a table in the ORNL plaza to the cargo bay on one orbit and returned it to the plaza on the next orbit without so much as one broken egg. The gutsiest test of all was when we duplicated it with a real human being, one of the contractors who developed the beam system. *Truly amazing!* The possibilities were endless. By the way, the human test subject was also not broken.

As we were busy with our training assignments, the civilian contingency began moving in and familiarizing themselves with their respective assignments. By that time the agrabots had planted a large variety of crops. The initial harvest was only months away. Pasture land was ready for the livestock. It was getting exciting now; this trip was really going to happen!

Increase in Natural Disasters—Assistant Director Samoa

Once personnel selection was completed, Tongo and I had time to get settled in our quarters. We had been working twelve hours a day and hadn't had much time for anything else. We were so focused on getting the ship ready for launch, we hadn't been following what was happening to the world. It was getting worse. Death rates were continuing to increase at an alarming rate. Deaths due to natural disasters were now the leading cause of death.

We vid comm'd our children frequently now and were surprised to see how much our grandchildren had grown. I felt guilty we weren't with them to see them grow from toddlers to little people.

So far, the Polynesian Islands Province had escaped any further problems. Fiji and the Cook Islands were pretty much recovered from the attack by Mother Nature. They still had the occasional aftershocks fortunately none leading to further deaths and the volcanic action had subsided. Unfortunately, the rest of the world hadn't been so fortunate. It seemed every place on Earth was undergoing some form of life-threatening trauma. Was it ever going to end?

Then it ended. Over a period of a few weeks, everything seemed to be trending toward normalcy with no more earthquakes or hurricanes or tornadoes, no more volcanoes erupting, no tsunamis nor flooded rivers. Weather patterns were changing back to how they had been decades ago. How could that be?

So-called experts reported what we had experienced was just a period of adjustments. Something to do with the tectonic plates moving to relieve stress. Tongo said all the hand waving meant they really didn't have a clue why it had begun or why it had stopped. Whatever the cause, it was a blessing.

Part 2
The First Generation

Leaving Earth—Commodore Gary Dagan

I sat in my captain's chair watching the monitors, attempting to appear calm. In reality, my stomach was churning. Malinda was standing beside me and laid a reassuring hand on my arm. I could see the slightest smile on her lips as we checked the data readouts. Ten minutes to go before we lit up the ion drive and began our voyage.

It seemed like we had been doing this for a very long time however it was really only a few years. Earlier today, *Hope* had been christened with the traditional bottle of champagne. Everyone aboard who wasn't busy with work responsibilities was watching the dedication on vid screens all over the ship. The current Secretary General of the AWN made a speech, congratulating everyone. Various religious leaders blessed our mission. Of course, all of these people were on Earth however when the secretary general pulled the trigger on a hand grip in front of the general assembly, a magnum of the finest champagne was launched pneumatically from a platform on the hanger next to *Hope*. It shot across the short distance to the hull of the ship, impacting just aft of the dedication plaque. The bottle shattered into a million pieces, the champagne vaporizing and flash freezing into crystals sparkling in the lights from the vid cams. I wondered if the champagne was a bit brash or possibly obtuse.

Five minutes until launch.

An ion drive vessel doesn't break orbit in the same manner as the old chemical powered rockets of centuries ago or even the more recent nuclear thermal rockets. When Apollo 11 launched from Earth, the three astronauts were subjected to 4-G thrust which would place them in LEO traveling at a velocity of 17,500 mph. Since *Hope* was already in orbit, we avoided that.

For the Apollo 11 capsule to break Earth's gravitational pull, the third stage chemical rocket, the J-2, began with a thrust of 0.6-Gs and increased to a little more than 1.4-Gs over about six minutes before the engine shut down and the capsule was free from Earth's gravitational attraction. They flew a zero-G ballistic trajectory to the moon before firing a rocket to place them in a lunar orbit, a trip of about 240,000 miles.

Hope would fire up the EM ion drive in less than five minutes and gradually ramp up thrust to a maximum of 0.1 G. In doing so, *Hope* would begin an outwardly spiraling orbit around Earth until it reached the escape velocity of 25,000 mph at which point, we need to be pointed toward Alpha Centauri. Once we reached a thrust of 0.1 G, we would continue to accelerate to a cruise velocity of five percent c. Which would take us six months. At that point, we would decrease our thrust to a level needed to maintain cruise speed.

The clock continued to count down. When it reached five seconds, everyone began to count down along with it. At zero, there was the slightest tremor throughout the ship as the ion drive came on line. We were on our way!

For the next four hours, I had the con and Malinda checked with all the critical system's leaders to get status reports as the ion drive continued to ramp up. It was tradition when a spaceship was launched for the first time its crew felt they had to behave...how should I describe it...maybe the word *quirkily* would describe it best. I looked forward to see how my crew would behave.

Hope's First Shift—Captain Malinda Dagan

My first stop was with the leader of Flight Ops who was about ten feet away from my husband. All of Flight Ops was located on the bridge while the other system ops were separately quartered. Marine Lt. Col. Jason Kuhn saw me coming, said something to one of his crew and a new image appeared on the large forward-facing vid screen. It was a picture of the constellation Centaurus, close to the Southern Cross. It had a bright blue circle surrounding a very bright star in the constellation. A flashing message next to the star kept repeating, *Target…Target…Target…*

"That had better be Alpha Centauri you've got circled, Colonel," I said.

"Yes ma'am. It most certainly is. Projected ETA is 100 years. We are so glad to finally be on our way. I thought those disaster drills would never end," he replied.

"I know it's only been a few minutes so I'll check back with you at the end of my rounds for a sitrep." I started to walk away then turned back and said to him, "If we get to full thrust before I get back, please com me."

"Roger that, sir."

I left the bridge. My next stop was Propulsion, "How are the fires burning Pris?" I asked the officer in charge, Commander Priscilla Hoyt.

"Hot and true, Commodore," she answered.

This is going to take some explaining. Please bear with me. On a ship, any ship, the commander of the ship is always called captain, no matter what their rank might be. No one else is called captain, only the commander of the ship. My rank is captain. Gary is officially the ship's captain, so as a courtesy, I'm bumped to the next highest rank, therefore I would be referred to as commodore. Gary, whose rank is commodore is called captain and as his XO, my rank is captain I'm called commodore. I know it's confusing however tradition must be upheld. At least that's what the admirals tell us.

"Everything is in the green. If it remains green, we should be at target thrust in 25.325 minutes, mark." Pris said with a hint of a smile on her face.

"Perhaps you could be more precise?" I asked, returning her smile.

"Sorry sir, that's the best I can do at the moment. I'll try harder next time."

"Carry on, Commander.

"Aye aye, sir."

Maybe more explanation is needed. When speaking with a superior officer, the formal address is sir. It doesn't matter if the officer is a woman or a man, sir is always accepted. A less formal way of addressing a woman officer would be to use the word ma'am". This is usually reserved for when both parties are of equal rank. That's my last protocol lesson for today.

Adjacent to Propulsion was Power Systems. They were responsible for all the fusion reactors on the ship and there were a ton of them. They supplied all the power to the ship. Propulsion had three dedicated reactors. Only two were used at any given time. They were the largest reactors by far on the ship. The smaller reactors powered all our environmental systems and computers as well as everything else that needed power sources. We had twice as many spare reactors in storage, some were scheduled as replacements to meet the ship's needs, the rest were targeted for the new colony on Proxima-b.

The leader of Power Systems was Dr. Cullum MacGregor, a contractor from ORNL, previously the leader of their Fusion Reactor R&D group. He was proud of his heritage and loved to flaunt his Scottish brogue. When I entered his domain, I was surprised to see him dressed in a kilt with all the trimmings. "Aye lassie, tis so gud a yah to visit our humble abode. What brung yah here?" he said in greeting. "How be yah this fine day?"

I quickly looked around and noticed that all of his crew were wearing kilts, even Kim Jong Li, a man of Korean descent. "Is this a costume party?" I asked.

"Nay, lassie," he answered, "More a display of tradition and solidarity."

"Do you maintain all the traditions of kilt wearing?" I asked, referring indirectly to the rule that no respectable Scotsman would ever wear an undergarment when they were dressed in their kilt.

Dr. MacGregor smiled broadly, nodding his head vigorously, then said, "Aye, lassie. We all be Scotsmen here today." He paused for a moment then added with a twinkle in his eye, "Would the Commodore like a wee peak to confirm traditions are followed?"

"Thanks for the opportunity, Doctor. Perhaps another time. I have other stops to make and I'm running late. Perhaps you can tell me how your reactors are performing."

He made a show of scanning all the readouts before he turned and said, "They be fine, lassie. All in the green. Humming along and in it for the long haul."

"Good to hear. I'll inform the captain. He will be pleased." I gave him a curtsy, turned and walked out. Not sure why I did that.

I heard him say as I walked down the hall to the next stop, "There goes a fine brath of a girl."

As I walked down the corridor, my com chimed. "This is the XO."

"XO, we are now at one tenth G."

"Thank you, Colonel. XO out."

I continued on and made stops at Environmental Systems, Astrogation and Information Systems. Everything was going well. No glitches discovered. I returned to the bridge and reported in to my Captain/Husband. I noticed a slight lean to those standing. The lean was caused by the linear thrust of the ion drive and would be with us for about half a year. Once we reach cruise speed, the leaning would stop.

"Sitrep, XO," he said.

"All critical systems are in the green. Has security reported any accidents caused by the thrust shift?" I asked.

"Not yet," he answered. "Just some minor shifting of things not secured to the deck. The governor has invited me to take a brief tour of the barrel, to see first-hand how people are handling it. XO, you've got the con until I get back. I plan to be gone a few hours."

"Roger that, Captain. Enjoy your tour."

<u>Tour—Governor Anita Ataksak</u>

I met the Captain at the closest tube station and we got aboard a two-person mag-lev car. "Captain, do you have any preference as to where we should go first?" I asked.

He shook his head and said, "Not really, Governor. This will be my first time outside of the Navy facilities. Wherever you want to go is fine with me."

I turned to the display panel and said, "Surface Tube 6 to mid-habitat station, slow cruise." Then I turned back to the captain as our car began to accelerate slowly from the tube station at the forward end of the habitat where the Navy facilities and civilian government offices resided. "I have to confess this is only my third trip since I transferred to *Hope.*"

As we moved out of the station we were suddenly 'outside,' with a full view of the inside barrel. It was breathtaking! We could see the entire four miles to the aft end. The central tube-shaft on which the habitat spun was prominently visible. That shaft was almost a hundred feet in diameter and fabricated from a combination of carbon fiber and plastisteel. Inside the tube were four sets of mag-lev tracks as well as conduits for our power, information and environmental systems. Three Sun Rings circled the central shaft giving even 'sunlight' to the entire inside surface. In a few hours when we begin transitioning to evening, the suns would dim and become three Mini Moons, which would vary in brightness to simulate the changing phases of Earth's moon. Twinkling laser lights would simulate stars rotating the same way the constellations rotate during the night on Earth.

Five spoked wheels encircled the habitat from forward to aft in equal intervals. There were six spokes to each wheel. The spoke tubes were only fifty feet in diameter; they also accommodated mag-lev tracks as well as all the conduits.

When we reached the mid-habitat station, our car diverted to the drop off track where we left the car and walked along a platform to an exit that opened into our central park. We hadn't talked much during our ride; we were both busy taking in all the sights. Now that we were outside, we stood turning slowly completely around in a circle, trying not to miss anything. It completely took my breath away!

I noticed it appeared the captain was now watching the people in the park rather than the landscape. It reminded me of vids of Central Park in old New York City before the flood destroyed it.

We continued our walk a short distance to a restaurant with outside seating. "Are you hungry, Captain?" I asked. "I hope so, I'm starving."

We were seated by a hostess who placed us at a table that had a terrific view of the lake and the waterfall that fed it.

"Have you eaten here before?" asked the captain.

"Yes," I answered. "It's my favorite restaurant on the ship as far as I'm concerned. They have the best whale blubber I've ever tasted. You'll have to try it."

As I anticipated, he looked up quickly from his menu. His mouth was open as if he wanted to say something however couldn't remember the question. I tried to keep a straight face; that lasted a few seconds then I burst out laughing.

He laid his menu down, closed his mouth and shook his head. His look of shock turned to a huge smile, "Wow! You really got me on that one. I thought the Intuits were a more stoic people."

"We are, for the most part. However, you have to remember, I'm only part Inuit. A substantial part of me is joker."

We ordered our food, not whale blubber, and it was promptly served. As we ate, I asked why he appeared to be watching the people in the park as we came out of the tube station.

"I wanted to see if there was any noticeable effects of the ion drive coming on line," he answered.

"Is there?" I asked.

"No, thank heavens," he answered as he picked up our water pitcher and began to refill my glass. "Watch this."

He held the pitcher about a foot above the glass and began to pour. At first, I didn't notice anything then it became obvious. Instead of flowing straight down from the pitcher to the glass, the water seemed to be flowing in a spiraling path. Now it was my turn to be surprised.

"How did it do that!?" I asked. "Are you related to a shaman or a witch doctor?"

He chuckled briefly and answered, "No such luck. It's called the Coriolis Effect. It's caused by two or more gravity fields operating at the same time. When we started the ion drive to accelerate us to cruise speed it resulted in this Coriolis Effect. I was looking to see if the people in the park were having any problems walking or standing. I didn't notice any one stumbling or falling down. Did you?"

I shook my head. "No not at all." She paused then added, "I want to thank you for your demonstration. I won't freak out when I pour myself a beer and see it doing loop-de-loops."

"Once we reach cruising speed, it will be even less noticeable," he replied.

We finished our meal and took a walk down by the lake. This was the first chance I had to speak with my co-leader of the ship. I think we were both glad to have the opportunity to get to know each other a little better. We sat at a bench close to the falls and we noticed a small boy walking with his parents, studying the falls.

"Do you see it, Daddy? Do you?" the boy asked excitedly. "The water is falling in little curlicues on the way down. Don't you see it? It's like someone is stirring the water as it goes down."

The father looked closely, then shook his head. "Sorry, Todd. All I see is what we always see. Just water going over the cliff."

"But, but…" he sputtered. He stamped his foot in frustration. "How can you not see the curlicues!?"

I got up quickly and approached the boy and his father. "Hello," I said to the family. "I have to tell you, Todd is right. There *are* curlicues. It's very hard to see. Your son must have a keen eye to see them. It's caused by something called the Coriolis Effect."

The father looked skeptical however when I handed him my business card with the title of **GOVERNOR** written on it in bold capital letters he smiled and thanked me. As they walked away, I heard his mother say, "Maybe we can look up Coriolis on your computer to see what that is." The boy was smiling as he took his mother's hand and began skipping as they headed home.

By the time we returned to our home tube station, our Mini Moons were out and the stars were twinkling. We said our goodbyes for what I thought was a very productive afternoon. Before the captain left, he said to me, "I'd love for you to meet my wife. Maybe you could tell her about how much you love whale blubber."

On Our Way—Commodore Gary Dagan

After a few days of slowly spiraling away from Earth, we attained escape velocity. Our Astrogation Ops group had our course plotted to Alpha Centauri. No longer would we be traveling in an expanding spiral around Earth. From now on we would be traveling in a straight line towards the Alpha Centauri cluster. More accurately, we were on a course to where the cluster would be in roughly a hundred years from now. There is always some relative motion between stars and that had to be accounted for in charting our course.

Always looking for an excuse to party, the Quartermaster was given the assignment for a Dining In. For those of you unfamiliar with military tradition, a Dining In is a formal dinner party where all the Navy personnel wear their dress uniforms and of course, their significant others would dress accordingly. Many toasts would be made and excellent food would be served. A band made up from our musically inclined crew members would provide the music and dancing was encouraged.

In addition to the Navy personnel, we invited some of the ship's high-ranking contractors as well as the Governor and her staff.

Those crew members who drew the short straw provided a skeleton crew to keep the ship running while the rest of us partied ourselves into oblivion. Of course, these unlucky souls were exempt from duty when the next Dining In was held.

The Dining In began promptly at 2000 hours with a reception line made up of *Hope's* high-ranking officers. Tradition dictated that the ship's captain was always the last in line with the lowest ranking officer at the beginning of the line.

As the doors opened, I realized how much I was looking forward to this gathering. It was going to be the first chance many of us had to relax and unwind since the crew selection began almost two years ago. I looked down the line and noticed Dr. Van Der Geist and her husband working their way through the introductions. A few minutes later, the Governor and her husband entered the line. Malinda told me she was looking forward to meeting the Governor. We were all so busy we hadn't found time to get together with her and her husband until now.

Once the introductions were over, we mingled with everyone, sampling appetizers and sipping flutes of champagne. I introduced Malinda to the Governor and her husband. His name was Arnold and he was the head of the Planning Commission for Growth and Population Control; a very important organization to ensure our population growth was maintained at a rate that we could sustain. His organization determined who could have children and when they could have them. They had to consider food and air usage as well as planning for the next generation of all the different civilian and military positions. The more he talked about it, the more impressed I was, as I learned how complicated his job was.

I was surprised to find out he also determined the number of pets our passengers could have. Pets were limited to dogs and cats and the same rules applied to how many were permitted. It was optional and required the family units that wanted pets had to make a request. Only one pet per family and breeding was tightly controlled as it was with people.

A tone softly rang indicating it was time to take our seats for dinner. There were six of us at the head table: Melinda and me, Judy Van Der Geist and her husband, Karl who was our contractor in charge of our extensive computer system and Anita Ataksak and her husband, Arnold. A legion of servers appeared from the extensive galley bearing dome-covered plates and placed them in front of everyone as *Hope's* chaplain approached the rostrum.

When the conversations subsided, the Chaplain said, "Please bow your heads for a moment of prayer," he paused briefly then began, "Dear Lord, our creator and sustainer of the universe, we come before you tonight as we begin our journey to a distant star. We ask for your blessing in this endeavor. Please guide us in this task and have mercy on those we leave behind…Amen"

As we looked up from the prayer, the servers came from behind us an removed the covers from the first course of our dinner.

The Governor looked down at her plate with a confused expression, then she broke into hysterical laughter. Everyone else was looking at their shrimp cocktails; the Governor was staring at a lump of white…something. "It's whale blubber, isn't it? Where did you ever get this?" She leaned forward and sniffed the mound of fat. "It *is* whale blubber, fresh whale blubber. This is impossible, how could you ever get this aboard *Hope*?

Many were standing, looking at the Governor's plate and laughing. The Governor's face was a bright red, a mixture of embarrassment and from laughing so much. She looked at me and said, "How in the world did you get this on board?"

I smiled and answered her, "Back in the mid twentieth century, there was an American Navy organization whose official name was the Construction Battalion, CB for short. They were better known as the Sea Bees. They specialized in building runways for military aircraft on remote islands in the Pacific during what was called World War II. It seemed they could build an airport almost overnight, their motto was: *The difficult we do immediately. The impossible takes a little longer.* That's all I have to say on the matter."

The evening couldn't have gone any better. The food was delicious; the Governor made everyone at the head table taste the whale blubber. Apparently, it was an acquired taste. The entertainment was outstanding; the newly formed orchestra played all kinds of music, from old time rock and roll to romantic ballads. I think Malinda and I danced to every song they played. Thank heavens for the ten-minute breaks between sets.

Towards the end of the evening, the interior lights were dimmed and curtains covering the large floor to ceiling windows looking out on the habitat were opened presenting a fantastic view of nighttime over our city. We could see the Mini Moons and the twinkling stars and even the lights from some of the residences as we slow danced to very romantic songs that almost everyone knew. Many of us were singing along to the lyrics as the last song was played.

It was a night we would always remember. It was a taste of normalcy we all needed.

First Harvest—Governor Anita Ataksak

Three months into our journey, our crops were ready for harvest. We had been living on a year's supply of stored food which had been brought aboard *Hope* just before our departure. The grains, fruits, and vegetables were harvested and made available to augment the stored food.

During the time our crops were growing to maturity, some fertile chicken eggs also reached maturity and thousands of chicks were being born. They began laying their own eggs for our consumption and additional eggs were fertilized to increase egg production.

Our crop of meat animals was the last to reach maturity however we survived nicely on the meat brought on board just before we left. Milk cows and goats were also producing adequate quantities, a portion of which was turned into milk products like cheese, yogurt and my favorite, ice cream. A pleasant change from whale blubber. I never did find out how our captain got that on board.

Once the harvest was completed, we had another party, actually, more like a gathering. This time for the ship's entire population. It was held outside in one of the recently harvested fields. It lasted two days with a big dance in the evening of the first day. It was kind of like a farmer's market with a party thrown in.

The stored food had been adequate for our needs for the first three months of our voyage and should last us for the next nine months however let's face it; nothing beats the taste of fresh fruits, vegetables and breads made from freshly harvested wheat, barley and rye.

Apparently there had also been a crop of hops which I hadn't known about and a micro-brewery turned out an excellent brew that was touted as a cross between beer and ale. They were calling it *Beale*. Very tasty! Unfortunately, we were limited to only one *Beale* per adult. They gave some lame excuse that production wasn't yet up to full capacity; they expected an unlimited supply during the next three months.

The gathering gave those of us who worked in offices most of the time a chance to get out and see the rest of *Hope*. Even the Navy was encouraged to attend and it appeared they did so in large groups.

The evening of the first day, when the Mini Suns set and the Mini Moons shined brightly, it was our equivalent of a full Earth moon. A dance floor was set up in one of the freshly harvested fields and a good old country band began tuning up. They consisted of five musicians, some of whom I recognized from the Dining In; there was a guitar player, a base player, a drummer, a banjo picker and a harmonica player who doubled on the accordion and all of them could really sing country western tunes (or so I'm told. Inuit as a nation aren't too much into country western music).

The first song was a rock-a-billy tune whose name I don't remember. Arnold pulled me out onto the dance floor and began to do something he called shuckin and jiving. Who knew he could dance to this music?

The song lasted at least five minutes and I was exhausted trying to copy all the gyrations my husband was making. We both never stopped laughing. By the end of the song, I told Arnold I needed to catch my breath.

He smiled and called me ma'am with a southern drawl and grabbed Samoa by the arm as she walked by with Tongo and began dancing with her as the band began another song. Not to be out done, I jumped up and grabbed Tongo and we headed out onto the dance floor.

My husband was wearing cowboy boots; Tongo was barefoot, wearing shorts and a sleeveless shirt which showed off his Polynesian tattoos. He normally wore his hair in what I think was called a horse tail. Tonight his hair was down around his shoulders. When the music began, he jumped up into the air and gave a shout and landed in a crouch and began slapping himself on his arms and legs. Then he stuck out his tongue at me.

I had been standing completely still, in mild shock by Tongo's antics but when he stuck his tongue out at me, I felt I had no choice. I leaned forward and stuck my tongue out at him only further, then began slapping him on the arms. He took a step back, then stepped towards me shouting something unpronounceable and slapped me on my arm.

I shouted back and we began slapping and shouting and raising our legs and stomping our feet, sticking our tongues out and wagging them at each other between shouts.

When the music ended, I noticed we were surrounded by all the dancers who were also stomping and clapping and shouting. A few were even wagging their tongues at us. I looked at my arms then at Tongo's, they were bright red form the slapping. I thought I could identify a red hand print on my upper arm.

Tongo walked up to me in the midst of the cheering crowd and gave me a huge hug as he whispered in my ear, "You may be Inuit however in your heart, you are Polynesian. Thank you for the dance, Governor."

He stepped back and took his wife's hand. I think Arnold was too embarrassed by my performance to join me.

I had no idea country western dancing could be so much fun.

The gathering ended the next day. As soon as the custodial bots had cleaned up the farmland, the agrabots began preparing the soil for the next crops. Soil preparation consisted of taking soil samples and measuring the nutrient and microorganism levels. Different crops had specific soil requirements to maximize crop yields. After every harvest, each field was evaluated and nutrient microorganism levels adjusted as required. That work was performed for each field by the agrabots. Once a field was treated, they remained dormant for at least a week to cook, an agriculture term that means the time it takes for the nutrients and microorganisms to work their way throughout the soil. Once the soil was cooked, the agrabots planted new seeds and monitored crop growth.

This process permitted harvests every four Earth-months. In addition to producing food, these crops also produced oxygen and consumed excess carbon dioxide; a part of the photosynthesis process. The tree forests also contributed to oxygen generation and carbon dioxide removal, however, harvesting trees and reforesting is not scheduled until the next generation, at least 25 years from now.

<u>Reaching Cruise Speed—Commodore Dagan</u>

It's been about six months since we left Earth and as we approached cruise speed, five percent of the speed of light (c), several changes were made in rapid succession. The first was to cut down on our thrust level. We shut down our port ion drive and reduced thrust on the starboard drive to a level that maintained a velocity of five percent c.

Some of you may be thinking we should have been able to shut down both engines and maintain cruise speed by the inertia we achieved during acceleration. If we were traveling in a complete vacuum, you would be correct. Fortunately, space is not a vacuum. It is full of all types of stuff, like atoms and molecules, microscopic specks of dust and the very occasional larger object. When traveling at our cruise speed there are a substantial amount of these particles impinging on our ship, resulting in a drag force that would slow us down and eventually stop the ship if we didn't counteract the drag force.

Another thing to consider is if these particles were permitted to hit the ship, not only would it slow the ship down, it would result in severe erosion of the ship's structure, damaging it to the point of destruction. To counteract the erosion, the ship is protected by a shield that wraps the entire ship in a protective force field which prevented any of the particles from hitting critical parts of the ship.

I know some of you were paying attention and would like to ask the obvious question: *Why did you say it was fortunate space is not a vacuum?* The answer to that question is: we need to collect a substantial amount of these particles in order to complete our mission. Which prompts the next obvious next two questions: *Why do we need space particles and how are we going to collect them?*

The answer to the first of the questions is that we used up almost all of our propulsion fluid accelerating from orbital speed to cruise speed. We don't have enough to get us to Alpha Centauri. The majority of the particles we gather will be used to replenish our propulsion fluid. A smaller percentage will help to replenish our oxygen supply for breathable air. Once we capture the particles, we can separate out the oxygen and direct it to our environmental system to make sure we have breathable air for the entire mission.

The answer to the second question is we will collect the space particles by using ram scoops. Three ram scoops are now in position and being used to capture the particles and bring them on board.

There was some risk, an acceptable level of risk, to deploy the ram scoops. We had to shut down a small portion of our shields while the scoops were being deployed. Depending on the density of the space particles we could have experienced unacceptable erosion. The good news is we were able to deploy the scoops in less than an hour and sensors revealed a very limited amount of erosion took place.

At the present time everything is working as designed. The amount of space material we are collecting is within two percent of what was estimated. We are currently processing the space material and slowly refilling our propulsion fluid tanks. Once they are filled, we will begin redirecting the oxygen molecules to the environmental system.

This was a major milestone in our mission and I'm happy to announce we passed it with flying colors. Accommodations will be awarded to the crew members who were involved with the air scoop deployment. A big *Well Done* to all involved. To show my personal appreciation, free Beale to all off-duty crew members between 1800 and 1900 hours. That is all.

First Year Annual Report—Governor Anita Ataksak

It is my pleasure to announce the birth of six new passengers who were born during the last two weeks in our Civilian Medical Center (CMC), babies and mothers are all doing well. Only 994 more needed to complete our full compliment. There's no rush since we have 99 years left for our trip. I've been informed that two Navy babies are expected soon. At the end of the month, we are planning a joint baby shower party for both civilian and Navy newborns. More information on that event to follow.

A summary of our education efforts will be given below. As a lead in I want to say we are just getting started in our schools. We have some excellent teachers who are working tirelessly to provide outstanding educations to our second generation on *Hope*. We will continue to strive to prepare everyone to carry on with *Hope's* mission.

Day Care

As of today, we have 15 preschoolers in our day care program. All of the children born on Earth have adapted well to our habitat environment.

Kindergarten through Senior High School

We have a total of 527 students in this category; 342 are in K through 6th grade. These students will definitely be part of the second generation. The junior and senior high school students are on the cusp. The older students, especially those slotted for critical positions, will be considered part of the first generation. Most of the younger students will be decided on a case-by-case basis.

I want to clarify something; there is no hard and fast law that says on a specific date the first generation ends and the second begins. We have no plans to space all of the old people of the first generation and install the second generation in their place. That would be ludicrous. We will have a gradual transition over a period of at least ten years. As long as the people of the first generation are willing and able to perform their assigned tasks, they will not be asked to step down. Some may decide to mentor their replacements for several years before they decide to fully retire.

College—Undergraduate and Graduate

Currently basic undergraduate college courses are being offered and taught by a core of certified professors. As graduate needs arise in different disciplines, we will provide one-on-one experts in the chosen fields incorporating vid course lessons as well. At the present time we have 407 undergraduate students, many of whom are taking online courses. We have 15 graduate-level students majoring in mathematics and the sciences. We also have 21 students in our medical school, looking to become medical, dental or veterinarian doctors. Each student is assigned to a practicing doctor who determines when the student is ready to practice their medical arts on their own.

Trade Schools

A number of trade schools are offered, being taught by journeymen in specific trades. Many of the students are already journeymen in one trade desiring to expand their skill sets in related trades. A total of 351 are registered in four different trades.

<u>Damage Control Report—Ensign Gerald Frakes</u>

At T+ 5 years, 3 months, 17 hours and 25.7 minutes since launch, *Hope* experienced a hull breach at 0351 hours. I was the officer of the deck (OOD) with nine minutes of my shift left before I was to be relieved. Space debris penetrated both the ship's shield and the habitat hull at 105 feet aft of Ring 3 approximately half way between Spokes 3 and 4. The debris imbedded itself in one of the unoccupied apartments on the other side of the habitat. No one was injured.

Maintenance bots were able to patch the hole in the hull without any significant loss of atmospheric pressure. The debris penetrated pasture land and two sheep were struck by it and killed. The remains of the debris have been taken to the lab for analysis. An investigation is planned as to why these particular objects were not detected in time for our defensive lasers to vaporize it prior to striking the ship. More information will follow as it becomes available.

<u>Analysis of Hull Breach—Commodore Gary Dagan</u>

I was upset. This wasn't supposed to happen and I wanted answers as to why it did. If things had worked the way they were supposed to, our advanced detection system should have identified the space junk in time for our laser cannons to vaporize it. It should never have gotten close to our shields, let alone penetrate the shields and still have enough energy to cause a hull breach and essentially destroy an apartment building. Thank God the apartment was empty, otherwise we would have lost human beings in addition to the sheep. *This cannot happen again!*

Commander Reynolds didn't look happy as he sat down across from several of the bridge officers. The commander was the leader of the Astrogation Ops group. He addressed me directly. "Captain, I have some startling and disturbing information to share with you. The space debris that struck our ship was very small, about the size of a golf ball. The extensive damage it caused to the apartment building was very unusual. It indicates that the debris was traveling at an incredible velocity. We have preliminary data that indicates when the debris hit our shield, it was traveling close to twenty percent c. That is why our detection system wasn't able to acquire the target fast enough to allow the laser cannons to vaporize it."

There was total silence in the room for several seconds, then Malinda replied in a disapproving voice, "That's impossible! This far out in deep space with no strong gravity field present to accelerate it, it should have been floating out there with very little velocity of its own. At best, the closing velocity couldn't exceed the ship's velocity of five percent c."

"That's correct, XO." Commander Reynolds replied calmly. "A spectrographic analysis of the remains of the debris revealed how this could happen. The material consisted of high-strength plastisteel. That particular alloy blend was used throughout the construction of the drones that were sent to gather data on Proxima-b. Those drones were cruising at fifty percent c and many of them failed to reach their target. We checked our data bases and discovered several of the drones were destroyed while traveling at full speed. It's been a few years since those explosions, which accounts for the degradation of speed from fifty percent c down to around fifteen percent. That would result in a closing speed of twenty percent."

When the Commander stopped speaking, the room went silent. Everyone was considering what he had just revealed. What he said seemed plausible to me. Could there be some other explanation?

I looked around the room at my staff. All I saw were blank expressions staring back at me. "So, what you are telling us is there is no way to defend against a repeat of this type of incident?" I asked.

Reynolds shrugged his shoulders and replied, "No, not really… the good news is the probability of a recurrence of this type of incident is infinitesimally small. We're talking on the order of billions-to-one odds."

"Why am I not reassured, Commander?" I asked, then turned to my staff and said, "I want our best minds working on how to prevent a similar attack. Reconvene in one week."

<u>Follow-up Meeting–Commodore Gary Dagan</u>

The night before our meeting, I had a nightmare. I dreamt I was on board the Sky One Habitat, peacefully orbiting Earth. It was early evening and Sky One's artificial moons were shining brightly in the night sky. Malinda and I were sitting on our veranda enjoying a drink before retiring for the evening. The air was cool and the slight breeze was chilling. Melinda pulled her sweater around her shoulders. It was simulated late autumn and the foliage in the forest was already turning shades of red and yellow. We were planning our trip through the garden forest the next day.

Suddenly, a shudder went through our apartment following by the shriek of metal being ripped apart. We were both petrified by fear as we felt the wind beginning to blow faster as it spilled out through a huge tear in Sky One's hull. We were caught up in the gale force wind, pulled from our veranda and sucked toward the gaping hole in the far end of the habitat. I could see the stars, the real stars, as our atmosphere rushed out into space carrying us and all the people on Sky One to our deaths. I attempted to scream but the air was too thin. The last thing I remember, was my body exploding as it entered the vacuum of space.

I was screaming as I woke with a start, attempting to gulp deep breaths of air into my lungs. Malinda had been shaking my arm attempting to wake me. Slowly, I sat up on the edge of the bed trembling; Malinda got up and turned on a small lamp and went into the bathroom. I looked at the chrono above the bed and it read 0217 hours. She handed me a glass of water and told me to sip it and sat beside me, putting her arm around my shoulder to comfort me.

"Was that a nightmare or a leg cramp? I've never heard you scream like that before. Are you alright?" she asked.

I nodded my head, the nightmare beginning to fade. "I dreamt we were on Sky One when it was destroyed. We got sucked out into space and exploded. We went from sitting on our balcony having a drink to dying excruciating deaths in about thirty seconds." I paused as I began to return to normal. "Sorry I scared you."

I took another sip as she rubbed my back and asked, "Do you remember what you were screaming?"

I turned to look at her. "I was talking? I thought I was just screaming."

She shook her head. "No, I heard you very clearly. You were screaming 'more gravity, more gravity,' over and over until you woke up. Have any idea what that means?"

I shook my head. "No, I feel exhausted. I want to go back to sleep. I'll sleep on it and see if it makes more sense in the morning."

I crawled back into bed, gave Malinda a hug and a kiss on the cheek and was asleep in less than a minute.

When I woke up the next morning, I had no idea why I had been shouting 'more gravity!' In the back of my mind, I had the feeling it was important. I was looking forward to seeing what my officers had come up with.

We reconvened in the conference room adjacent to the bridge at 0900 hours. Commander Reynolds led the presentation. Several suggestions seemed promising however the technical experts who were also invited kept shaking their heads and gave very good reasons why those approaches wouldn't work. After thirty minutes we ran out of ideas.

Suddenly, I had the beginning of an idea. I'm no expert when it comes to shields however I wanted to see if I could expand on my idea.

"Commander Reynolds, did our surveillance equipment ever detect the debris from the drone?"

"Yes sir, it did," he answered. "We acquired the target 1.2 seconds before it struck the ship. Unfortunately, that was insufficient time for the laser cannons to take a shot."

"How much time does it take for the lasers to find a target and take their shot?"

He looked at one of the officers who was responsible for ship defense. "At least twice that amount of time, with no guarantee of a hit on target. To get a guarantee kill shot would take more like 5 seconds."

"I see, thank you. Commander how much increase in our shield strength would it have taken to deflect the debris?"

He looked at the contractor who was involved with the design of the shields. The contractor said, "Give me a minute to determine that, please." He began rapidly feeding numbers into his com unit. Two minutes later, he said, "It would have taken ten times more repulsive power in the shields to deflect that debris. The power requirements would be astronomical. We'd have to shunt almost all of the fusion power to the shields at the expense of all the other power needs."

"Thank you. Let me ask you another question. Would it be possible to ramp up the shields to ten times the standard repulsive power within less than a second?"

The man spoke into his com again and replied, "We could do it in about half a second."

"If we were to spike the repulsive power to ten times normal, then chop the power back to the standard level how long would it take for the repulsive power to return to standard?" I asked.

There was an audible beep and he looked at his display. A smile began to spread across his face as he said, "Even with the power at normal setting, the shield strength would decay slowly, from ten to fifteen seconds."

"Can we connect the computer control system to automatically spike the shield strength to ten times normal, then do a reversed spike of the power to normal without blowing out our power sources or cause any of our essential systems to drop off line?"

The man's smile turned into a huge grin as he said, "Yes sir, I believe we can make that happen."

There was spontaneous cheering from everyone in the conference room. When it subsided to a dull roar, I asked, "How soon can we set this up and test it?"

Commander Reynolds replied to my question. "We will begin working on this right away. It should be relatively simple to connect our detection system to the shield system." He looked at his men and asked, "How quickly can we test out the captain's elegant solution to our problem?"

The answer was a week to ten days. I gave the order and dismissed the group. Commander Reynolds and Malinda were the last to leave. The Commander paused at the doorway, turned back to me and asked. "How did you come up with such a simple solution to a very difficult problem?"

With a straight face, I answered, "It came to me in a vision."

Malinda snorted and said, "As I recall it was more like a nightmare but hey, whatever works."

Two weeks later we had our shields upgraded and operational. Five years later we were able to see it in action when another piece of drone was deflected off our shields back into space without so much as a scratch to *Hope's* hull. So much for the billions-to-one odds!

Beginning of the End-- Lieutenant Alicia Legleu

I began my Navy career aboard *Hope*. I graduated second in my class at the Space Academy nine years ago and received my commission as an Ensign in the Navy. It was recommended I apply for one of the generation ships by a UPNA Senator who was also a retired Navy Admiral. It turns out he and Vice Admiral Amanda Jackson had been classmates at the Academy.

The Senator (who shall remain nameless) told me in no uncertain terms his recommendation wouldn't guarantee my selection however he felt confident with my performance at the Academy and the military background of my family, there was a good chance I would be selected.

I had six bothers, all older than me, all of whom had served in one military branch or another and most had been involved in combat. I had lost one brother to war the others had survived. Eventually most of them passed away by one natural disaster or another. My father had served and survived his war unfortunately he and my mother were also lost. They were killed in a flashflood of the Santa Cruz river of unheard-of proportions near the New Arizona/Sonora border while I was at the Academy. My only living relative was my retired brother, Colonel Pedro Legleu.

Pedro enthusiastically recommended I apply. Based on his and the Senator's recommendation, I applied to both *Faith* and *Hope*. I was chosen by *Hope* and never looked back. I lost Pedro to prostate cancer before I left for training aboard the ship.

As an Ensign, my duties as a communication officer were to make sure all forms of coms from or to *Hope* were received. Due to privacy rules, I wasn't permitted to view any of the messages, either personal or official ship coms. This wasn't a problem for me, because while we were in Earth orbit there were so many transmissions, my main concern was having sufficient band width to accommodate all the com traffic. Fortunately, the work load was divided between five other crewmen: another Ensign, a Chief Warrant Officer and three

First Class Petty Officers. While in orbit, the vid coms were always live, with only the slightest of lags as the ship moved around the Earth. Of course, we used comsats to relay messages when we were out of line-of-sight with the parties involved; essentially it was just like vid comming from someone across town or the world.

After we left orbit and got further away from Earth, things changed. We could no longer do live coms. We had to record our messages, queue them up, then send burst transmissions to Earth where they were downloaded, decrypted when necessary and finally routed to the designated recipient. Between my training onboard *Hope* and the time it took to transition to burst communications, almost two years had elapsed. Just before the transition, I was promoted to Lieutenant JG (Junior Grade).

It took time for some of our users to understand the process for preparing a burst transmission. Training classes were set up for those having difficulties. The most often asked question was: "How long will it take to get a reply to my message?" Of course, the answer to that question depended on how far we were from Earth and would change as time went on. After five years of travel, it took about two months for a message from *Hope* to reach Earth and depending on how quickly the receiving party returned the message, it would take more than two months to receive a reply because the ship was continuously moving farther away from our home planet. At five years from Earth, you could expect around five months from when your message was sent until you received a reply. It will only get worse as we continue our mission. When we are half way to Alpha Centauri, it will take four years for a round trip message, eight years once we arrive at our destination.

I know it sounds ridiculous however our coms are limited by the speed of light, at least they are now. Maybe someday, some brilliant scientist or engineer will invent a way to bypass this barrier unfortunately in our present situation we are limited to the speed of light.

At seven years after we left Earth orbit, I was promoted to full Lieutenant with five people reporting to me. I was given a security clearance of Secret.

That entitled me to be read into certain decrypted coms. Once a week, the captain called a meeting of all those who needed to know what was considered not to be made known by the rest of the ship, at least at the present time.

For the most part, it was pretty boring. I wasn't sure why most of it was even classified. Far be it from me to complain; they served taquitos for snacks during the meetings; the best I had ever had since leaving my home in Nogales.

Everything was going smoothly aboard *Hope* for the next couple of years. Based on the reports I saw regarding the ship's performance, everything was nominal. This included the civilian world as well. Schools were now full of students at every level, food production was operating above nominal and our food storage area was almost full, which permitted us to leave several fields fallow for a season. Recreation turn-out was at an all-time high with both individual and team sports running at capacity with waiting lists. It wasn't utopia by any means however there certainly was no poverty in sight.

Then, in our last security meeting, the other shoe fell. The news from Earth wasn't good. The natural disasters had started up again. The most concerning of all was a new disease, a fatal airborne virus was discovered somewhere in the Asian Countries. Some reports said it was discovered in Mongolia, others in Nepal. There had been no communications originating from within those two provinces for a few days. The boarders to all neighboring provinces were sealed until further notice. The International Health Organization (IHO) was planning to send out teams to inspect tomorrow. That message was almost five months old when it reached *Hope*. Captain Dagan ordered none of this information was to be shared with the ship's personnel until he personally approved it for release.

From then on, the security council held a meeting every day. I was responsible for decrypting and presenting the latest new reports to the group. By our next meeting, both Dr. Van Der Geist, the leader of the civilian contractors, and Governor Ataksak were both given Secret clearances.

The news reports received the following day showed a vid from a drone aircraft flying over Kathmandu, the capitol of Nepal. The vids were horrifying to watch. Every scene showed literally thousands of people dead in the streets.

Drones landed and bots were deployed to enter the buildings to search for survivors. There were none. An entire city of over a million people had died within a 48-hour period.

Everyone in the conference room sat quietly, shocked at what they had just seen. Tears were running down the faces of many of us, myself included. I had seen the vids as I decrypted the feeds and I cried then. I cried again in the conference room along with the others. I cried every time I watched it. Over the next few days, I watched it as other cities in the Asian Countries fell to what was being called The Plague. It appeared the extinction event had descended upon the Earth. God save us.

However that didn't happen. Over the next few months, The Plague spread rapidly. Despite mankind's best efforts, The Plague touched everywhere mankind lived. As we moved into the tenth year of our journey, the vids from Earth ceased. The last one we saw, was from a man sitting at his news desk somewhere in Mid America. He was sick, deathly sick but he managed to say the following: "To all of you on the generation ships bound for Proxima-b, you are mankind's last hope for existence. Here on Earth, God's finger of death has touched us all, saved and sinner alike. I pray you are safe from his wrath. God speed to you all." With those final words he breathed his last breath and pitched forward onto his desk.

We continued to stare blankly at the vid screen; some of us sobbing, others sitting staring at the man's corpse, their faces frozen in shock. I don't know how long we sat there. After what seemed like an eternity, our captain broke the silence.

"This meeting is adjourned, please return to your rooms without speaking to anyone. We will put together an announcement to present to all the ship's personnel within 24 hours." His voice was so firm and soothing. I couldn't imagine where his strength came from. All I knew is he was exactly the right man to see us through the beginning of this mission.

The Announcement—Commodore Gary Dagan

An all-hands notice was broadcast throughout the ship the day before we were to make the announcement. At 0900 hours the next day we broadcast my message on all vid screens. It was done live. The ship was placed on autopilot for the short time it would take to notify everyone as to what had happened on Earth and what we were going to do moving forward.

The XO and a few key crew members who had viewed the vid of the last transmission from Earth volunteered to also be on the bridge with Malinda.

Governor Ataksak and I were seated in the conference room facing a vid com recorder. Promptly at 0900 hours a chime sounded and I began.

"Ladies and Gentleman, We come to you today with heavy hearts. Yesterday we received a transmission from Earth that I will share with you shortly however we feel the need to prepare you for what you will see.

"A pandemic has spread across the Earth in what is called an extinction event. It has ravaged every country in our world. Because of our distance from Earth, what we saw in the last transmission happened over five months ago on Earth. It took that long for the message to reach us.

"I'm sure many of you have received vid coms from family and friends regarding The Plague. It is not our policy to censor coms for any reason. Several weeks ago, messages from Earth stopped being sent or received. We did receive messages from the Admiralty unfortunately there was so much contradictory information, we decided it was best to wait until we were sure of what was happening before sharing with you. Now we are sure. Civilization on Earth has ended."

At that point we played the last vid com from Earth. When it was finished and the picture of the news man lying dead on his desk faded to black, I continued, "As most of you know, I believe there is a

God, our creator and sustainer. In every instance He unleashed his wrath on unbelievers or unrepentant sinners, -He always left a few, a remnant to begin again. Take Noah for example; the Bible says that God destroyed every living thing that walked the face of the Earth except for eight people, four men and four women. From those eight people the population of the Earth has soared to over ten billion souls. From time to time there have been tragedies, like wars and plagues that have killed so many of us but we as a race have always survived. I believe human kind will also survive this tragedy, this plague, as well."

Tears began running down my checks, I didn't wipe them away. "*Hope* and our sister ship *Faith* were apply named. For we must have faith in our creator that He will again provide a remnant. We hope those of us on the generation ships will start a colony on a new world where human kind will flourish.

"When our ships return to Earth, almost two hundred years from now, I believe we will find another remnant. Our descendants will join with Earth survivors to rebuild another civilization.

"I want to leave you with this thought, human kind will prevail, our ship will survive and so will our people. May God bless us all."

I turned to Governor Ataksak and she presented information regarding the memorial services we would be holding the next day. She also presented information regarding grief counseling for any and all who felt they would benefit from it. Malinda and I were at the top of that list.

<u>Mourning Our Children—Samoa</u>

We knew when we boarded *Hope* we would never be with our children again. Of course, we would stay in contact and we cherished our time together over the vid com. However, it wasn't the same as being able to touch them again, to hold my grandchildren in my arms, to smell their sweetness and be able to kiss their cheeks.

When it seemed the natural disasters were subsiding, most people thought things were returning to normal. There was even talk about canceling the construction of the generation ships. Many felt the money for constructing the ships could be better spent rebuilding Earth's infrastructure. Others stood firm in the belief we were just experiencing a brief respite from the natural disasters. Their position was Mother Nature was only pausing to take a deep breath before unleashing another round of chaos.

Still others felt we had almost completed construction of the ships. The funding for the projects was already mostly spent. We should finish what we started just in case the disasters resumed or another event that we couldn't imagine yet might occur. Of course, if they didn't resume, we would then start rebuilding no matter what was decided about the generation ships.

The latter position prevailed and both ships being constructed in the United Provinces of North America were launched on their missions to Proxima-b.

I believed most people on Earth truly believed the disasters were a thing of the past. So-called experts presented theories which, in their opinion, proved the devastation was caused by the tectonic plates shifting to reduce the tremendous stress they had been under. The earthquakes, volcanoes, violent weather and diseases that followed all occurred as a result of the plate adjustment. Now that the adjustments had been made, we had nothing to worry about for thousands of years. It sounded reasonable, perhaps even logical. Unfortunately, it wasn't true.

We started getting indications things were going bad again several months ago. They were experiencing tremors in the Polynesian provinces. A few weeks later our son reported smoke was seen rising out of the supposedly dormant Olotele volcano. They were considering relocating to the other side of the island just in case things got worse.

When we asked about The Plague, they said as far as they knew, there were no cases reported on Samoa. Two days later, in their next message, they said several people in their neighborhood had died from The Plague and they were evacuating everyone to a 'safe place.

Their message was garbled but I could tell they were frightened. They were being ushered out of their home by people dressed in hazmat suits. Our son managed to choke out a short message, "We all love you, Mom and Dad but this looks like the end. Pray for us."

It was the last time we heard from them. Tongo and I replayed the message over and over. We paused the vid com so we could see it in more detail. They were dying, all of them, the children too. They had the same look as the news reporter just before he died.

Tongo and I were inconsolable. I wanted to pray to God they would survive. Tongo reminded me gently their vid com was months old. They were already gone.

Parents aren't supposed to outlive their children. It's just not right. I couldn't live with the anguish I was feeling. I wanted to kill myself so I could be with them. I had to be sedated and put on suicide watch. Poor, poor Tongo. He had to handle his own grief from the death of our children as well as take care of his crazy wife. I will always love him for his strength. I knew how much pain I must have caused him.

It took months before I could be taken off the meds. Tongo was with me the whole time. Without him, I wouldn't have survived. It took that long for me to realize how selfish I was. I wasn't the only one on *Hope* who had similar problems. Unfortunately, their grief had led to rebellion.

<u>Riots–Security Chief Lieutenant Greg Donaldson</u>

A substantial number of the ship's personnel, both Navy and civilian, demanded that we return to Earth. They felt we needed to support those who survived The Plague. Their demand was met with a resounding **No.**

Both Captain Dagan and Governor Ataksak were adamant *Hope* would continue its voyage to Proxima-b and complete its mission of establishing a colony. They gave the following reasons for their decision:

- The vid com message we received from the news feed was more than five months old. Based on news reports, most of Earth's population had already died from The Plague.
- Even in the event of there being a substantial number of survivors, our medical personnel, as good as they are, weren't trained to find a cure for The Plague. The experts on Earth weren't able to find a cure; it is doubtful we could be of any help.
- We were sent on this mission specifically to preserve human life in the event of such an extinction event. If we returned, it is very likely we would also die from The Plague and the human race would cease to exist.

Their comments seemed to appease most of the ship's personnel...however not all of them. All of the Navy crew who had protested recanted. Several were having a very difficult time grieving and were placed on medical leave. All of them returned to duty within a month. Unfortunately, a substantial number of the civilians took another approach; they began rioting. They attempted to destroy or at least damage, critical parts of the ship, thinking it would result in the ship having to return to Earth for repairs.

The rioting lasted two nights and some damage was reported. None of the damage was done to any of the critical parts. However, our microbrewery was burned to the ground.

A fire on a ship, any ship, can be disastrous; on a spaceship it can be deadly. Our oxygen supply is limited and a fire consumes oxygen at an incredible rate. On *Hope*, we have the ability to enrich our atmospheric oxygen from what we capture with our ram scoops however if the fire had been allowed to spread, the ram scooped oxygen wouldn't have been enough to ensure the needed oxygen content in the ship's atmosphere.

Our first duty was to put out the fire. We used bots and drones to attack the fire and some of my security team were also called to assist.

Three of the rioters attacked two of my troops and began beating them unmercifully. When one of them attempted to escape, one of the rioters turned the torch he had used to start the microbrewery fire on the escaping crew member, burning her to death. The other Navy crewmember was beaten into unconsciousness by the other two attackers before we could get help to him. He died on the way to the infirmary.

All three attackers were apprehended by troops from my security team and placed in the brig to await the captain's pleasure (or in this case, his extreme displeasure).

The Court Martial—Captain Gary Dagan

A tribunal of Governor Ataksak, my XO, Commodore Malinda Dagan and myself, sat in judgment of the three rioters who had been charged with killing two Navy personnel. It was vid comm'd live to the entire ship.

A security team of three men and three women escorted the rioters, each charged with two counts of murder. They were seated at separate tables facing the tribunal and shackled to a large eye bolt in the center of each table.

Before I could make my opening comments, the rioter at the middle table spoke up, "Hey! Where is our lawyer? I know my rights and I'm entitled to be represented by a lawyer."

I stared at him for a second. He had an arrogant, defiant expression on his face. There was no remorse for starting the fire or killing two human beings. I spoke to one of his security guards, "If this man speaks out again without being asked a question first, gag him." I glanced at the other security guards. "The same goes for the other two."

The middle rioter jumped up and started to protest before he was slammed back into his chair by both of his security guards and a gag was put securely over his mouth. The other two rioters had watched dumbfounded then turned away and sat quietly.

I sat and stared at each one of them in turn. The one in the middle glared at me with a look of rage burning in him. The other two didn't meet my gaze; they sat with downcast eyes.

"Let me be very clear about what is happening here. This is a court martial, not a trial. As captain of this ship, I alone have the authority to decide the fate of everyone on board *Hope,* both military and civilian. This has been the standard for every ship that has sailed the seas and also for those spaceships that travel between planets."

I turned to the governor and said, "Governor Ataksak, would you confirm what I just said to the prisoners?"

She nodded and turned to the prisoners and said, "The captain of this ship has full legal authority over everyone on *Hope.* He decides if you are entitled to have a lawyer or to have a jury to decide your fate. He is within his rights to choose your fate all by himself. In this case he has opted for a Tribunal. We three will decide your fate after the evidence is made public. Nod if you understand what I have just said."

Two of the prisoners nodded, the gagged one just sat glaring at me. We stared back. After a few minutes he gave the slightest of nods.

Evidence was presented. There was vid cam coverage of every move the three prisoners had made from starting the fire, the beating to death of one security officer to the burning of the other security officer. It also included the capture of the three prisoners. From start to finish everything was recorded. There was no possible doubt as to what happened that night and who was responsible. It took roughly twenty minutes to review the data from several different vid cams.

"We are done examining the evidence," I said. "The Tribunal will now decide your fate." All three of us voted guilty. The next vote was to determine the punishment.

The XO said, "I believe the punishment should fit the crime. I would like to see him," she gestured to the middle prisoner, "burned to death. The other two beaten to death by security guards."

I noticed the Governor nodded her head in agreement. A shiver ran through me at the thought. I agreed with them in principle however I couldn't agree with them in reality. "I believe the punishment should fit the crime, and in this case, I also vote for the death penalty." I paused and stared at each one of them as I added, "We are not the animals you have become. However we can't tolerate your behavior. Regardless of how appealing it might be for the prisoners to experience the agony of the deaths they visited upon our security people, I rule all three of them to be spaced, ejected from our ship without a pressure suit. May God have mercy on your souls. There will be no mercy from me. Security teams, please escort the prisoners to the hatch for execution."

It was a short walk from the Court Martial chamber to the exterior hatch room. All three men were thrown into the hatch at the same time. The hatch was sealed behind them. As the captain of the ship, I could have delegated the task of opening the outer door which would suck them out into the vacuum of space. However, I felt it was my responsibility. I knew vid cams were trained on me as I approached the control panel. Vid cams were also trained on the three murderers. It was necessary to record the execution so there were no doubts that justice had been done. I pressed the button and the outer door slid smoothly back. The three men shot out into space, one tried to grab the door frame but to no avail. They all died within a few seconds.

I returned to our quarters to find Malinda waiting for me. She was crying and I discovered I was too. We hugged each other tightly. Sometimes it's a real bitch to be in charge. This was certainly one of those times.

The Next Ten Years—Commodore Gary Dagan

It took a considerable amount of time for the people of *Hope* to get back to normal. Some never made it. The loss of the two security team members and the execution of their murderers were the first deaths aboard the ship. During the first few months afterwards, we had five suicides. Their ages varied from people in their early twenties who couldn't deal with the deaths of their parents back on Earth, to those in their later years who couldn't deal with the death of their children. We've had two additional suicides during the last ten years and seven attempted suicides. That's the bad news.

The good news is; there's lots of good news. The fact there haven't been any further riots is at the top of the list, right along with the ship's performance. *Hope* has been operating efficiently for twenty years. Shield strength hasn't diminished, ion drive performance has been maintained. We have two ion drive units and once we attained our cruise velocity, we were able to shut down one drive unit and operate on a single unit at a reduced thrust to maintain our desired cruise speed. We switched drive units on an annual basis to maintain the same operational times on both drives. We examined each drive when it shut down and no potential problems were noted. We will continue this procedure throughout our voyage until we begin our braking maneuver and begin orbiting Proxima-b.

Astrogation reports that the Alpha Centauri cluster is still where it should be and we are on course with an ETA of eighty years.

Our ram scoops are working perfectly so far. The oxygen content of the scooped material has been higher than estimated which has resulted in a twenty percent excess in our oxygen supply. We have a similar excess in our propulsion fluid supply.

Hope's population has grown to 4,500 during our twenty years in space. It is estimated we will reach full capacity in the middle of the second generation.

Habitat City, the name chosen for our town during a recent contest, is thriving and I'm happy to report the microbrewery was rebuilt and we have an unlimited supply of Beale.

Stepping Down—Commodore Gary Dagan

I received an encrypted, classified vid com from Vice Admiral Amanda Jackson eight years into our voyage. It was classified Top Secret-Your Eyes Only. I told my XO she had the com and immediately went to my ready room, just aft of the bridge, locking the door behind me. It was orders for me from the Admiral. I read it through three times then placed it in my safe and locked it away until a few days ago.

Paraphrasing the Admiral's orders, it said when we were 25 years from Earth, I was to be promoted to Rear Admiral and step down as captain of *Hope.* I was to become an unofficial aide to Malinda. In addition, I was going to begin evaluating our crew to determine who should become the ship's leaders when Malinda and the other original crew still on the job stepped down.

Malinda was to be promoted to Commodore and become captain of *Hope* for five additional years. Then she was to be promoted to Rear Admiral and we were both required to become mentors for the new Navy personnel that would become responsible for the operation of the ship. Once Malinda had stepped down, Generation 1 was officially over and Generation 2 had begun.

I wasn't to share this information with anyone, including Malinda, until I had reached my 25th anniversary as *Hope's* captain. At that time, only she was to be read in and she would assume command. Her first order of business would be for her to select her XO (with my assistance, of course).

When my 25th anniversary arrived, I called Malinda into my ready room and showed her Vice Admiral Jackson's orders. At first, her eyes grew wide then as she continued to read, tears formed in the corner of her eyes. When she had finished reading, she looked at me with a wistful smile then grabbed me in a bear hug that took my breath away. When she released her grip and stepped back, she said, "I never thought I would say this but here goes. I love you Rear Admiral."

Then she grabbed me again, this time without further damage to my spine and kissed me like when we were much younger. It brought back fond memories to us both.

We sat at the ready room conference table and discussed who we thought would make a good XO for her. We both agreed we needed to lock someone in before we announced our promotions and her advancement to captain.

We narrowed it down to two candidates: Marine Lt. Col. Jason Kuhn, Leader of Flight Operations and Commander Priscilla Hoyt, Leader of Propulsion Systems. Before we made any decisions, we needed to be sure there were strong candidates within their respective groups to consider as their replacements. We did a quick search of our personnel database and both of us came to the same conclusion, each leader had several strong candidates who could take over the leader roles.

Then we came to a stumbling block. Malinda wanted Commander Hoyt as her XO. I favored Lt Col. Kuhn. We kicked around the reasons for our preferences. In the final analysis, it was her decision as the new ship's captain.

We invited Commander Hoyt into our ready room, read her into the Vice Admiral's orders and told her she was being considered for the new XO position. We thought she would jump at the opportunity; we were very surprised when she rejected our offer.

"I'm sorry," she said. "I can't thank you enough for considering me for the position however I'm a propulsion specialist, more specifically an EM ion drive specialist. I am so thankful to have this job and I consider it the highlight of my career. I have no aspirations to move beyond what I am currently doing."

She paused for a moment, then said, "I hope you won't think of me as arrogant but I would recommend you consider Lt. Col. Kuhn for the position. He's been on the bridge and had the opportunity to observe you two in action every day. I'm sure he's very well qualified for XO."

I noticed Malinda turning her head slowly toward me. I quickly began looking around the room at anything except her. After a brief moment, she turned back toward Commander Hoyt and said, "Thank you for your comments, Pris. Also, for your recommendation of Jason. This conversation with you is considered privileged information and shouldn't be discussed with anyone. Do you understand?"

"Yes Captain, Commodore." She stood, saluted us both and left the ready room.

We called in Lt. Col. Kuhn and made him the XO offer. Without hesitation he accepted. We asked him to give us at least two names of people from his group whom we could considered for his replacement as Flight Ops Leader. He said he would have it within the hour.

At 0800 hours the next day, we made our announcements. A promotion party was planned for that evening at 1930 hours in the crew's mess hall. The Governor and her council were also invited.

At 1300 hours we discovered an oversight; we forgot to stock the insignias for promotions. Fortunately, our Information System Leader said we could fabricate the shoulder bars and stars required for both Rear Admiral and Commodore and any other insignia we might need in the future. A program was sent to one of our 3-D printers and in practically no time at all, our stars and bars were ready for the party.

At 1915 hours, the reception line formed just inside the double doors leading to the crew's mess hall. Promotion parties were always formal. It was a tradition I looked forward to, especially this one since I realized it would be my last.

The reception line began with the lowest rank first, then worked its way to the highest rank, that would be me. There were three civilians in the line, Dr. Van Der Geist, the leader of our contractors assigned to the Navy, Dr. MacGregor, Leader of our Power System group and Governor Ataksak. We took our places and chatted briefly. At exactly 1930 hours, the doors to the crew's mess swung open and the party began.

Military parties have a protocol that is usually followed to the minute: 10 minutes for introductions, 15 minutes for cocktails and *hors d'oeuvres,* 45 minutes for dinner, including toasts, 20 minutes for awards, announcements and vids, 60 minutes for music, dancing and socializing. Each part of the party is announced by a chime or soft tone.

When the first tone sounded, the reception line dissolved and servers emerged from the galley bringing trays of snacks and flutes of champagne. Malinda and I mingled with as many of the attendees as possible during the fifteen minutes, then took our seat at the head table once the second chime sounded. I was seated at the middle of the table with Malinda on my left, on my right was Governor Ataksak and on her right was her husband, Arnold. Just before dinner was served, Anita leaned over and whispered in my ear, "There better not be any whale blubber at this dinner. Once was hysterical, a second time would be really embarrassing."

I stifled a laugh and turned to her. "I promise, there is no more whale blubber on the ship, unless you smuggled some aboard." Changing the subject I said, "I am so looking forward to seeing you and Tongo dancing again."

She managed to mostly suppress a giggle, then hit me in the arm playfully. She must have hit me in a nerve because my entire arm went numb. Her husband shook his head and began scolding her in a language I couldn't understand. Apparently, her love tap was intended to momentarily paralyze my arm. This woman was just full of surprises.

Dinner was wonderful, the toasts were also very well done. Dr. Judy Van Der Geist gave her toast in Dutch. Not be out done, Dr. Cullum MacGregor, dressed in his most formal kilt, made his toast in Gaelic, the language of his native Scotland.

When dinner ended, the people from the head table stood and walked to the rostrum behind them. It was another tradition to take pictures of the senior officers and leaders of any ship. *Hope* would follow that tradition and this was the first of many still-vids that would be made of all six generations of *Hope's* crews. These pictures would be hung in chronological order in the hallway behind the bridge, leading to the large conference room.

Once the still-vids were taken, everyone left the rostrum except Malinda, Jason Kuhn and myself. Governor Ataksak approached the rostrum with three boxes in her hand. She turned to face the audience and said, "If anyone has ever earned a promotion, it is these two, fine people. They have led us on this great quest that we are on to save the human race. Anyone can be a decent leader when times are good. it takes great skill and compassion to get through hard times. I don't have to tell you about our hard times, we lived through them. Without their leadership, their dedication to our mission, without them setting the example for all of us to follow, we may not have survived to this day.

"I am so happy to be allowed to be part of their promotion. Lt. Col. Jason Kuhn, please step forward." Jason stepped forward with his wife. The Governor handed the box to Malinda who removed two silver eagles from the box and handed one to his wife. As the two women removed the silver oak leaves from his shoulder boards and began attaching the eagles, I recited the following, "Lt. Col Kuhn, for exemplary performance in your duties as the Leader of Flight Control and your time in rank you are here by promoted to full colonel. In addition, you are assigned as the new executive officer of *Hope*." There was polite applause and his wife gave the XO a kiss as they stepped down off the rostrum.

The Governor opened the second box and took out two silver stars. She gave one to me and kept one for herself. I spoke up again. "Captain Malinda Dagan, for exemplary performance in your duties as Executive Officer and your time in rank you are here by promoted to the rank of Commodore and appointed Captain of the generation starship *Hope*." The Governor and I removed the silver eagles from her shoulder boards and replaced them with a silver star on each shoulder. I then took the liberty of kissing my wife as the audience stood and applauded loudly for the new commander of the ship.

The Governor opened the last box and removed the two double stars form the box. She kept one and the new captain took the other. They removed the single silver stars from each shoulder board and the Governor turned to the audience and said in a firm voice, "Commodore Gary Dagan, for exemplary performance in your duties as captain of this ship and for your time in rank as commodore you are hereby promoted to Rear Admiral. In your new assignment you will be responsible for preparing the crew for the second generation and ensuring a smooth transition. We all thank you for your outstanding performance in making an idea into a reality. We are all blessed to have had you as *Hope's* first captain."

The applause was thunderous and lasted for several minutes. When it had subsided, I faced the audience and looked out over all the smiling faces, then began. "Thank you for the applause. This has been a dream assignment for me and my wife as well. I thought I understood what I was getting into when I accepted the assignment however I really had no idea what would be involved. In the normal military you get assignments that lasts four to eight years; no assignment I have ever heard of lasted 25 years. The only way I survived this tour is by having the very best crew in the entire world, working together for the common goal. And not just any goal; the most incredible goal anyone could ever imagine: the first ever starship traveling for a hundred years to establish a colony on another planet. When I first looked at the mission goals, I thought someone had slipped me a science fiction novel. Now we all know it's a reality.

"The army of scientists and engineers who transformed the dream into a reality should be congratulated for their awesome effort in overcoming every roadblock that came up threatening the mission's success. Dr Judy Van Der Geist was indispensable in bringing all the elements of the design and turning them into this incredible generation ship.

"Before that could happen, we had to have champions to sell the idea to those that held the purse strings. The two people who made that happen are here with us today continuing to support our efforts in meeting mission requirements, Without Samoa and Tongo, both secretary generals of the Alliance of World Nations, convincing our world governments that for the sake of preserving the human race these ships were our only option, an idea would have remained a dream, never a reality.

"Would you three join us on the rostrum? Bear with me please, I'm almost finished."

Judy, Samoa and Tongo walked to the rostrum as I finished.

"I want to thank all of you. Each one of you has sacrificed to be here and have contributed so much of your lives to our mission. We still have a long way to go however I am confident those who come afterwards, those we teach and prepare, will complete our mission. Mankind will not perish because all of us will have the same vision, the same drive to survive."

I stopped for a beat and looked at all the faces. I saw their determination, their belief in success and their hope.

"May God bless us, everyone."

Five Years—Commodore Malinda Dagan

The last five years seemed to fly by. I was busier than ever. I had been a ship's captain before and knew what to expect. The main difference between being a ship's XO and her captain is responsibility. Both positions require you to be ready for anything at all hours of the day or night. However, all good captains train their XO to become good captains. They don't just assign them crummy tasks to keep them busy.

Fortunately, my captain, also my husband, was an excellent captain. I had also been a captain but gave up my command to be my husband's XO. Why would I do that, you may wonder. The answer is that once I became captain on another ship, we never saw each other. For the three years I was a captain, we only communicated by burst vid coms and even that was rare. Our ships were on different ship-times. When I was sleeping, he was on duty and vice versa.

A very unique situation occurred shortly after my three years as a captain. My XO was due for promotion to captain, he was very well qualified. Unfortunately for him, no captain slots were available. My husband had an XO who decided to retire. He was in his late sixties with a medical condition and wasn't interested in becoming a commander of a ship. I saw a remote possibility and decided to run it by my husband. He was very enthused with my plan

I submitted my recommendations to the Admiralty that my XO take command of my ship and when my husband's XO retired, I would transfer to his ship as his XO. I knew it was a long shot however my husband had some friends in the Admiralty and he unofficially ran it by them.

To our great surprise and joy, it was approved. Two months later, I transferred aboard his ship and became his XO for five years before he applied to be the commander of *Hope*. And as they say, the rest is history. One last comment; to my knowledge, we were the only husband and wife team to serve as Captain and XO aboard the same ship. And we did it not once but twice.

Once the transition had been made, Rear Admiral Dagan (I love the sound of that) immersed himself planning the move from our present group to those who would eventually replace us. The goal was to make it seamless, with the best qualified people moving into the most critical positions. Most people consider the next generation begins when the serving captain stands down and their replacement assumes command, however it's not that cut and dried. Those who hold other key positions may take up to ten years before they step down or they may step down several years before the new captain takes command. As long as a person is performing well and wants to stay they can stay.

This required numerous meetings with all the system leaders. He also met with the Governor and her staff to brainstorm the best approach for advancing the civilian population. It seemed he was busier with this new assignment than he was when he was *Hope's* captain.

During my time as *Hope's* captain, I had it pretty easy. Everyone knew their jobs and performed at a high level. The new XO was working out well. He was very smart and knew the ship from stem to stern (and old Navy term). He wasn't afraid to ask me questions when confronted by something new. I'm a little embarrassed to say that sometimes I didn't have the answer however I knew where to find them. The Rear Admiral was quick to help us both out.

During my command, several of our more elderly passengers passed away. When people first came aboard *Hope*, several were in their late fifties or early sixties. Thirty years later, they were in late eighties or early nineties. The health care aboard *Hope* was as good as it could get, including hospice care. We had trained personnel to assist those who needed help, both in their apartments or in our hospice clinics. They aided in whatever capacity that was needed. Eventually the end came.

Almost all of those who passed on were civilians. When someone was approaching the end, they were given two options as to how to deal with their remains; either cremation or ejection into space in what was called a coffin tube. We didn't have any provisions for burial. All our land area was used to grow crops and raise animals. We did have a small mausoleum where ashes could be displayed or if they had relatives aboard the ship, they could be kept in their apartments. It was a pretty even split between the two options.

The first passing occurred shortly after I took command. He was a 92-year-old farmer who had been retired for several years. Once he retired, he mentored young people who wished to become farmers or work with livestock. He had no relatives on *Hope* however many friends attended a brief memorial service to honor his contributions to our mission. He chose to be launched into space.

After the first passing it seemed like it opened the flood gates. By the end of my first year, we had 32 passing. By the end of my fourth year, it was up to 253. Our population growth slowed as a result. Fortunately the birth rate continued to climb so we were still on our projected total population curve.

Gary finished his succession plan for the Navy crew. Several young men from the civilian side signed up which helped immensely. It took him a little over three years for him to feel comfortable with his plan. He went over it with me and my XO in great detail. We were amazed to see the amount of effort he put into the planning.

I was glad to see him finish his work. He was now in his mid-eighties and he was really slowing down. Based on his annual physical, he was in good health however the change in him was noticeable, very noticeable.

I was slowing down too. I was seven years younger than him and in good health but I was looking forward to retirement. My XO was almost ready to assume the role as captain. In another year I was sure he would be ready.

One night, when my shift just ended, I turned over the command of the ship to the XO and returned to our quarters. Gary was waiting for me when the door opened. He was still dressed in his uniform, which was unusual, we both usually got into more casual clothes as soon as our shift ended. I looked over his shoulder into our living space and noticed the lights were very dim. The curtain was opened displaying Habitat City by night. I saw the Mini Moons and the twinkling stars. Then I noticed there were candles on the dinner table which was set with crystal goblets, fine china and silverware.

"What's all this for?" I asked.

"For my loving wife," he answered. "I finished up with my chores early and thought it would be nice to have a romantic dinner with my wife."

It was a wonderful surprise. He had ordered my favorite dinner, it was perfectly prepared and had just been delivered by the foodbot. We each had a glass of champagne and for dessert, fresh strawberries from the ship's gardens. When we were done with dinner, the foodbot cleared the table and left.

After the door had closed behind the bot, Gary said to our home computer system, "Alfred, play dance music, mix two." It began with what we called our song, then played all of our favorites. We danced to many of the songs and just sat and listened to the others as we looked out our window. We talked about all the good things that had happened during our lives and how blessed we were to get this assignment aboard *Hope*.

When the music was over, we went into the bedroom and got ready for bed. I was very tired, the last thing I remember was Gary holding me in his arms and whispering in my ear, "I love you Malinda, I've always loved you and I always will."

When I awoke the following morning, he had passed away. He had given me one more perfect night together. He must have sensed his time was short and he wanted me to know how much he loved me. I will always remember the last night we had together. I hope he knew I loved him just as much and always would.

There was a memorial service the following week following his cremation. There were so many people who admired Gary, so many speeches commemorating all his accomplishments. I barely heard any of them; I was lost in my own grief.

I tried to resume my duties as *Hope's* captain however I really wasn't up to the task. I had to step down and let my XO take command of the ship. I felt terribly guilty but I couldn't continue. It was like I was only partly there, the other part left with my husband.

I was having a difficult time sleeping. I would wake up calling for Gary, then it would hit me, he was gone. It was like a physical pain, like fighting a fight I knew I couldn't win. One night, as I finally fell asleep, I had a strange dream; one of those dreams that seemed like it was real.

I saw Gary sitting in the chair next to my bed. The curtains were opened and he was backlit by the light from the Mini Moons. He spoke to me softly, "Malinda, I'm so sorry your grieving is tearing you apart. I'm gone and you will be joining me soon. Then we will be together forever. Go to sleep, my love."

He stood and bent over me and kissed my cheek. Then he was gone and I fell into a deep sleep.

Part 3

The Second Generation

Updates—Captain Jason Kuhn

With the passing of Commodore Malinda Dagan, I was confirmed as the new captain. The commodore had made me acting captain after her husband passed away. She survived less than a month before she also passed. For most of that time, her grieving for her husband almost incapacitated her, however the last week of her life she seemed to me to be like her old self. She smiled a lot and interacted with the rest of the crew; she even gave me some constructive criticism on a few issues.

During the day before she passed, she suggested that I consider Commander Priscilla Hoyt for my XO. She said she might resist but told me to be firm. "Remind her it's in the best interest of the ship and its mission for her to step up." The next morning, she was gone.

A memorial service was conducted a week later and following Vice Admiral Jackson's orders, she was promoted to Rear Admiral, posthumously. Following her wishes, she was cremated and her urn was placed in the mausoleum next to her husband's.

The death of those two giants hit all of us hard. Many of us needed help to grieve and our counselors were working overtime. It seemed that with their passing, it opened the flood gates. Many of our other leaders passed away over the next two years. Dr. Van Der Geist and her husband were the next to pass, followed several months later by Governor Ataksak and her husband. A year after that, Dr. Cullum MacGregor passed. All of us thanked God that Rear Admiral Gary Dagan had done an outstanding job in putting together the succession plan. Because of it, I was able to convince Commander Hoyt to accept the position of XO.

It took the better part of two years for us to work out all (or most) of the kinks. After that, we were working like a well-oiled machine (an expression my grandfather taught me—most of today's machines don't need oil to run smoothly).

As for the status of *Hope,* she's also running like a well-oiled machine. After more than 30 years of operation there have been no breakdowns of any of our major systems. Even better, there hasn't been any measurable degradation of any of those major systems, with one important exception: the ram scoops. The part of the scoops that penetrated beyond our shields was eroding faster than projected. Our diagnostic team estimates failure within another five years. They reported the cause of the accelerated erosion was due to a higher concentration of space particles than estimated.

We weren't going to wait for the scoops to fail. Our maintenance team began replacement of the scoops' inlets within a week.

Hope has three ram scoops located at the aft end of the ship, placed equidistance apart around the ship's circumference. The scoops aren't attached to the habitat and don't rotate. Instead, they are attached to the stationary support frame at the ship's aft end and feed directly into collection tanks which process the collected space material. A small portion of the oxygen is routed to the atmospheric storage chamber, the majority of the space material is passed on to the propulsion drive-fluid tanks. These tanks are located adjacent to our ion drives.

Our protective shields completely envelope the ship however they don't rotate. Actually, there are five places where the shields don't cover: the exhaust from the two ion drives and the inlet to the three ram scoops.

The three shields which covered the ram scoops were of a specific design which permitted the scoop inlets to penetrate the shields. The design team assumed we might have to replace these parts, so they designed the shields to permit the scoop inlets to be retracted inside the shields and closed over the opening, providing protection to the scoops while the repairs took place. It was explained to me by the leader of the maintenance team Like this, "Think of the shield as a layer of gelatin with a straw (the scoop) sticking through it. When you pull the straw back out of the gelatin, it flows into the hole left by the straw and seals protecting the ship. When the repairs are complete, we push the straw back through the gelatin and we're back in business." It made sense to me.

The design for the replacement scoops were stored in our maintenance data bases and three were ordered to be fabricated with our industrial grade, 3-D printers. The maintenance leader, CWO Bill Wallace, recommended we apply a thicker layer of anti-erosion material to the scoop inlets, enough to ensure we make it to Alpha Centauri before we needed to do this again. I thought that was an excellent suggestion and signed off on his request.

Once the scoop inlets were fabricated, they were taken by maglev transports to an aft hatch. We shut down the ram scoops one at a time. The maintenance team retracted the scoop inlet, removed it from the scoop duct which ran to the collection tanks. Then they installed the new inlet onto the duct and extended it through the shield. Once they had determined structural integrity had been met, the inlet was opened and checked to ensure it was operating correctly. When we had all green lights, they moved onto the next scoop and then finally to the last one.

The entire process took about a week to complete. I was very impressed. It was the first time in over 30 years a team had gone EVA in a zero-gravity environment to perform a major repair of the ship.

A special awards night was conducted in the crew's mess hall which was well attended. Awards were handed out and everyone could have as much Beale as they wanted as long as it was no more than three mugs. It was the first time we had partied since we'd become *The Second Generation*. It wouldn't be the last.

<u>Habitat City—Governor Belinda Lopez</u>

It's been forty years since we left Earth orbit and I'm happy to announce Habitat City is thriving! In a few more years we should reach our population goal of five thousand. Population Control has been busy issuing baby permits to married couples. That was made possible by the increase in deaths over the last few years. I am also happy to say that none of those deaths were the result of accidents or illnesses, all were due to natural causes. One of our charter rules, established well before *Hope* launched from Earth, was we wouldn't hasten anyone's passing and except for the execution of three men convicted of murder thirty years ago, we have maintained that rule.

While I'm on the topic of crime, I want to mention our crime rate is essentially non-existent. I attribute that to two factors:

1. Our selection process weeded out any potential trouble makers and they have passed that positive trait down to their children.
2. Our security people, both Navy and civilian, have followed the rule friendly, but firm. None of our security people carry weapons. In fact, guns aren't permitted onboard. Firing a gun inside a spaceship would be suicidal.

That doesn't mean we don't have an occasional altercation however nothing which would be considered a felony. We don't have any prisons, just a few holding cells for the rare misdemeanor.

Enough about crime. Our city—actually more like a city-state rather than just a city, which justifies me being a governor instead of a mayor—is for the most part a very pleasant place to live. Everyone has work to do and when they retire, they become mentors for the future generation. In my opinion, it's one of the most critical functions in a retirement community. Of course, everyone goes to school, almost everyone continues to learn at college or trade schools. Every critical occupation has apprentice programs to support our needs.

However, we do have free time to enjoy non-work-related activities. We have a number of worship centers throughout the city as well as recreational facilities. Personally, I like to walk for exercise. I try to do at least one trip around the circumference of the habitat every day. That's a little over six miles, not that I do it all at once. I usually stop halfway around for a break at one of our many restaurants and enjoy something to drink while I converse with the patrons. After about thirty minutes, I continue around the loop to home.

Besides exercising, I've taken up painting. I began by copying still-vids, then moved on to scenes inside the city. My next step will be to try portraits. One of my aides asked when I would be painting nudes. He said he'd volunteer to pose for me. It made me feel all flustered inside just thinking about it. I told him I would consider it but it wouldn't be soon.

Shifting gears (someday, someone is going to have to explain to me what that means. What are gears and how do you shift them; *why would you want to?*), our farms and livestock ranches are keeping up with our quotas. Every spring we have a rodeo and every fall after harvest, we have a Fall Festival. Both events last a week. At my first rodeo after becoming governor, I was told I would have to ride a horse and participate in at least one event.

I declined the invitation. I'd never been on a horse; they are big and scary. The rodeo committee insisted; it was tradition for a new governor to ride a horse in the parade. I gave in to tradition.

The horse was enormous! I could tell he didn't like me. I couldn't get my foot up high enough to reach the stirrup so I had to stand on a box. When I started to swing my leg over his back, he turned his head and tried to bite my foot in the stirrup. I screamed, which scared the horse; he jumped and I fell backwards into the dirt. I wasn't happy.

Now I was determined. No two-thousand-pound monster was going to treat me like that! One of the cowboys held the horse's head and two other cowboys helped me into the saddle. Not trusting a tenderfoot (it wasn't my foot that felt tender), a cowgirl took the horse's bridle and led me around the arena as I waved at the cheering fans. I got off quickly and headed for the stands.

After a few words of dedication to the crowd, the rodeo began. I had to admit watching the events was very exciting, thrilling even. I couldn't believe anyone could stay on a bucking horse or would even want to. I was shocked to see one of my aides riding a bucking bronco. It was the same aide who wanted to pose nude for me. He only lasted a few seconds before he was flying through the air, landing on his butt and bouncing three times. What fun that must have been for him (tongue in cheek). However, he popped right up, dusted himself off and walked off waving his cowboy hat to the fans.

The last event was called calf decorating. It was limited to women over 18. Two women worked as a team. We would chase the calf, catch it (not as easy as it sounds), then one woman would grab its back legs and lift it up in the air while the second woman would slide on a pair of XXXL bloomers up its legs and over its back. The team which 'decorated' the calf in the shortest time was the winner.

There were four teams; my team would go last. My teammate was Commander Alicia Franklin. The first three teams made it look so easy and their times were very low. Obviously, they had done this before, perhaps many times. The commander and I had never even heard of this event let alone attempted it.

It was a disaster from the time the flag dropped. We chased that damn calf all over the arena. Finally, we decided to split up and managed to corner it. It tried to run again. Finally I lunged on its back, knocking it down. The commander grabbed its hind legs and pulled them off the ground. I jumped up, ran to the back side of the calf and began sliding the bloomer first up one leg, then the other. Meantime the calf had struggled to its feet. Just as I began to pull the bloomers over its tail, it let out with what sounded like a scream and pooped all over us. What a mess! What a filthy, stinking mess! I was covered in wet, stinking cow poop from my cowgirl hat to my cowgirl belt and all over my cowgirl shirt. That included my face and hands.

There was absolute silence in the arena, except for the screaming calf as it ran away from us terrorized by what we had done. We stood there, dripping warm cow poop, in shocked silence. Then the audience began laughing, more of a chuckle at first but quickly building to hysteria.

What could we do? Being the troopers that we were, we took off our cowgirl hats and waved then at the crowd, trying to smile without opening our mouths. Then as quickly as we could, walked off to the women's restroom, hoping and praying they had showers.

I have to say I find both the Rodeo and Harvest Festival alluring. However, If I had to choose one, I'd pick the Harvest Festival; an apple has never tried to bite me and I'm pretty sure a cucumber would never poop on me, especially in front of hundreds of people.

It just occurred to me I did this all wrong! I should have begun by introducing myself and giving the reader a little background to the path I took to become governor. Oh well. There's no time like the present.

I was among the first children born on *Hope*. My father, Paul Lopez, was an operator of one of the industrial 3-D printers. To the uneducated, that may seem like it's a menial job. It really isn't. My father has a PhD in manufacturing computer science with a specialty in computer programming. He was the lead operator when the replacement ram scoop inlets were fabricated. My mother, Enedina, was a very successful innovator of clothing manufacturing. She has several patents on the use of 3-D printer fabrication of clothing. She developed a process to build clothing out of a variety of synthetic materials that can feel like any type of natural fabric, like cotton or wool, even animal skin. One feature I particularly loved was the ability to change the color of the clothes. They can be changed in a twinkling of an eye. If my mom made me a dress I thought looked fabulous in black for eveningwear and I wanted the same dress in a different material and color, no problem. With simple voice commands, it changed into whatever color I wanted. It could have stripes or polka dots or fade from one color into another; whatever I desired. It could go from silk to cotton to wool or taffeta; whatever I wanted. *How does she do it? Magic!* Or maybe advanced science, I will never understand.

Once the dress or whatever piece of clothing you want, from uniforms to casual clothes, or swimwear to underwear; whatever you need, Mom can program and print it in about fifteen minutes. Oh, I almost forgot; she can fabricate footwear, from slippers to work boots. She made me my cowgirl outfit, including the boots and the belt with a big fancy buckle. Both my parents have recently retired and are now mentoring their replacements.

I attended elementary school and high school then, at the recommendation of Governor Ataksak, I went to college with a double major in political science and human relations. I was brought aboard the governor's team, along with several other possible replacement governor candidates. When she stepped down, she chose me as her replacement.

Governor Ataksak continued to mentor me for almost a year. Shortly after she stopped mentoring me, she passed away. When she told me she was discontinuing being my mentor, I panicked. I said I didn't feel ready; there was so much more I needed to learn. She just shook her head and said, "No Belinda, you are ready; readier than I was. Remember, a good governor listens to her people. However she has to decide what's best for all of them. I've seen you make the tough choices, not always the best choices but never bad choices. You will do fine." A week later she checked herself into hospice, three days later she passed.

I'm fortunate to be surrounded by very intelligent people who understand their responsibilities perfectly. At least in my opinion, they do. We don't always agree but once I've made my decision, they don't push back. In fact, they give it their best effort to make my way work. God bless them for that. Maybe that's what being like a well-oiled machine means.

One last thing before I sign off. I'm not married, my age is my own business. I would very much like to be married and have children soon. Governor Ataksak said being married to Arnold and having a family made her feel her life was complete. She suggested I put my name in with the matching service. I followed her suggestion and submitted my name yesterday. So far, I have only one response; it was my cowboy aide who wants to pose nude for me. I hope I get more responses soon.

Three months have passed since I wrote the above entry. During that time, several other men showed an interest in me as a marriage partner. None of them appealed to me. They were all very nice men, however I think they were hesitant about marriage because of my position. I believed the thought of being married to the highest civilian authority on *Hope* intimidated them.

My chief of staff, his name is Josh White, began to grow on me. He treated me like an equal in spite of my title. He was very smart, funny and not exactly good looking. He wasn't unattractive, perhaps rugged would be the better way to describe him. He was my senior aide, working closely with me every day and I felt very comfortable around him.

One evening, I decided to have him accompany me to a formal dinner. He was quick to accept and we had a great time. He impressed me by the way he interacted with the senior people at the dinner; he was very much at ease and friendly with everyone, regardless of their title.

Shortly after that, we began dating. Josh asked me out for our first real date the week after the formal dinner. It caught me off guard, however I agreed. We had a nice dinner at one of the restaurants at the park. After dinner we walked around the park and stopped at the waterfall. We ordered drinks at an outside club and talked for hours. When I told him I had early meetings the next day and should get going, he asked me to stay for a few more minutes. He had something important to say.

"I know this is kind of sudden," he said, "but I need to tell you something. I have admired you ever since I began working for you. You're a really incredible person. You're smart, beautiful and have this easy way of working with people. The longer I'm around you the more I admire you. I really admired the way you acted at the rodeo when the calf unloaded on you. Most people I know would have been scared to death to even try that calf decorating event. All the other teams had grown up on farms or ranches and were used to working with animals. You went out there with no experience, not knowing what to expect and got the worst of it.

"I grew up on a ranch and have gone to several rodeos. I've seen other people have the same thing happen to them and they were either comatose or in a rage. I even saw one woman grab a knife and try to kill the calf that crapped on her. Fortunately for the calf, she was disarmed.

"You took it in stride. You waved your hat to the crowd and even smiled. I'd never seen that reaction before. In that moment I knew I loved you and wanted to be your husband. So that's why I hacked your computer and deleted all the other men who wanted to date you. I left a few dorks so you wouldn't get suspicious. I want you all to myself."

I sat stunned. My first reaction was to get angry, maybe slap his face or fire him as my chief aide. However, I did none of those things. Instead, I began to smile. He looked relieved and returned my smile, took my hand and said, "I hope this means you don't hate me?"

I shook my head and replied, "I only hated you for a moment I don't doubt your sincerity. If you had waited to reveal your sabotage of other possible suitors, or worse, if I discovered on my own what you'd done, I may not have been so forgiving."

I paused for a moment. He began to frown and said, "Do I detect a 'but' coming?"

"Yes," I answered. "Before I commit to marriage, I want to know more about you and I will share my heritage with you. I really like you a lot, maybe even love you a little." I paused for a moment thinking the best way to word this. "I want to love you a lot more before I decide to get married. Is that okay with you?"

He was smiling again and answered, "Sure, that's fine with me." He squeezed my hand and asked, "Does that mean I can pose nude for you?"

I shook my head and replied, "Don't push it, cowboy."

We met socially several times a week to share our heritages and our pasts. I found out a distant grandparent of Josh was a slave who was brought from Africa centuries ago to the southern part of what used to be called the United States of America. Someone in his family was a genealogist who had documented his entire line from then to the present.

It seems there were periods of terrible barbarism throughout long years of our world's history. Entire types of people were slaughtered just because they were different. Because of their differences, they were considered inferior, not even accepted as human, in spite of scientific evidence that proved we were all the same. Certainly, there were great variations between individuals of each race. On the average, we were all the same, we were really all the same race of living beings.

It took decades, centuries, before ethnic cleansing was eliminated and people began to accept, then embrace, different types of people.

The ship's libraries were full of vids detailing what was called, The Era of Miscegenation. That began almost a hundred years before we left Earth. Now there are no longer white people, black people, brown people or yellow people. There are just people.

We were married almost two months ago. Governor Ataksak was right; I'm on my way to becoming complete. I'm married and one month pregnant. *Hallelujah and Amen!*

P.S. Josh finally got to pose nude for me.

<u>Communications –Commander Alicia Franklin</u>

During the past thirty years, I have been steadily working my way up the chain of command. When *Hope* left Earth, I was in my early twenties. My first assignment was to be part of the communications team. I was an ensign at the time. I was promoted to Lieutenant JG three years later and led one of the communication teams. Five years after that, I was promoted to Lieutenant and was assigned the position of communication systems leader with three teams reporting to me.

On a personal note, while I was a lieutenant, I met this man. His name was Guy Franklin and he was also a lieutenant working in the Propulsion Systems Group. Actually, I had met him before; we were in the same class at the Space Academy however there was no chemistry between us at that time. We only interacted at Academy functions and that wasn't often.

He came up to me during one of the Harvest Festivals. I didn't even recognize him at first. By the end of the evening we were dancing to slow songs. He was the perfect gentleman all evening long. When the evening was over, we held hands in the maglev back to the station and he walked me to my quarters and said goodnight. There was an awkward moment before he gave me a hug and kissed me on the cheek. Then he turned and walked back to his own quarters.

Once inside my room, I stood there with my back against the door feeling…I wasn't sure what I was feeling. It had been a really nice evening. I guess I was a little disappointed he didn't give me a kiss, a real kiss, one on the mouth.

I was startled out of my musing by a knock on my door. When I opened it, there stood Guy. Without saying a word, he stepped inside, picked me up and planted a very passionate kiss on my mouth. He kept kissing me as he carried me to my bed and laid me down. He was about to lie on top of me when my roommate interrupted, "Hi. I'm Michelle, Alicia's roommate. You guys must have had a terrific evening."

Guy let out a little squeak of surprise and stood up abruptly. "Yes, we did," he replied as I reclined on my bed, lipstick smeared all over my mouth and chin. "Well, I should be going now. Good evening ladies." With that he turned abruptly and left our room, closing the door quietly behind him.

Michelle just stared at me silently for a moment then we both started laughing hysterically. "What a great first date," I screamed between laughs.

We dated for three months. We were madly in love. We were married during the fourth month. That man changed my life forever! We now have two children, a girl and a boy.

Back to business. The Communication Systems Group is responsible for handling all communications, both within *Hope* and external to *Hope* as well. This involved not only directing com traffic to and from individuals on the ship but also communications with Earth and with *Faith,* our sister ship. In addition, I had responsibility for the techs who took care of maintenance on all our com system hardware and software.

When we were about ten years into our mission, the extinction event we had all feared became a reality; The Plague destroyed all civilization on Earth. I was a lieutenant at the time and as you can imagine, the coms went viral. Our com capabilities escalated exponentially until we had to prioritize, to ensure the most important messages reached the people in charge in a timely manner.

There were numerous coms between *Faith* and us. *Faith* had left Earth almost a year before us and was considerably farther from Earth than us. Based on the coms we received from *Faith,* she was on the verge of open rebellion to scrap their mission and return to Earth. Fortunately, that didn't happen unfortunately they did lose many people.

Since that incident, I was promoted twice, first to Lt. Commander and later to full Commander and leader of the Information Systems

Group. I now have responsibility for not only the com systems but also all the computer systems, including hardware, software and maintenance.

We have maintained com links with *Faith* on a routine basis. However, they're being a year ahead of us, it took 18 days for a message from *Faith* to reach us and another 18 days for any reply we made. Most of our coms were limited to the status of our respective ships, which included all changes to the chain of command.

Even though *Faith* is well into their second generation, there seems to be considerable unrest aboard our sister ship. Nothing specific, more of an undercurrent of grief over lost loved ones from The Plague. It appears there are several groups who continue to press for an immediate return to Earth. Of course, we will continue to monitor *Faith's* coms and keep our captain up to date on any changes in this situation.

<u>Halfway to Alpha Centauri—Captain Jason Kuhn</u>

It's been fifty years since we left Earth's orbit. Officially, we were halfway to our destination. However, Astrogation has informed me we passed the half-way distance mark a few years ago; the hundred years of flight-time was just a round-number estimate of the time it would take to reach the Alpha Centauri Cluster. Our actual target star is Proxima Centauri. More specifically, our ultimate goal is Proxima-b, an Earth-like planet which orbits Proxima Centauri.

We decided to have a half-way-there party to celebrate the occasion (even if it was a few years late.) The governor thought it was an excellent idea, provided there were no horses involved. She mentioned something about once bitten-twice shy. I'm not sure what she meant by that. She chose not to elaborate.

The governor put together a planning committee and gave them a week to present their ideas for the party. She told me she was delighted with their plans and gave them the go-ahead to make it happen. She even reluctantly approved children's pony rides.

The venue selected was located on one of the fallow fields adjacent to our timber forest. The trees had reached maturity several years ago and select trees were harvested for their lumber. The forest trees had grown to over a hundred feet tall and added considerably to our oxygen supply. To many, the contribution of lumber was a bonus and several log buildings were built near the edge of the forest. Those building were selected to house some of our party activities.

A dance floor was setup complete with a bandstand. Several musical groups performed during the party which lasted for three days. Each group focused on a specific type of music from various time periods in Earth's history. The intent was to have at least some music that would appeal to everyone's taste. They started with waltzes, moved on to jazz, from there to swing, then to rock and roll, heavy metal, hip hop, funk, bongo blast and finally, astral plane. They repeated this routine each day of the party.

Our microbrewery provided barrels of Beale and a relatively new distillery venture was producing stronger beverages.

There was food to meet the appeal of every conceivable taste. Harvest of fruits and vegetables had finished up a week before the party which contributed to delicious cuisine. There were meats from cattle, sheep, pork and a variety of seafood. Pasta, potato and rice-based dinners garnished with a wide variety of breads were served every evening. I almost forgot to mention the deserts: all types of cakes, pies, cookies, candy and ice creams were available.

It was a proper party. Everyone had a good time. Many told me it was a wonderful celebration that wouldn't be soon forgotten.

Unfortunately, the party was remembered not so much for the good time but for what followed. The day after the party ended, people began reporting to our various medical clinics with symptoms of food poisoning. It began harmlessly enough with mild discomfort, however it quickly escalated into something very severe. People began dying.

All of our medical clinics were suddenly at full capacity. It seemed to affect the children and our senior citizens the most. It took several weeks before it subsided and a full month before we were back to normal. For those who lost loved ones, they were a long way from normal. We lost several hundred people due to this event.

Our medical doctors were baffled for several weeks attempting to determine the cause of the poisoning. It finally was determined to be some new type of bacterial poison, a very virulent strain. It was traced to several of the foods served at the party. Our home-grown food wasn't to blame. It was discovered some of the food brought aboard *Hope* before we left Earth-orbit was to blame. That food was to be used during the first year of our voyage. It turned out not all of that food had been consumed; it had been stored and thought preserved, for fifty years. When it was discovered by the food prep team, they ran an inspection on it and the data said it was fine for consumption.

The mantra for our voyage was known by everyone aboard: DON'T WASTE ANYTHING. This also applied especially to our food. When the inspection of the stored food came back positive, it was thrown into the mix with our home-grown food. It turned out the equipment used to check the stored food was out of calibration and returned a false positive for consumption reading on several of the items. All of the stored food was consumed during the party, so it was difficult to determine exactly which foods were poisonous. The best guess was the seafood and pork products. Those who survived the poisoning reported they had eaten several helpings of both types of food over the three days. Of course, they also ate a wide variety of other food as well. There were also many people who ate the seafood and pork products and didn't get sick, so it's hard to know for sure.

The deaths of so many people were tragic however there were other matters to consider. Several of the older people who passed held important positions. Fortunately, on the Navy side, both my XO and myself survived. Both of us had mild cases and recovered within a few days. Various system leaders covered for us while we were unable to command.

On the civilian side, the governor and most of her ruling committee also survived. She didn't get poisoned, however two of her committee members got sick and one passed. Unfortunately, he was the leader of the Planning Commission and Population Control. He had been mentoring a young man to be his replacement. Hopefully, the governor can assist him to move into that role prematurely.

Compounding the problem is the passing of some of the children. Three of the older deceased children had been chosen to fill entry level positions in critical areas. New candidates needed to be selected and quickly brought up to speed.

Planning Interim Manager—Robert Bowman

As the new interim manager of the Planning and Population Control group, my first order of business was to determine who will be our civilian leaders for the next generation of *Hope.* Our captain will oversee a similar role for Navy personnel.

I served as one of three trainees for the position I now hold. The previous leader, Mr. Perry Hendrix (May God rest his soul), had mentored all three of us for about a year before he passed. Our governor and the leaders of her support organization chose me for the interim position.

Fortunately, our first captain and governor had the foresight to create an algorithm to assist me in this challenge. It considers all of the ship's personnel and determines three possible candidates for each of the ship's leadership positions. The program also considers the individual's desire to fill the slot. Once the three candidates are selected, they undergo an extensive evaluation by the ship's current leadership.

To best utilize the talents available on the ship, it is necessary to prioritize the positions, based on which are the most critical. Three tier levels were established. All the highest-level positions are scheduled to be filled first. The two candidates not selected are then thrown back into the pot and we begin again. This process is continued until all three tiers have been filled.

Every year we go through what has been called a mock draft. When I was a trainee, all three of us were involved in the last mock draft. It covered all three levels of tiers. What made it challenging was it had to be run numerous times to account for who was selected for the highest tier.

I know this sounds confusing, so let me use an example to help explain the process. Let's say we have three candidates who are being considered for a highest tier position. We'll call them A, B, and C. Assume A is selected. Then what happens to B and C? There are two possible paths; they can be placed in the pool for a second-tier position or be added as a candidate for another highest tier in a different discipline.

Then you have to do it all over again with B being selected for the highest tier position, then again with C.

The number of iterations expands exponentially and takes a considerable amount of time to complete but it ensures we get the most qualified people in the most critical positions.

Fortunately, only a few critical positions lost potential candidates to the poison; it took the better part of six months to reestablish a completed revision to the third generation succession plan. I heard the Navy had completed their succession plan about the same time.

<u>Mentoring the Next Captain—Captain Jason Kuhn</u>

It has been fifty-nine years since *Hope* left Earth's orbit and began our voyage to a distant star. Approximately a year from now, the Third Generation crew will take command of the generation starship *Hope.*

I am currently mentoring two candidates. One will be the captain and the other their executive officer. My current XO, Commander Priscilla Hoyt, is assisting me in the mentoring process. Both of us have decided to step down next year and become advisors to the crew in whatever capacity the new captain chooses.

I was recently approached by my XO and she reminded me I haven't made any formal disclosure about our relationship. *How could that have possibly slipped my mind!?* I don't want to say I forgot or I was too busy. That would only lead to trouble. I prefer to say we want to maintain privacy about our off-duty lives. It was the best excuse I could think of on short notice.

For the sake of peace in the family, I would like to publicly announce the commander, my XO, and I were married about a year after we took command of *Hope.* We have two adult children who have no interest in the Navy. They are very busy with their businesses in Habitat City. Both are married and we currently have three grandchildren with a fourth on the way. That concludes any personal family information I wish to disclose.

I'm happy to announce that both candidates are doing very well in their preparation to become ship's captain. As an example of my trust in their abilities, I've already given them command of the ship from time to time, mostly on grave shift. Also, they have led various safety drills and performed them within the specified time constraints. At the present time, it would be difficult to choose a captain.

I needed a way to test them where it wouldn't seem like a test; more like a real emergency, something that would get their adrenaline flowing. I couldn't let the rest of the crew know either. They needed to think it was a real emergency as well.

My XO and I brain stormed ideas. It had to appear life threatening or at least mission threatening. We spent several days hashing over possible tests when we were off duty.

On the second day, Pris told me a story from her family history that she thought might apply to our situation. She had a distant relative who was an instructor pilot back in the twentieth century. He had a student who did everything correctly. One of the inflight tests was a simulated engine shut down. It was called the Inflight Engine Shutdown Drill. This was during the days of combustion engines that burned gasoline and had propellers; well before electric aircraft motors. The gasoline engines used spark plugs to ignite the fuel. The spark plugs got their energy from something called a magneto.

There were three things the pilot could do to determine why an engine stopped working:

1. The plane was out of gasoline.
2. The fuel line from the fuel tank to the engine was inadvertently shut off.
3. The magnetos were inadvertently shut off.

A fourth reason was an engine failure. If the engine broke the plane became a glider and the pilot had to quickly find an emergency landing site.

It wasn't hard to know if you had an engine failure, however it was very easy to check if one of the other three things could have resulted in the engine shutting down. It took just a few seconds to check all three.

The engine shutdown drill was usually done by taking the aircraft to about 5,000 feet above ground level (AGL) over farmland or empty fields (locations of emergency landing sites). Then the instructor would pull back the throttle to idle. The student would immediately configure the aircraft for the slowest decent glide, then run their checks. They would first check the fuel tank gauge to see if the tank was empty. If the fuel tank was empty, they had to land in the best emergency landing site available. If the tanks had gasoline, they would then check to see if the fuel line valve was open or closed. If the valve was closed, they would open it, restart the engine and go on their merry way. If the valve was opened, they would check if the magnetos were turned on. If they had been inadvertently turned off, a good student would turn them on and restart the engine and proceed to their destination. If the magnetos were already on, it was time for an emergency landing.

At the end of the test, if everything checked out they would either return the throttle to cruise or, at the discretion of the instructor, leave the throttle set to idle and set up for an emergency landing, aborting the actual landing and climbing back to cruise altitude.

My XO's relative told the story about how this cocky student who always did everything correctly was faced with a new challenge. They were flying along, practicing some maneuvers when the instructor reached down between the seat and closed the fuel line valve. The engine continued to run for about two minutes using the fuel left in the line. Then it shut down abruptly. When the propeller stopped spinning, the student looked at the instructor with terror in his eyes and yelled into the now quiet cockpit, "What happened?"

The instructor replied in a calm voice, "Your engine shut down. Remember your drill procedure."

The student nodded his head and began his checks. He placed his finger on the fuel gauge and said, "Fuel tank over half full." Then he stuck his hand down between the seats and touched the closed fuel shut off valve and said, "Fuel line valve open." His hand went to the magneto switch. "Mags on."

He paused for a beat then looked at the instructor and said with panic in his voice, "What do we do now?"

"Repeat the drill again," answered the instructor.

The student repeated the drill two more times. Each time he touched the closed fuel line valve, he would say "Open." By then the plane was approaching 500 feet AGL over and empty field. "I can't do this," whined the student. "You land the airplane, please."

"No," replied the instructor. "I shut off the fuel line valve. Open it and takes us back to the airport."

The XO finished the story by saying, "According to the memoirs of my flight instructor relative, the student never flew again."

I had sat there listening in rapt attention, captivated by the story. When Pris finished, I said to her, "Thank you. I think I have the perfect test for our two candidates."

Special Drill—XO, Commander Priscilla Hoyt

Captain Kuhn had me put together the final test for the two candidates for *Hope's* new Captain. It would also determine who would become the new XO. The first candidate was Commander Björn Sjöblom, the current leader of Propulsion Systems. The second candidate would be Commander Britt-Marie Andersson, the current leader of Power Systems. Coincidentally, both trace their ancestry back to the Scandinavian Provinces of the European Commonwealth, however their great grandparents migrated to the United Provinces of North America almost two hundred years ago.

Björn was in his mid-thirties when he was first considered for the position of ship's captain. His ship-born parents had no military experience. His father was a civilian professor at our university specializing in rocket propulsion systems. Björn didn't attend the ship's Space Academy. He received military training at our university. He received his PhD from *Hope* University with an emphasis on ion drive technology. He was commissioned as an ensign and went on active duty in the Propulsion Systems group.

Britt-Marie was also in her mid-thirties when her name came up as a possible candidate for captain. She attended the Space Academy and graduated with dual majors: nuclear engineering and human resources. She was commissioned ensign and assigned to the Power Systems group. Her father was also a Space Academy graduate and served in the Power Systems group. He retired from the service after 20 years of duty at the rank of Lieutenant Commander. Her mother served on the governor's committee for ten years prior to her retirement. Both her parents are currently acting as mentors.

The test consists of the following: approximately one month from now, there will be an event they must deal with. The thrust from our EM ion drives is gradually decreasing. If it continues to decay at the present rate, we should be able to make it to Proxima-b. No one knows if the decay in thrust is caused by some problem in the drive system or in the power system that is used to ionize the propulsion fluid. Or it could be a weakness in the magnetic field that accelerates the ionized particles to over five percent c.

All the propulsion and power system data inform us everything is operating at nominal levels, our thrust isn't declining. However, Astrogation says we are slowing down which they attribute to a decline in thrust.

The only people who will know there is no real problem are myself, the captain and the Astrogation leader; we are sworn to secrecy during the drill. The drill will run one month regardless of if a solution is discovered or not.

Captain Kuhn called both candidates into the conference room to brief them on their new assignment. He laid out the stated problem, told them they needed to work together as well as separately and had the full cooperation of everyone on the ship to help them solve this problem. It must be solved as soon as possible. He left them in the conference room to plan on how to begin approaching the problem.

"Well, Commander Andersson," said Commander Sjöblom, "this is quite a challenge. I think we may be busy for quite some time. How do you think we should proceed?"

"Call me Britt-Marie when we are alone. May I call you Björn?"

"Of course. I think it will be better to not maintain a formal relationship as we work together to resolve this problem."

Britt-Marie nodded her head in agreement. "I know we haven't had much time working together; we each had our own responsibilities however now we must become a team."

Björn said, "I agree. I think we should have a team name."

"I hadn't thought about a team name," replied Britt-Marie. "What name do you propose?"

"Our ancestry is from Scandinavia, how about we call our team, The Vikings?"

Britt-Marie smiled. "An excellent choice. From now on we are The Vikings."

"Well, that's one problem solved," said Björn. "Perhaps we should move on to bigger issues."

Meeting-Astrogation—Commander Björn Sjöblom

Britt-Marie and I decided to first meet with Commander Shojiro Koyama, the leader of the Astrogation Group. He was expecting us and had a very detailed presentation. "The math is pretty simple really. We take a fix on the Alpha Centauri Cluster then measure the distance of the cluster from *Hope*. We do this every day at the same time. We can use a very simple equation to determine the ship's speed:

Velocity = Change in Distance / Time Between Measurements

"Ever since we reached a cruise velocity of five percent c, we have applied that equation to determine the ship's velocity every day for almost sixty years. Every day it has shown the ship has maintained exactly five percent to six decimal places until two weeks ago. The data now shows a steady decline.

"Of course, we recalibrated all of our instruments to make sure we weren't experiencing any measurement drift. None was detected. We use three different types of instruments to measure both our distance from the star cluster as well as the way we measure time. All three approaches are exactly the same up to nine-digit accuracy for both time and distance measurements, no drift and no errors."

Britt-Marie spoke up, "Have you tried using another target star, perhaps perturbations in the orbit of our target star could result in misleading results. By the way, which of the three stars which make up the Alpha Centauri cluster do you target?"

Commander Koyama stared at Britt-Marie for a second before responding. Perhaps he was annoyed at her questioning his measurement methods. "Commander Andersson, let me answer your last question first. When we left Earth's orbit, we were over four light years away from the cluster. At that distance we had no option other than to make our measurement on the brightest of the three stars, Alpha Centauri-A. It is fifty percent brighter than B and hundreds of times brighter than Proxima. We are currently approximately 1.7 light years from A. And just so you know, orbital perturbations of stars in the cluster are insignificant compared to our current distance from them.

"To answer your first question, yes, we have used another star relatively close to the cluster and its movement relative to our ship has been measured. We have calculated the same reduction in *Hope's* velocity. If there are no further questions, I need to get…"

"I have a last question, actually, more of a request," I said, interrupting Commander Koyama before he dismissed us. "Could you authorize us to access your databases?"

There was a long pause before Koyama answered. When he did both Britt-Marie and I could sense his anger. "Why would you want access to something you couldn't possibly understand? Do you have any knowledge of the algorithms we use to analyze our data? I am concerned you might inadvertently damage our software. Therefore, your request is denied."

He stared into my eyes and then Britt-Marie's and said, "Our meeting is over. Good luck on determining the cause of the degradation of the ship's thrust. We need to rectify this problem as soon as possible."

As we walked out of Koyama's office, Britt-Marie said, "He's hiding something."

"My feelings exactly," I replied.

Power System Meeting—Commander Britt-Marie Andersson

Björn and I decided to split up to make our initial examination of the respective groups we used to manage. He had the Propulsion Systems Group and I, the Power Systems Group.

I was welcomed by my interim replacement as group leader, Lt. Commander Stewart MacGregor, grandson of my former leader, Cullum MacGregor. I noticed he wasn't wearing a kilt.

We spent several hours reviewing our reactors' performance data. After what I considered a very thorough study, I concluded the reactors weren't the cause of the reduction in thrust. Each of the two reactors (one for each EM ion drives) were continuing to perform as they did the day we throttled back to our cruise power setting, almost 60 years ago.

The Power Systems Group was responsible for three features of the EM ion drives: the first was providing power to the pumps which supplied the propulsion fluid to the drives; secondly, they provided power for the ionization of the propulsion fluid; and lastly, they supplied power to generate the magnetic field used to accelerate the electrons of the ionized propulsion fluid to provide the thrust necessary to maintain the ship's cruise speed of five percent c. Any variation in the power supplied to anyone of the three subsystems would result in a variation in the thrust.

Stewart and I reviewed the supplied power to each of these subsystems over the last 59 years. We also checked the measurement systems which were used to control the needed power supplies. Both of us agreed everything was working exactly as it was designed to do.

I asked Stewart, "What are we missing?"

He was staring at the bulkhead, his mind focusing on the problem. "The only thing I can think of are the computers that control everything. Maybe there was a software upgrade that had some type of glitch which would account for the thrust degradation. That's the only thing I can think of."

I thanked him for his time and told him I would check with the Information Systems Group to see if there had been any recent software upgrades. Before I did that, I wanted to check with Björn to see what he had found out from the Propulsion Systems Group.

Propulsion Systems Meeting—Commander Björn Sjöblom

While Britt-Marie was meeting with the interim leader of the Power Systems Group I was conducting my own meeting with my old group from Propulsion Systems. My interim replacement (and to my way of thinking, the next generation leader of the group), was Lt. Commander Gloria Li. She was also a very close associate of mine whom I believed was very competent. As I expected, she had a very detailed presentation plan of all the features her group had checked on prior to my arrival.

By way of greeting, she said, "It's about time you came to see me and your other grunts."

I forgot to mention she was also a jokester. "I've been very busy with the captain's candidate evaluation program. However, I was confident you had everything under control. Perhaps my confidence was misplaced, what have you done to my ion drives?" I said returning her jesting manner.

Her face went blank for a moment, then she said something in Mandarin that I couldn't understand but assumed was profane.

"All joking aside, Gloria. Do you have any idea what's happening? Do you think it might be some kind of problem with the drives?"

"Absolutely not, boss man. Our drives are still at optimum. I'd bet my life it's not a propulsion problem."

We sat down at the conference table and went over every possible propulsion problem we could think of and between the two of us, that was a long list, a very long list.

We looked at each and every one of the items on Gloria's list. By the way, her list was longer than mine. She was very thorough in spite of her jokes. We looked at damage to the magnetic field generators, deterioration of the ejector nozzles, leakage between the working fluid pumps and the magnetic fields, damage to the thrust measurement system and on and on as the hours rolled by until we came to the end of the list.

We sat there quietly, trying to think of what we might have missed. I asked, "Have you done an external examination of the exhaust system?"

She nodded her head and answered, "Yes, we had maintenance bots all over the aft end of the ship making vids of everything. No visible damage anywhere."

"What about the ram scoops? It hasn't been too long since the inlet nozzles were replaced. Could they have any effect on thrust?" I asked.

"I don't see how," she replied.

"What about the composition of the propulsion fluid, has it changed recently?"

Gloria looked down at her list, then up at me. "It's not on my list. To answer your question, yes, it could have an impact. If the space material the ram scoops supply to the fluid tanks changes significantly, it could easily affect the thrust. Damn, boss. No wonder you're going to be captain. I'll have my team…actually, still your team, on this right away. I'll have an answer for you first thing tomorrow. In the meantime, I'll keep thinking about what else I may have missed."

I headed back to the captain's conference room to meet with Britt-Marie and compare our findings. Captain Kuhn and the XO were expecting a briefing after dinner.

Briefing the Captain and XO—Commander Björn Sjöblom

Britt-Marie and I had decided we would alternate who would lead the briefing for the Captain and XO. They were to be held every evening. We flipped the coin and I lost so I led the first briefing. Of course, Britt-Marie was encouraged to add additional information.

I went over what we had done on our first day of the assignment, recounting our meetings with Astrogation, Power Systems and Propulsion Systems. I started presenting the detailed information but hesitated when the captain raised his hand to stop me. He said, "I don't want the details of what you both did. I'm only interested in the results and what you plan to do tomorrow."

"Yes sir," I replied. "I'll take them in order. Astrogation is convinced his data is accurate and *Hope* is slowing down."

Again, the captain raised his had to stop me. "Don't rehash what I already know. Results?"

I was beginning to become annoyed at the captain's interruptions. "Both Britt-Marie and I believe that Commander Shojiro Koyama is hiding something from us."

"Why would you think that?" the captain interrupted again.

"Because he refused to grant us access to the Astrogation data base," I answered, struggling to keep a calm voice.

"Why would you want access to his data base?"

"To verify his findings."

"That would be a waste of your time, Commander. Move on."

I got the feeling Commander Koyama wasn't the only person hiding something. I kept my mouth shut and let Britt-Marie continue the briefing.

She told them she had one action item regarding the Power Systems Group. She was going to check with Information Systems to see if there had been any recent upgrades to the software that controlled the Power Systems reactors.

The Captain held up his hand. "Another waste of time. Do either of you have anything else to tell us?"

I stepped up again and told him about checking on the propulsion fluid composition having a possible impact on the thrust. The Captain looked at the XO and shook his head. Then he turned back to us and said, "Your briefing was a waste of our time. Frankly, I'm disappointed in your lack of progress. Perhaps you're not candidate material after all. You are both dismissed."

We both stood, saluted and left the conference room. Never in my life had I wanted to slap someone so badly.

We returned to our conference room to discuss what we should do next. I was barely in control of my emotions. I could sense Britt-Marie was feeling the same way. While she went to the restroom, I sat at the table for a whole ten seconds. I was filled with such anger-energy I had to do something. I stood up and walked around the room at a brisk pace in an attempt to burn off some of the anger. I was doing jumping-jacks when she returned.

She smiled at me and said, "Does that work for you? I slammed the door to the stall about a dozen times before I could calm down. I have never seen our captain act so…so…" She couldn't find the right word so she just gave up, shrugged her shoulders and sat down at the table. After I finished my hundredth jumping jack, I sat down with her.

We sat quietly for a few moments just starring off into space. We both began to speak at the same time. We both stopped and said in unison, "I'm sorry…" We started to giggle; it had broken the tension we had been feeling.

Britt-Marie gestured for me to speak first, "Do you think the captain's behavior towards us was unusual?" I said.

"Absolutely," she answered. "I've never seen him act that way toward any of his subordinates. I'm surprised the XO didn't attempt to calm him down."

"Exactly!" I exclaimed. "The XO has never been shy about interrupting him when she thinks he's off track." I paused, then added, "Do you think their rude behavior was planned in advance? It seemed to me they were intentionally trying to make us angry."

"Why would they do that?" she asked.

"I'm not sure," I answered. "It's just one more piece to the puzzle we are tasked to solve." I took a deep breath and let it out slowly, then added, "We are the Vikings. We will conquer our anger and find the solution."

Before we could continue, the emergency klaxon began to blare loudly along with red flashing lights.

"All hands, report to the bridge, this isn't a drill." The order repeated over and over as we bolted from the conference area and headed for the bridge. We were joined by most of the on-duty crew however the captain and XO were nowhere to be found.

"Cancel the alarm," I yelled and immediately the klaxon and flashing red lights stopped. "State the nature of the emergency," I said in a calmer voice.

A computerized voice answered, "The EM ion drive has shut down."

Everyone stood speechless for a moment. I found my voice and asked, "What is the location of the captain and XO?"

The answer came back immediately, "Neither the captain nor the XO are available."

"What does that mean?" someone screamed.

"They aren't on the ship," came the computer's reply.

A cold chill ran down my back. Britt-Marie spoke in a calm voice that masked the fear I was sure we shared. "All system leaders, report to you stations and get our drives back on line as soon as possible. Until the captain and XO return, Commander Sjöblom and I have command of the ship."

I looked at Britt-Marie and said, "We need to do a complete shut down and restart. I'm going to Propulsion Systems while you go to Power Systems. Keep in touch."

I ran to my left and Britt-Marie ran to the right. On my way, I yelled, "Computer, I want a continuous search for the captain and the XO with a status update every five minutes. As acting captain, you are to disregard any and all attempts to mask their locations. Confirm orders."

"Roger acting captain, I will run a continuous search for the captain and XO and give you a status check every five minutes."

I slowed to a stop. "What about the part where you will disregard any and all attempts to mask the location of the captain and XO?"

There was no response. "Connect me to Commander Alicia Franklin immediately."

"The Information Systems Leader is currently off-line."

"Priority override. Emergency request."

There was no answer.

When I arrived at Propulsion Systems, Commander Li met me. She was obviously distraught. "What's happening? Everything is shut down. When I attempt a restart, nothing works."

I did a quick scan of the control board; all I saw were red lights. "Begin manual shut down immediately. When completed, begin a manual reboot of the entire system. Let me know how it goes."

I turned and ran to the Information Systems bay. Commander Franklin was in her office looking at one of her monitors. "Commander, our com system is either being hacked or it's been corrupted. It refuses to accept emergency orders."

She stood up abruptly, "That's impossible!"

"I thought so too. I believe the Captain is running some type of drill to determine how well we know our systems. I recommend you ask your computer for the location of the Captain and XO. I suggest you invoke your administrative authorization if you need to. This is very important. Let me know how it works out."

I ran out of Information Systems and headed to Power Systems. I noticed half the control board was dark and as I watched the red lights were turning dark. When Britt-Marie saw me, she said, "The only thing that works is to manually shut everything down, one subsystem at a time."

"Yes, I'm having Propulsion do the same thing. Our com system has either been hacked or corrupted. I've got Commander Franklin working on it. Until I get notified it's fixed you need to send a runner to let me know how things are progressing. I'm heading back to Propulsion now."

When I got back to Propulsion the control panel was completely dark. "Waiting on you, boss," said Gloria. "Do you want us to manually bring the subsystems online?"

"You need to coordinate with Power Systems, don't you? Let me check with Information Systems to see if they have the com system operational yet."

"No worries, boss. We have our own com system set up between Power and us. We can have everything ready to fire up an hour from now."

"Really?!" I said, "In that case, Gloria, get to it." As I turned to leave to check with Information Systems, I saw an aide standing next to Gloria with a portable handheld backup com unit acting as a relay between the two groups. Very innovative.

When I arrived, Commander Franklin asked me a question. "Do you want the good news first or the bad news?"

"I really need some good news, please," I answered.

She smiled and said, "We located the captain and the XO. They are in Shuttle Tango in the forward shuttle bay. It seems they forgot to shut off their locator pins. The bad news is it will take us a little longer to have our com systems back on line."

I thanked her and went to Security. CWO Zipowicz was on duty and I ordered him to go to the forward shuttle bay and remove Captain Kuhn and Commander Hoyt from Shuttle Tango and lock them in the brig until further notice. They weren't allowed any visitors.

The CWO raised his eyebrows and said in firm voice, "What would the charges be, Commander?"

"Treason!" I answered in my own firm voice.

<u>The Hearing–Interim Captain Sjöblom</u>

"All rise," said the yeoman as Britt-Marie and I entered the conference room and took our seats. Seated next to us was *Hope's* governor. Seated against the wall were all the leaders and acting leaders of *Hope's* system's groups.

"Please have the detainees brought in," I said in my firmest voice.

The doors to the conference room swung open and a detail from our security group led in three shackled detainees and sat them down at a table facing us. The security team assumed the position of attention directly behind the detainees.

"Please identify the detainees, yeoman," ordered Britt-Marie.

The yeoman stood again and said, "Captain Jason Kuhn, Commander Priscilla Hoyt and Commander Shojiro Koyama."

"And what crimes are they charged with?" she asked.

"The captain and Commander Hoyt are charged with treason. Commander Koyama is charged with accessory to treason," he said in a firm voice.

"Last question," Britt-Marie paused for a moment, then asked, "What is the penalty for treason?"

The yeoman turned to look at all three detainees and said with a sneer," The only penalty for treason and accessory to treason is…*death.*"

Britt-Marie turned toward the detainees. "How do you plead," she asked?

As the captain began to stand up, he yelled at us, "Stop this farce right no…"

The security officer pushed the captain back into his seat and placed a gag in his mouth.

I turned to the system's leaders and asked, "How do you find the detainees, guilty or not guilty?"

Every one of them held a fist out in front of their body and one at a time gave the thumbs down sign.

"Before we pronounce your verdicts, we need to ask the captain and XO one question. Your fate hinges on your answer. Which one of us will be captain after you retire and which one will be the XO?" I gestured to the security officer to ungag the captain.

"Before you answer, we would like to remind you we solved the unsolvable problem you put before us in only three days instead of the month you had allotted us, in spite of your hindrances and rude behavior. The ship is now operating at optimum performance and all communication systems are back online. We couldn't have accomplished this without the extraordinary effort by the crews of Performance and Power Systems and the assistance of the Information Systems Group.

"We need your answer in five minutes. If you chose not to answer, we'll space all three of you out the nearest hatch." I smiled broadly as I said that. Britt-Marie also smiled.

Part 4

The Third Generation

Change of Command—Captain Björn Sjöblom

It's been 61 years since we left Earth's orbit. Captain Kuhn and Commander Hoyt stepped down shortly after our hearing a year ago. They are both mentoring our future commanders and doing a fine job based on the reports I've seen.

At the treason hearing, they selected me to be the captain of the third-generation crew and offered the position of XO to Britt-Marie. I was shocked when she declined the position. I had grown quite found of her during our candidate phase and was looking forward to working together. Initially, I thought she was disappointed she wasn't selected as captain. it turns out that wasn't the case.

Unbeknownst to me, she was also interested in becoming the third-generation governor. She had been contacted by Governor Lopez prior to her selection as one of the two captain candidates. The governor was the one who suggested if she wasn't selected as captain, she should consider becoming a candidate for governor.

Obviously, the other two governor candidates thought it unfair she be considered at such a late date. However, the governor responded by telling them her primary goal was to select the best possible person for governor.

Six months later, Britt-Marie was selected. Governor Lopez commented that it was critical to the overall success of the mission for *Hope's* naval commander and the governor to be able to work closely together after they arrived at Proxima-b. She believed her experience of working with me as a captain candidate proved we could work together well. The other two candidates had no such experience.

I thought it was a very good choice. And in the interest of working closely together, we were married shortly after her appointment. I think we both knew we were fated to be married. After all, we *are* the Vikings.

Our Work Cut Out For Us—Governor Britt-Marie Sjöblom

I believe the third generation will be the most challenging of all the generations that have come before or will come after us. Not only will we have to continue our trip for the next 30 years, we will also have to accomplish several critical tasks in order to have a successful mission. I would venture to say the vast majority of those tasks were identified before *Hope* left Earth's orbit. All of those tasks fall into one of six categories:

1. Establish an orbit at Proxima-b.
2. Refurbish *Hope* for the return trip to Earth.
3. Determine the best location for the Colony.
4. Select those who will establish the Colony.
5. Establish the Colony.
6. Determine the leaders of the fourth generation to begin the return trip to Earth.

The first three tasks will come under the command of Captain Sjöblom. The next two tasks will fall under my command and the last task will be handled jointly by the captain and myself.

Each one of these tasks have numerous subtasks that need to be accomplished. Let's take the first task as an example. Approximately six months out from the planet Proxima-b, the ship will need to decelerate from our cruise speed of five percent c to maneuvering speed. In order to accomplish this subtask, the ion drives will be shut down and maneuvering rockets mounted on the frame of the ship will be used to turn the ship 180 degrees. This will place the ion drives facing into the direction of travel.

This procedure is estimated to take several weeks so as to not cause unacceptable levels of Coriolis Effect on Habitat City's artificial gravity. Once completed there is concern the exhaust nozzles of the ion drives could be damaged by space material. Therefore, we need to extend the shields beyond the nozzle exits until we are ready to fire up the drives.

We will also need to use several of our onboard drones to make exterior checks of the ship prior to restarting the drives. These drones will stay within the extended shields to avoid the effects of high relative velocity space material. In addition to our drones, we have a total of sixty shuttles on board. Thirty in the forward shuttle bays and another thirty in the aft bay. Their main function will be to ferry the new colonists and supplies down to the surface of Proxima-b. At the present time we have no qualified shuttle pilots on board. We will have to train them using flight simulators well before we make orbit around the new planet.

Astrogation will play a very important role in determining our path to Proxima-b. An added complication is that *Faith* will also be approaching Proxima-b at nearly the same time. The goal is to establish the same orbital paths for both ships, thirty to forty-five minutes apart. This will provide a safety margin when shipping people and supplies to the surface from both ships.

Orbit insertion will be handled by *Hope's* Flight Operations group. Simulation drills will commence a month before actual insertion begins. Three separate crews will be trained for this function.

Each of the six major tasks have numerous subtasks that need to be accomplished if we are to accomplish our mission. These tasks are in addition to maintain growing our food, manufacturing all sorts of products, maintaining our living areas and living our lives. When we arrive in orbit, we expect to have a population of 5,000 people. Once the colony people are sent to the surface, our population will decline to half that number. Yet we will still have the same day-to-day requirements. We plan to rebuild our population base during our journey back to Earth.

Plan & Train, Plan & Train—Captain Björn Sjöblom

The first five years of my command was just getting used to the routine of the ship. It wasn't a difficult transition however it did include a lot of details I hadn't been aware of. One of those details was the ship's log. Whoever had command of the ship was required to record specific details, such as their name and rank, the time they assumed command and when they were relieved, with a quick summary of their activities. Anything that had occurred out of the ordinary during their watch was to be recorded in detail.

As captain, one of my duties was to determine the watch list. Our watches were ordinarily four hours in duration then four hours off, followed by another four hours and you were done for the day. Of course, as captain, I was to be available during the entire twenty-four hours every day.

Our watch rotation was usually the same every day. First watch began at 0800 hours and ended at 1200 hours. I chose to cover the first watch. I was relieved of command by the XO and he had the con until 1600 hours, then I relieved him and assumed command until 2000 hours. The XO would then resume command from 2000 hours until 2400 hours. The last two watches were when the ship was least busy and I would assign a variety of junior officers to those two watches to give them command experience.

Since Britt-Marie had declined the XO position, I had to select a new XO. I chose a young lieutenant commander named Alexander White. He was very impressive; I think his age held him back from the original selection process. He was one of those rare individuals who had bounced around between several of the critical systems groups. He began taking military classes while in *Hope* University but transferred to Space Academy for the last two years of school. He graduated tenth overall in his graduating class of fifty-three cadets and was commissioned as an ensign.

His first assignment was in the Power Systems group. At the end of his first year, he was selected for the Outstanding Ensign of the Year award and promoted to lieutenant JG. A few months later, a slot opened up in the Propulsion Systems group in the area of his senior cadet project. That project had boosted his class rating from twenty-two to ten. I remembered him well from his outstanding performance in one of the groups I had led. Two years after joining my group he received a promotion to lieutenant by our then Propulsion System Leader, Jason Kuhn, who had nothing but praise for the young man.

After another year in Propulsion Systems, he was stolen (Captain Kuhn's recollection, not mine) by Shojiro Koyama, the Astrogation Group Leader. It seems they had become close friends when Lieutenant White joined a martial arts class being taught by Commander Koyama in his off-duty time.

Three years after that change of assignment, he was promoted to Lt. Commander (LCMD) by Commander Koyama. It appears when Commander Koyama's involvement with Captain Kuhn's inappropriate actions were made public, there was a falling out between Mr. White and Commander Koyama. LCMD White left the Astrogation Group at that point and volunteered for Security Detail where he could put his martial arts training to practical use.

When I approached him regarding the XO position six months later, he snapped it up in a heartbeat. It was one of my best decisions, LCMD White has been an excellent assistant.

A normal day for me was to be on the bridge at 0800 hours and checking the status of the ship. At 1200 hours the XO would assume command for the second watch while I would meet with the governor, also known as my wife and fellow Viking.

We'd have a working lunch for about a couple of hours, mainly discussing the order in which our planning should proceed. It took us a couple of months before we were satisfied with our joint plan, at which point we would run it by her planning department for their comments. It took us about three and a half months before everyone was satisfied. Then we took our plan and compared it to the original plan created over sixty years ago before *Hope* left Earth's orbit.

The old plan and our new plan were pretty much in agreement and only required a few tweaks before we announced, "We Have the Plan!"

<u>Colony Members—Governor Britt-Marie Sjöblom</u>

Fifteen years into the third generation we began executing our plan for selection of those who would become members of Proxima-b's colony. This process was handled by my Planning Commission and Population Control department. It should be mentioned the vast majority of those who were selected came from our civilian ranks, only a few came from the military. We were to select approximately 2,500 of the 5,000 of *Hope's* total population to become colonists, leaving only 2,500 to repopulate *Hope* when it began its return voyage to Earth.

Some may think it strange but we began our selection process by determining who would remain on *Hope*. We needed to ensure that we had enough skilled people to maintain the integrity of the ship. We had to cut out a lot of the recreational positions or at least plan for people who could handle more than one specialty. Those couples who were selected to remain on *Hope* were given approval to have more children as quickly as possible which would result in teenage children being available to assist with some of the activities when the colonists left the ship.

Those who were selected came from a pool of people with specific skill sets required to build and sustain the colony. Priority was given to married couples with children above the age of sixteen.

There were some exceptions to this policy, of course. These weren't hard and fast rules, only guidelines for our initial selection process. The actual selection process wouldn't be completed until the colony infrastructure was completed and *Hope* was prepared to return to Earth. This was estimated to be two years after we established orbit around Proxima-b.

The last step of the selection process came after training was completed. We over selected around 3,000 people. I forgot to mention, for the most part all of those selected were volunteers. To get these volunteers we held meetings with information regarding what life on the colony would be like. We had some really great vid footage from the inspection drones sent out many decades ago of possible colony sites. It showed rivers and lakes, beautiful mountains with snowcapped peaks. There wasn't any noticeable vegetation, however computer-generated images showed how the land could be made fertile and crops and forests could be grown. It also depicted how the colony buildings would be constructed before the colonists would transition to stay on the surface. They also mentioned how the majority of *Hope* and *Faith's* people would all assist in the construction processes leaving only a skeleton crew on each ship until everything was completed. After the sales pitch, we had more than 3,000 volunteers.

There were requirements for a vast variety of skilled construction positions: operators of heavy equipment, electricians, plumbers and loads and loads of specialized assembly workers to name a few. Much of the building sections were already stored aboard the two starships in modules that could be easily and quickly assembled. What didn't exist as modules was fabricated on the ships by 3-D printers. The programs for the printers were generated well before we left Earth.

In discussions with my husband, the Viking Captain, he informed me the Navy would contribute to two areas of specialization: shuttle pilots and transport beam operators.

He told me, "To set a good example, I will join with those who want to be pilots in the flight training on the simulators. We can't actually fly the shuttles until we are in orbit around Proxima-b. If we tried to launch a shuttle while we are traveling at high speed, it would be destroyed immediately after it penetrated our shields. It would be like playing arcade games again. You remember how good I was at those games don't you?"

"Not really, I thought they were silly games for a PhD to be playing. I thought you had forgotten all about playing vid games," I answered.

"Not at all, my love," he replied. "Every few days, after we finish our lunch, I don my virtual reality helmet and gloves and play my favorite game."

"And what is this favorite game you play, little boy?"
"Why, Viking Raiders of course!"

Simulations—Captain Björn Sjöblom

Pilot Training

Some of you may be wondering why we need human operators for the shuttles and the transport beam. Don't we have sophisticated autopilots that operate the equipment better than a human?

Good questions. My answer is we need both. When we are operating under very well-known parameters, an autopilot is usually sufficient. AI controlled flights can handle almost any type of flight requirements however I will always require a human pilot to be in our shuttles. It gives me a sense of security to know if the autopilot malfunctions, the pilot can take over. Many will call me old fashioned but who knows how well our shuttles have survived this one hundred-year trip. Of course, we will inspect each shuttle from top to bottom before we ever take them out of the shuttle bay.

The same goes for the transport beam, except I have no idea how it works. Therefore, I want someone I can shout at if something goes wrong.

Before we began our simulator training, all the pilot candidates made a visit to the hanger bays and had a chance to check out all of the various shuttles. We have three shuttle configurations; however, the flight controls are the same for each configuration.

The largest shuttle, known as the transport model, can seat up to 100 passengers plus a pilot and copilot. Both shuttle bays have ten transports. The next size shuttle holds 30 passengers: a full platoon of battle-ready Marines, plus pilot and copilot. We call this model our assault shuttle and we have five in each bay. Lastly, we have the scout model which has only ten seats including the pilot. We assume the scout model will be the most used model during the construction of the colony, ferrying people from one location to another, as well as for scouting the terrain surrounding the colony site. The scout model can also accommodate a squad of Space Marines if needed.

We have a Light Brigade of Space Marines aboard *Hope* which serves as the ship's security detail. The Light Brigade is commanded by Major Thomas Bruce and has two companies of a hundred soldiers each commanded by Marine Captains. Each company is divided into four platoons made up of twenty-five troops. The platoons are led by both first and second lieutenants. The Space Marines have first priority for the assault shuttles; they can also be used for other operations.

A total of twenty-five Space Marines were selected for flight training. When the marines were on mission related duty, their pilots would fly the shuttles.

In addition to the twenty-five marines selected to begin flight simulator training, two hundred civilians also volunteered. Before we stepped into the simulators, I wanted each of them to see what they would be flying, assuming they passed the simulator training.

I took the entire group to the forward shuttle bay and turned them loose. They were like little kids with new toys. The chief warrant officer in charge of the shuttle bay gave a brief safety briefing, then they were on their own exploring everything they could get their hands on.

I had been on this tour along with the XO a few days before so I just stood and watched the chaos. Each of the thirty shuttles had a warrant officer or petty officer standing by the shuttles' wide-open hatches. The reactors that drove the shuttles and supplied power to all their equipment had been powered down for safety reasons. Instead, power cables ran to each shuttle from a portable generator unit that drove all the bells and whistles but not the propulsion system.

Each of the trainees had the option of sitting in the pilot seat of at least one shuttle for ten minutes. Every one of the trainees chose that option for as many shuttles as they could. I could see the enthusiasm on their faces. There's something about flying that's in the blood of adventurous people that can't be explained. All I knew was when the

XO and I sat in the pilot's seat and touched all the controls, I was hooked for the rest of my life.

I've read stories of the long-ago pilots and what they went through. One quote stuck in my mind. "Flying is hours and hours of complete boredom, punctuated by moments of stark terror however I would never consider giving it up."

Simulator training began the next week. First there were several weeks of what the trainer referred to as book learning. I'm not sure why since there were no books used in the class, just vid pads. We learned about all the systems aboard the shuttles, then all the safety procedures, next came how to launch and recover from the shuttle bay, how that differed from taking off and landing on the ground, the procedure for communicating with Flight Control and on and on and on.

There were tests that followed each topic of learning. If you didn't score 100% you had a second chance to test again. If you failed your retest (100% was needed) you washed out of the program even before you saw a simulator. However, coaches were available to assist in your preparation for the retest. The washout rate was very low.

Those who passed the book learning moved on to the simulators. The simulators were an exact copy of the shuttle cockpit area. There was a total of ten simulators and they operated ten hours a day, six days a week. Each trainee had a one-hour training session every other day. On the off days, they were to read the flight simulator training manual to prepare them for the next simulator lesson. They had to pass a test on what they read before they were allowed to enter the simulator. The training manual consisted of fifty lessons. That meant simulator training lasted seventeen weeks, almost four months. There was more to come.

The simulators gave our pilot candidates some necessary experience, however there was a limit on what they could do. In my opinion a major limitation was you can't simulate G loading in our basic simulators. Before the drone era, the best fighter aircraft were limited to 9-G loads. Drones were designed to operate at G loads two to three times that number. One antiaircraft missile was designed to accelerate at 100-Gs. The 9 G design limit was based on what a human pilot could withstand.

Even with the most sophisticated G-suits, most fighter pilots would pass out immediately when subjected to a 9-G load. At G loads greater than six or seven it was almost impossible for the pilot to move their arms to fly the aircraft and the brain function diminished quickly as G loads increased.

To give our potential shuttle pilots a taste of G loads we used a centrifuge. Our forefathers were wise enough to design one which could be built with our 3-D printers. Actually, the printer created all the parts required for the centrifuge and it was assembled by our construction team.

The design consisted of two long arms with a cockpit capsule on the end of each arm. A ring collar, nicknamed the donut, encircled the habitat's central tube near the forward end with the arms extending a hundred feet, one arm pointing straight up, the other straight down. Electric motors were used to spin the entire assembly around the central tube.

Two pilot candidates took a maglev car up a spoke from the surface to the central tube which is always in a zero G condition. They would float to hatches on each side of the central tube, open the hatches and pull themselves along the arms until they arrived at their respective cockpit capsules. These capsules were an exact replica of a shuttle cockpit with the exception of the monitoring equipment used to measure each pilot candidate's vital signs. Once the monitoring equipment was online, baseline measurements were made by our medical staff and the tests began.

The large view screen in each capsule showed a view of the interior of the hanger bay. As the centrifuge began to spin, the feel of gravity began to increase. When it reached 1-G it stopped accelerating and the vitals were checked again.

To give the same type of gravity effect they would feel in an actual launch from the shuttle bay, each capsule was very slowly tilted upward and the rotational speed increased to 1.5-Gs. The view screen showed them exiting the hanger bay into space. They were to execute an immediate right turn by banking the shuttle to the right to avoid other shuttles that would be exiting behind them. When each pilot was set to go, the capsule rotated to simulate the turn and the G load increased to 2-Gs.

The entire simulation was based on flying the shuttle from *Hope's* hanger bay down to the surface of Proxima-b, executing a vertical landing, then simulate a vertical takeoff and climb at 4-Gs into space and land in *Hope's* forward shuttle bay. Assuming all their vitals were in the green they would repeat the procedure with variations, like air turbulence during atmospheric flight, night missions, thunderstorms and so on.

Each session in the centrifuge lasted about thirty minutes. During each session the missions varied, eventually increasing the maximum G loads they would be exposed to. Each pilot was expected to train at least twice a week, no more than four times a week. They logged each mission on E-pads and reviewed them with their flight instructors. Award certificates were handed out for operations at 6-Gs and 8-Gs. The centrifuge missions continued until we began our deceleration maneuvers, about six months before we began orbiting Proxima-b.

Once *Hope* decelerated to slow maneuvering speed, actual flights were made in the shuttles. To become certified to carry passengers, each pilot had to have at least a hundred hours of flight time. The highest rated pilots were always the pilots in command, the others served as copilots. I am happy to say I was in the top one hundred.

Transport Beam Training

I have to admit, I know very little about the transport beam. I feel it borders on magic, a very good magic. It allows us to transport very heavy loads from an orbiting ship to a planet's surface. It can handle huge pieces of equipment weighing up to fifty tons to packages as small as a book. All it takes is a laser beam and some magic cloth.

It reminds me of an ancient story my grandfather would read to me when I was a wee tike. The story is called *Jack and the Bean Stalk*. It's a tale about a young boy taking a milk cow into his village to sell it when a gnome approached him and convinced him to give him the cow in exchange for some magic beans. When the boy's father found out what his son had done, he was enraged, threw the beans out the window and sent the boy to bed without supper. In the morning, when they arose and looked out the window, the magic beans had grown into a huge bean stock which had grown into the clouds. If you wish to know any more of the story you may read it yourself. I found it quite enchanting.

In our case, it's not magic beans, it's magic cloth; cloth with tiny wires made of a very rare and secret material. The cloth itself is also woven from a secret fabric using a *very* secret process. It has a very attractive powder blue color.

When you wrap any object in this blue cloth and shine a laser beam on it, you can move the object anywhere you can see, like from an orbiting space ship to a place on the ground. Or vice versa; if you shine the laser on an object on the ground covered with the secret blue cloth, you can transport it into the ship.

The object can be people too, just as long as they are wearing a hooded jumpsuit made from the magic blue cloth. When the laser touches them, they can be moved wherever the beam operator chooses.

Some of you may be asking, 'What type of laser is used to move these objects covered in magic blue cloth?' The answer is... wait for it...IT'S A SECRET!!! Are you surprised?

Anyway, the entire beaming operation is computer controlled. The operator inputs target coordinates and touches the article to be transported with the secret laser beam, pushes a button and *voilà* another successful transport is made.

Of course, the operator training is very extensive. When I asked if I could learn it, I was told no, *It's a secret.*

Change to Our Flight Plan—Lieutenant Chang Liu

A month ago, I was on night watch, the 0000 to 0400 hours shift, believed to be the crappiest watch of all. At that time of night there wasn't much to do. Most of the crew were sleeping and only a skeleton crew remained on duty.

To keep from falling asleep, I decided to review the procedure for slowing the ship down from our cruise speed of five percent c to maneuvering speed. The more I read, the more complicated it seemed to me. The plan indicated we were to shut down the ion drive, extend the shields to cover the drive exhausts, rotate the ship 180 degrees using the maneuvering rockets, retract the shields to expose the drive exhausts, restart the ion drives and decelerate the ship to maneuvering speed.

I thought there had to be a less complicated way to slow the ship down. Then it came to me. *Why not shut down the drives and let the drag of space material slow us down? I thought to myself, it couldn't be that simple, could it?* I needed to see if there was enough drag from the space material to slow us down within a reasonable amount of time.

It was pretty easy to determine the amount of drag on the ship. It was equal to the amount of thrust needed to maintain our cruise speed. Of course, as the ship slowed, the drag would be reduced, so I had to take that into account. I created a simple algorithm and plugged in the variable values; in a few nanoseconds, my ePad gave me the answer: 13 months, 6 days, 3 hours and 12.6 minutes (give or take a few days). I rechecked the math and decided to tell my commander it would take a little over 13 months.

When my watch was over at 0400 hours, I took a short nap. Promptly at 0830, hours I approached Commander Olga (as she preferred to be called). I waited until she finished her first cup of coffee and then asked to speak to her.

As succinctly as I could, I explained my suggestion, handing her my ePad so she could check my algorithm and math. When she was done, she handed me back my ePad and just stared at me for a very uncomfortable moment. Without speaking to me she picked up her com unit and asked for the captain.

"Captain this is Olga. I have a lieutenant here who has an idea you might want to consider. Could you spare us a few minutes of your time?" There was a short pause, followed by, "Yes sir. 0900 hours would be fine. We'll see you then."

We arrived at the captain's chair promptly at 0900 hours. He smiled at her and looked quizzically at me, then turned back to Commander Olga and said, "What have you got for me Olga?"

"Captain, this is Lieutenant Chang Liu. He has a suggestion he'd like to run by you. I think you'll find it interesting."

I spent the next ten minutes explaining my idea. During that time, the captain didn't say a word. When I was done, he turned to my boss and said, "Well, Olga. This sounds promising. Do you think it will work?"

I felt a sinking feeling in the pit of my stomach until Commander Olga replied to the captain, "Absolutely, sir. I wouldn't have bothered you with a bad idea."

The captain smiled at her and then turned to me and said, "Outstanding work, Lieutenant. I want Information Systems to take a look at your calculations however your principles are sound. It's such a simple solution, I wonder why no one else ever thought of it."

A week later, Information Systems gave it their approval. At the monthly awards dinner, I received an award for the best new idea of the month. It turned out the night watch wasn't so bad after all.

<u>Fabrication Begins—Governor Britt-Marie Sjöblom</u>

Twenty years into the third generation, we began fabrication of some of the equipment we would be needing for the initial landing on Proxima-b, well not exactly the initial landing. First there will be survey crews and scouting expeditions of the area around the colony site. Those would be day trips, with everyone returning to their respective ships two hundred miles above in orbit for eating and sleeping.

The first equipment needed on the planet would be rock crushers. The individual components of the rock crushers needed to be fabricated, then assembled and finally tested before they could be beamed down to the planet's surface.

Survey reports from the drones decades ago revealed most of the planet's surface consisted of very large boulders. One might think that wouldn't be a good thing; actually, it's perfect. The boulders lie on top of virtually flat rocky planes, which are perfect for the foundation of our buildings as well as the base for our crops.

The boulders on the land designated for building needed to be cleared by our transport beam and deposited onto potential farmland. Then the rock crushers take over.

The rock crushers break down the boulders into smaller rocks which in turn need to be converted into even smaller rock particles. The end product is a coarse sand that is mixed with water and nutrients to turn it into soil. The soil is then spread over the flat rock surface three feet deep and allowed to 'cook.' After three months of 'cooking,' we will begin planting crops.

There are three different machines which need to be fabricated in order to produce soil ready to plant: rock crushers, pulverizers and spreaders. A minimum of four of each type need to be built. This requires the fabrication of hundreds of components. Once our 3-D printers are programmed, they'll 'print' all the components of a rock crusher, then move on to the pulverizer, followed by the spreader. Assembly commences as soon as all components of a given machine are fabricated. Once a set of machines has been assembled, they're to be tested, then packaged for transport to the surface. This process will be repeated until all four sets of machines are packaged.

In order to complete this task in a timely manner, a dozen 3-D printers of various capacities are required. We had six printers in operation when we began and six additional printers were taken from storage and activated.

The various raw materials required for the fabrication were transferred by robo-transporters to the manufacturing sites from our material storage facilities.

At the present time we are fabricating the components of the first rock crusher.

<u>Deceleration—Captain Björn Sjöblom</u>

We were fifteen months away from orbiting Proxima-b when we began our deceleration from five percent c. We followed Lieutenant Liu's suggestion and shut down our ion drive to let the drag force of the space material slow us down. It turns out his calculations were dead on. It took a little over fourteen months to reach our maneuvering speed. Thanks to the excellent mapping out of our course by Astrogation, we were only a month away from our destination!

The star Proxima Centauri was now a large red ball of light in our vid screens. We could actually see the shadow of Proxima-b as it moved across the face of its sun. The excitement in the ship had grown steadily during the deceleration process. I think the most excited people were the shuttle pilots; they couldn't wait to begin flying, really flying! Of course, I was one of the most excited.

I wanted to be the first one to fly out of the shuttle bay, however my wife and *Hope's* Squadron Commander vetoed me. The Squadron Commander said it was tradition the pilot who had the highest score in flight training be given that honor. My Viking wife said it would be better if I let all those who scored higher than me to go before I did. She was right of course. I had let my emotions get the best of me. I finally gave in to their 'recommendations.' That meant I was the ninety third person to fly a shuttle. I was assigned to fly the scout model. By the time it was my turn to fly, the shuttle had already been flown twice by pilots who had scored higher than me.

Once I was inside the shuttle, I no longer cared. My bruised ego made a miraculous recovery while I was strapping in and went through my preflight checklist. I had two passengers with me on the flight. It was unusual to have passengers on a pilot's first flight. It was recommended they have a couple of solo flights to familiarize themselves with the shuttle. However, I was special (or so they told me). I was almost finished with my checklist when Britt-Marie climbed aboard and took the seat next to me. She was followed by the squadron commander who took the seat behind me.

I smiled at them both then said, "Thanks for wishing me a good flight however you need to leave now. I'm almost ready to launch."

Britt-Marie smiled back and said, "We're going with you."

I frowned and turned to the squadron commander, "Please don't make me order you off the flight. I want to make my first flight a solo just like the other pilots."

He shook his head and replied, "Sorry Captain, you aren't like all the other pilots. You're the captain of the starship and as such you are required to be accompanied by a backup pilot."

I turned back to glare at Britt-Marie and said, "What about her? She's not a backup pilot. She's the governor. She's too important to go flying around the universe with an inexperienced pilot."

Britt-Marie, a normally good-natured woman, turned to me and her smile became a slight frown. Then she spoke to me in a burst of Swedish that lasted for only a few moments. She didn't raise her voice or shout at me. She remained calm as she said things that would remove paint from a wall and make my blonde hair curl in the process. I will not bother to translate, I'm sure it would remove much of the sting her comments carried in Swedish.

I turned from her toward the forward view screen without saying a word, pushed the button to close and seal the hatch, brought the shuttle to a low hover and slowly moved out of the bay, then turned the shuttle forward and accelerated at a 2-G rate.

I took the shuttle through a series of programmed maneuvers, never exceeding 3-Gs. Thirty minutes later, I landed the shuttle back in the forward bay. As we disembarked from the shuttle, I noticed Britt-Marie wobbled a bit as she walked out of the bay. Inside, I smirked a little. *Serves you right,* I thought to myself.

Colony Personnel—Lieutenant Governor Malcolm Cole

My responsibilities as lieutenant governor are focused entirely on preparing for colonization. The governor has delegated to me all activities required to prepare for moving the colonists off of *Hope* to the colony site. Those activities include, but aren't limited to:

Onboard Ship Activities Prior to Landing

- Selecting the colonist.
- Training the colonists and ship's construction teams.
- Selection of the colony site.
- Overseeing the construction of housing and office modules aboard *Hope*.
- Overseeing the growing, processing and packaging of colony food supply for one year.
- Overseeing of clothing and accessories manufacturing and packaging for colonists.
- Overseeing fabrication and assembly of heavy equipment needed for construction.
- Ensure all equipment, supplies and building modules are transported to the surface.

Planet Side Activities

- Clearing space for living quarters and office buildings.
- Ensuring all electrical, water and waste services are available to all buildings.
- Assembly of living quarters and office buildings modules.
- Oversee the setting up of farmland and pastures.
- Establish a ruling council for the colony.

I had joined the Colony Planning Team at the age of 25. I was 32 when *Hope* began to orbit Proxima-b. By that time, I had become the lieutenant governor and was also selected to become the Chairman of the Ruling Council. I would accompany the 5,000 original colonists to populate Proxima-b. While I was aboard ship, I gave Governor Sjöblom weekly updates on where we stood with regard to the plan. She played a major role in overcoming any obstacles I encountered. When I moved to the colony, I would be on my own to make all the major decisions.

Once the colony members were selected—a very complicated task, using incredibly complicated algorithms (complicated for me. Math was never my strong suit. Neither was computer programming)—the training began.

I was amazed at how detailed our ancestors were in providing training material for each discipline required to begin our colony. All the trainees had to do was fire up their ePad, enter their discipline code, wait a few minutes for the program to download, then follow a step-by-step set of instruction on how to be a plumber or an electrician or an equipment operator. It wasn't just boring text, there were audio segments and vid clips which showed how to accomplish every conceivable problem that could occur.

As great as 'book learning' is, we also had literally dozens of mentors to help with the training. Most of the mentors had years, if not decades, doing the same things the colonists would need to do.

I was reassured each one of the colonists would be well trained before they would ever reach Proxima-b. I reported all this to Governor Sjöblom who appeared delighted.

Another major undertaking involved growing an excess amount of food during the two years we were in orbit. Our goal was to produce enough food to feed the colonists for one year while they got the colony up and going. This was the same thing that happened aboard *Hope* when they departed Earth. Until the farms and pastures of Habitat City had matured, the initial passengers lived off the stored food supplied by Earth's farms and pastures. *Faith* had a similar program. The goal was for each ship to produce enough food to feed 2,500 people for one year.

In addition to the food program, a program to supply clothes and accessories began when we began orbiting.

Both of these efforts were on schedule. Food and clothes and accessories would be packaged up and placed in appropriate storage areas within *Hope*. When the colonists began to migrate from the ships to the *Colony City* (the name the colonists had chosen for their new home) those items would be transferred to storage areas there.

Conversations with *Faith*–Communications Officer LCMD Marvin Eide

As we approached the end of our journey to Proxima-b, the com traffic between our two ships increased greatly. Recently, *Faith's* captain notified us he was still a year ahead of us. He suggested he use that year to search Alpha Centauri-A/B to see if they could discover any planets that might be more favorable for colonization than Proxima-b. Now that they were approaching so close to the Alpha Centauri cluster, they had a much better chance of making that discovery. If they discovered what he considered to be a more favorable planet we could rendezvous at the new planet. If they didn't find anything worthwhile, we would rendezvous at Proxima-b as originally planned.

Captain Sjöblom consulted with his staff before concluding it was a worthwhile endeavor. We contacted *Faith* and wished them good hunting.

There were several additional exchanges of coms while *Faith* undertook her search. When the year was completed, they sent a summary of their search results. They had discovered several additional planets, some with indications of microscopic life forms however none were better for colonization than Proxima-b.

Rendezvous at Proxima-b was scheduled for three months later.

<u>Choosing the Site—Lieutenant Governor Malcolm Cole</u>

I was surprised when I was selected to cover this report. I thought either the captain or the governor would handle it. They said they wanted me to handle all reports regarding the colony. Selection of the site was an important part of establishing the colony, therefore they wanted me to make the report. However, both of them indicated they would contribute to the report where they saw fit. Let me begin.

Once *Hope* and *Faith* were synced up in orbit, the first order of business was to determine the best site for the colony. We knew from very old data the sweet spot on the planet was close to the equator. Actually, we would only scan any possible colony sites that were within plus or minus thirty degrees latitude from the equator. Farther north or south would be unacceptably cold.

We spent the first three months in orbit making detailed topographical scans of all the land within the sweet spot band. At the end of the scanning three potential sites were chosen. All three sites were located on relatively flat planes positioned between low mountain ranges. Each site was located close to great fresh water supplies; two had rivers and one was next to a lake.

The next step was to send out shuttle teams to determine which one of the three sites was the best choice. Three assault shuttles were used to ferry the survey teams to the various locations. The assault shuttle had the capacity to carry up to thirty people; only twenty were selected to make up each team. One shuttle was from *Faith.* That team examined the lake-side site. The other two locations, the ones near the rivers, were examined by *Hope.*   Eight of the team members were Space Marines who were tasked with supplying security to the remainder of the party. The other twelve were scientists and technicians who would take precise measurements of the complete area, take core samples to determine the composition of the rock surfaces and boulders, determine the quality of the water supply, and a hundred other things that needed to be known. The extra space on the shuttles was used to store all the cases of equipment that would be needed to evaluate the sites.

The mission was to last no longer than a week. The evaluations were all made during daylight hours. The teams returned during twilight each day and additional technicians onboard the starships ran the analyses of the collected data.

I would vary which of the shuttles I would take so I would have a feel for both sites. When I entered the shuttle the second day, I was surprised to see Captain Sjöblom in the copilot's seat, going through a preflight check list on his ePad.

He looked up at me as I took the seat behind the pilot and smiled, "Good morning, Lieutenant Governor or should I refer to you as Chairman now that we're exploring the planet's surface?"

"Why don't you just call me Malcolm, Captain. I didn't know you were going to be the copilot on this flight," I replied.

He put a finger to his lips and made a soft shushing sound. "It's a secret," he whispered softly. "Please don't tell the governor. I just had to be one of the first to land on Proxima-b."

I smiled at him and replied, "My lips are sealed, Captain. Enjoy the ride."

A Marine sergeant was the last passenger to come aboard. The pilot closed and sealed the hatch. "Everyone belted in?" he asked. A frivolous question since the display on his panel would indicate if anyone didn't have the safety harness belted however one I'm sure protocol demanded.

Flight Command had us wait for a few moments until we were at the correct orbital position for the quickest flight to the location we were scouting out. His loud baritone voice finally announced, "Assault Shuttle 7, you are cleared to launch. Good hunting."

"Roger, Flight Command, Assault Shuttle 7, launching," replied our pilot and we eased out of the shuttle bay, executed a quick maneuver to clear us from the orbiting ship and began our decent. When we entered the atmosphere, we encountered some light turbulence (or chop as the pilots call it) but thanks to our pilot and of course his onboard computer-controlled autopilot, our trip was uneventful. I really enjoyed the large vid screen that let us watch as we broke out of the clouds and got our first view of the terrain below.

The pilot took command of the ship as we reached 1000 AGL (pilot talk for Above Ground Level) and flew us over an almost flat valley between two low mountain ranges which ran for miles. Right in the middle was a large river. I'm not talking about Mississippi or Nile river wide, maybe a hundred feet wide or so. It definitely had fast flowing water which I was told had its origin in a spring somewhere up in one of the mountains.

As we approached the possible colony site, the pilot slowed down to give us a better look. The most prominent thing I noticed was the number of large boulders. They were everywhere, the biggest ones as big as a three-story building, with estimated weights of two or three hundred tons. Fortunately, those were the exceptions. The vast majority were on average ten to fifteen feet high, weighing maybe as much as fifty tons.

After our initial pass, the pilot turned us around and we flew back to where the other shuttle had already landed. There were a lot of people all over the area. Our pilot brought us down for a vertical landing as gentle as a feather, shut down the drive and opened the hatch. We got out and got to work, well most of us did. The captain and I were mainly observers and there was a lot to see.

As we walked over to the river, the captain commented, "The riverbed seems to have been carved in solid rock just by the flow of the water. To accomplish that must mean this is a very old place, perhaps ancient would be a better description."

One of the geologists was standing nearby and overheard the captain's comments. He said, "You're right, Captain but the water has a pretty high silt content made up of small pieces of rock broken off by the fast-flowing water. That would increase the abrasiveness of the flow."

The day passed quickly. As we boarded our shuttle to return to the ship, the captain was very excited, "The pilot said I could fly us back to *Hope*. I can't wait for launch time."

After we lifted off and accelerated into a 2-G climb, I began reviewing my notes on the day's activities. Not as easy as it sounds when you have a small elephant sitting on your chest. My overall impression was that surely this was an alien world. Instead of a blue sky, it was a faint pink. The air had a slightly strange odor, not unpleasant, just different. There wasn't any vegetation, not one blade of grass, not one weed; just rocks, rocks and rocks and more rocks. I knew it would look different after the terraforming was complete; it was only mildly depressing.

The only thing I thought was all right was the water. Water samples had been analyzed indicating it was okay for us to drink from a large storage barrel. So, I filled my cup from a spigot at the bottom of the barrel. The cup was made from a clear, transparent plastic and the water had no sediment at all, it was crystal clear. It smelled okay and I finally got up the courage to taste it. Surprise, surprise, it tasted just like water from home or at least water from *Hope*. For some reason, after taking a large drink, I didn't feel depressed anymore.

When we landed in the forward shuttle bay, the governor was waiting for us. She wasn't smiling. Since both pilot and copilot have to go through a shutdown procedure which takes a few minutes, they remained on board while the rest of us left the shuttle and headed into the main part of the ship. I avoided looking at the governor and she seemed to be concentrating on waiting for her husband. I walked at a brisk pace to ensure I wasn't present for the coming encounter.

Once all of the survey data was analyzed, we were ready to make a site selection. The first site to be eliminated was the one by the lake. It turns out the lake was toxic. One of the streams feeding the lake had a high level of a toxic mineral I'd never heard of. It ended up polluting the lake.

The other two sites were very comparable. Each had rivers that would run through the center of town which would provide a more than adequate water supply to the colony. Unfortunately, the seasonal variation in the water quantity might be a problem. Much of the water for one river would be from mountain snow melt. The mountains were close to the proposed colony site however if there was a mild snow fall it could result in an insufficient water supply. Therefore, the site the captain and I had visited was selected.

The next step was to lay out a plan view of the colony site on top of the topographical data and make whatever adjustments were required. The detailed planning resulted in determining which rocks were to be moved to create a level foundation on which to build Colony City. It was also determined which rocks were to be used to create farmland and pastures.

The following step was to send down transporter beams and rock crushers to get the party started.

Transport Beams—Lieutenant Governor Cole

Before we could send down the transport beams we needed to assemble the two support towers where they would be mounted. Each ship would first transport down the components that made up the towers. A shuttle from each of the orbiting ships ferried crews who would perform the assemblies of the towers, one in the area of the city and one in the farmland.

Hope sent their powder blue cloth covered package to the city site and *Faith* beamed theirs to the farmland. It took several days for them to anchor the bases of the towers to the bedrock and then another two days to assemble the tower modules. The finished products were ten stories tall, awaiting the transport beams.

The transport beam components were sent down from each ship to a location close to their support towers. A new team assembled the beams which were then loaded on transport shuttles which took the assemblies to the top of the towers and lowered them into place where they were secured to the towers.

Once installed they were tested, demonstrating they could lift boulders and move them to wherever they needed to be relocated. It took a total of two weeks before both towers were certified for operations.

Once certified, they were put into immediate use. The plan was to accumulate boulders into specific areas so the rock crushers and pulverizers could do their work.

It took two additional weeks before the *Hope* transport beam had cleared most of the boulders from what would be the foundation for apartments and office buildings. Of course, the boulders that weighed in excess of fifty tons had to wait for the rock crushers to break them up into smaller boulders before we could move them.

The *Faith* transport beam positioned boulders on the farmland in close proximity to one another so the rock crushers didn't have to be moved too far to get to their next assigned rock.

It took a little less than a month from the time the shuttle assembly crew landed in the shuttles until everything was ready for the rock crushers.

<u>Sometimes Bad Things Happen—Captain Eric Jackson Commander of *Faith*</u>

Faith had been selected to send down the first rock crusher, *Hope* was to send theirs a week later. The assembled rock crusher had been placed on a pallet and covered with the secret powder blue cloth that would allow us to use the ship's transport beam to deliver it to the farmland.

The rock crusher, together with its pallet, weighed thirty tons, well within the fifty-ton limit. It was moved from its prep room to the transport launch room on a maglev platform twenty minutes before it would begin its journey to the surface of Proxima-b.

Hours before this an assault shuttle from *Faith* was launched from our aft shuttle bay loaded with a crew of technicians responsible for unpacking the rock crusher and getting it ready to go to work. The foreman of the crew was in constant contact with the transport beam operator. The foreman notified him he had put the homing beacon in the proper location and activated it. He also told him the target area was clear of any debris and they were ready for launch.

The beam operator acknowledged the homing signal and said they would launch in ten minutes. He also said there were thick clouds over the target area and they wouldn't see the package until it broke through the clouds.

Ten minutes later the rock crusher launched and began its twenty-minute trip to the target area. When the package was at an altitude to 10,000 feet and just entering the clouds, power to the beam went off line. The rock crusher was just beginning its deceleration for landing when it was suddenly in freefall, its velocity increasing.

When it burst through the bottom of the cloud layer it was a fiery red bomb. The beam operator began screaming into his com to the crew chief, "Abort! Abort! It's in freefall! Get the hell out of there!"

The package hit the rocky surface like a meteor. The kinetic energy of the impact was like an earthquake. The flat rock surface of the landing zone was shattered into stone bullets that found too many targets. Eight of my crew died that day. Eight of my crew were killed. Eight good men and women under my command, people whom I had worked with and considered my friends were gone…forever. Two more died once they were back aboard the ship.

Red lights were flashing on the bridge and klaxons were blaring. An emergency shuttle was launched immediately from the front shuttle bay with medics aboard to save those who were injured and return them to the ship. They also brought back the bodies of those who didn't survive.

An immediate investigation sought to determine how this could possibly happen. All our systems had triple redundancy to prevent this type of system failure. We needed to find out how it happened and how to correct it or we wouldn't be able to use our beam transport again. That in turn would severely impact the building of Colony City.

It took two days for an inspection team to discover the answer. When I heard their report, my knees buckled. I had to sit down to keep from falling. It was sabotage! It wasn't a failure of any equipment. It was caused by another member of the ship or maybe several members of the crew.

I made an announcement to the entire ship. "This is your captain speaking. We have discovered that the failure of our transport beam wasn't caused by any equipment malfunction. It was caused by one or more of the ship's crew. Whoever they are, they are responsible for the deaths of ten precious human beings. I want you to know, my highest priority is to find out the names of the cowards, the murderers, who took part in this unspeakable action…and make sure they never do it again."

As part of our investigation, we came across some com messages that indicated we had several insurrectionists aboard. Way back in the first generation, there was an uprising caused by knowledge of The Plague. A sizeable number of people wanted us to return to Earth in an attempt to help find an answer to the disease. It almost led to a mutiny however the rebellion was put down and *Faith* continued on her way. Apparently, those who shared those rebellious feelings went underground through the next two generations.

Several days later, we got a break. One of the saboteurs came forward. She was held in our temporary brig. Her confession was recorded. "We never intended for anyone to die. I'm so sorry so many were sacrificed. We only wanted to give you an excuse to back out of this insane idea of setting up a colony on a foreign world. You must know it will never work. The only way to save humanity is to return to Earth, humanity's only true home. It makes more sense to return now since The Plague has to have run its course. Instead of sending half our population to a doomed existence on this rock, we should turn around and head for home as fast as we can."

She identified the others of her group, assuming we would be merciful. Once they told us how they went about shutting off the power to the transport beam, a court martial was held. They were found guilty of treason and murder and sentenced to death. I believed their punishment should fit their crime. They were covered in the magic blue cloth and sent down to the surface on the repaired transport beam. Ten thousand feet above the target area we shut off the power and let them all fall to their deaths. I believe justice was served.

<u>Rock Crusher—Lieutenant Governor Malcolm Cole</u>

While *Faith* was having their problems, *Hope* was moving on with our plan. We successfully beamed our first rock crusher to the area where the apartments and office buildings would be assembled. The crew chief began the process of taking the biggest boulders and making them into 'bite sized boulders the crusher can get its teeth into' (the crew chief's words, not mine).

Built into the rock crusher was a high-energy construction laser which could be used to split off sections of the largest boulders. The laser can be used in one of three different modes of operation: single shot, percussion and trepanning. Single shot is what the name implies; a single burst of laser energy is directed at the rock. This method works best when a fault line in the rock is visible. Percussion uses multiple single shot pulses at the same target. This process is needed to split very thick rock. Trepanning is a slicing motion of the laser beam, 'like carving a turkey' (again, the crew chief's terminology).

Optical sensors in the rock crusher scan the boulder and the computer decides how best to split the rock. A small, on board transport beam then picks up the smaller boulders and delivers them to the rock crusher inlet. The finished product was a pile of rocks no bigger than the size of a basketball. Those rocks would then be sent to the pulverizer to be turned into course sand.

When operating at normal operating speed the noise level is ear splitting. Ear protection is required. Also, when the boulders are being split by the laser, the smaller pieces sometimes become lethal projectiles. Therefore, when the rock crusher is doing its thing, the crew chief and his crew are located behind protective shields. Robo cams provide close up vids of the activities and real time data is transmitted to the crew's ePads. The crew chief holds the kill switch which immediately shuts down the operation if a serious problem occurs.

Fortunately, our first rock crusher has performed flawlessly since it went to work. About two weeks after it began making boulders into small rocks, our first pulverizer was transported down from *Hope.*

At the end of each day the operation is shut down and the crew returns to *Hope.*

Foundations–Lieutenant Governor Malcolm Cole

Before we could assemble apartments and office buildings, it was necessary to ensure access of critical systems. The first order was to sweep and level the rock surface the structures would be attached to. Then the floor plan of the entire city was laid out. Attachment points of all of the required services (fresh water, waste removal and electrical power supply) were determined and installed.

To ensure an adequate fresh water supply, a reservoir was constructed and a portion of the river was diverted to fill and maintain it. Water was pumped every evening to a water tower to provide enough water pressure to maintain the proper flow to buildings. Grooves were cut in the foundation rock and supply pipes laid in running to every building complex.

Waste removal was similarly prepared that would direct the waste water and its contents to a large city septic tank for treatment.

Electricity would be supplied by a series of fusion reactor powered generators strategically placed around all potential building areas.

All these services were put in and tested prior to any building assembly beginning. It took several teams of technicians working for three months to complete this phase of Colony City construction.

During those three months, survey teams expanded their examination of the surrounding area. They mapped all the terrain within a fifty-mile radius of what would be city center. That took them up into the mountain ranges on the east and west side of the city and followed the river fifty-miles upstream and down-stream to ensure there wouldn't be any potential blockage points which could cause an insufficient flow of water into the city or a flooding of the city if the river was blocked downstream.

During these surveys, geologist discovered rich veins of iron and copper in the mountains. Exploration of the river uncovered potential blockage sites which were cleared. We were ready to start putting buildings together.

<u>Preparing Farmland—Captain Eric Jackson of *Faith*</u>

After a short delay to mourn for our fallen crew, *Faith* began their establishment of the farmland and pastures. Rock crushers, pulverizers and spreaders were delivered to the rural area adjacent to Colony City.

The rock crushers were amazing to watch. It reminded me of the old vids of giant gorillas fighting against prehistoric monsters. They dwarfed the human creatures who were scurrying around trying their best not to be stepped on or smushed by the giant feet of the monsters.

The rock crusher was the loudest of the three types of machines. As each rock was crushed it sounded like a series of detonations. I expected to see the rock crusher blown apart by the exploding boulders and rocks. The pulverizers were much quieter. They were designed to take the rocks from the crusher and turn them into a course sand. A side effect of this process was a repeating huffing sound followed by exhausting a puff of air. Some inventive individual gave the machines the nicknames of Huff and Puff. It caught on with the techs and of course the children loved it. Children's vids were produced and shown to the small ones living in both starships.

The spreaders were the quietest of all. They took the course sand from Huff and Puff, mixed it with water and nutrients to form a pasty like substance which was spread three feet deep on the prepared rock surface. The surface was prepared by drilling deep holes in the rock to allow for adequate drainage. Once the paste was in place it was left for three months to cook while other fields were being similarly prepared.

After three months of developing, the fields had transitioned to soil and were planted with grass as the first crop. After another few months green fields were beginning to pop up all over the farm area.

It took over a year to get all of the farmland and pastures ready to plant other crops. A variety of crops were planted on the farmland as a test to see how well they would grow. It was crucial for the colony to grow their own food as quickly as possible. They had to be self-sustaining within one more year. If they couldn't, the colony wouldn't survive.

Hope Returns to Earth—Captain Björn Sjöblom

While things were going smoothly down on the planet, we began getting *Hope* into shipshape for the return trip to Earth. Between Malcolm and Governor Britt-Marie (I really like the sound of that), they have handled everything needed for getting the onboard colonists ready for their move to their new homes on Colony City. At the same time, they are preparing to manage Habitat City with a much smaller population than they have ever had. I'm sure they will fill you in on both those endeavors shortly.

As the Captain of *Hope* (soon to be retiring), my current focus is making sure the ship is completely refurbished and ready to leave orbit. My XO has provided me a to-do list; it fell on me to decide which items needed to be addressed first.

I decided replacement of the EM ion drive system came first. That entailed several sub tasks as listed below:

- Replace the fusion reactors dedicated to the drive system.
- Replace the ion drives.
- Inspect and refurbish the ram scoops.
- Inspect and refurbish the propulsion fluid tanks and pumps.
- Fill the propulsion fluid tanks with water from Proxima-b.
- Make test runs of the new drive systems.

The list the XO gave me had 22 items and I added a few more. Each item had several sub tasks similar to the propulsion system. We had many of the replacement parts in the ship's storage; the replacement parts we didn't bring with us from Earth were fabricated by our 3-D printers.

In addition to the list I'd received from the XO, I also requested lists from all of the critical systems leaders. After I'd checked their lists and approved most of the items they felt needed to be upgraded or replaced, they were authorized to proceed.

The combined lists had several hundred items; it was going to take most of the year to get them completed.

<u>Buildings Are Assembled—Lieutenant Governor Malcolm Cole</u>

Once all the prep work was completed, the next step was construction of the living spaces. We lumped them into apartments and office buildings as we talk about them but it really includes more than that. Worship centers, restaurants, entertainment venues and recreation centers were also included. All of these had been fabricated as modules upon the two starships then beamed down to a central site on pallets. The local transport beam then picked up individual pallets and deposited them to each construction site where the construction crews began their assembly process.

The apartment buildings went up first. Each apartment was a two-bedroom unit with provision for expansion to three bedrooms. Each complex was three stories high with five hundred apartments. *Hope* and *Faith* each contributed four apartment complexes which provided for the five thousand colonists as well as population growth.

At the same time the apartments were being assembled, other construction teams were assembling the office buildings. The name office buildings may be misleading. The term covers every type of building except a residence even storage units and fabrication facilities.

The majority of the new colonists were Christians, however other religions were well represented. There were Jews, Muslims and Buddhists along with a few other faiths. To the best of my knowledge there were no atheists, perhaps a few agnostics. I am happy to report there was little or no religious conflicts between the various faiths. They shared the worship center on the starships just as they will share the center in Colony City.

This was a major activity and it took over six months to complete. The next step was to send furniture and appliances which were fabricated aboard the ships and install them in the various buildings.

The packaged starship food was also sent down and stored as well as clothing and accessories. This took another three months. At that point, we were ready to start bringing the colonists down to their new home.

<u>Transition to Proxima-b—Captain Eric Jackson</u>

While *Hope* construction teams were assembling Colony City buildings, the crews from *Faith* were busy planting. A large variety of vegetables, fruits and grains were planted. As soon as the pasture land was considered ready for livestock, animals were placed in large containers covered with the powder blue cloth and transported to the pastures. At first, only the livestock from *Faith* was transported. *Hope's* transporter beam was busy moving furniture and food. As soon as they completed that task, they began sending their livestock as well.

The vegetables, fruits and grains had two growing seasons per year and the starships were to remain until one successful harvest had passed. We had to be sure the colony was on its way to becoming self-sufficient.

Everything was in place and ready to receive the colonists. *Faith* was the lead starship in orbit around the colony planet. *Hope* trailed us by thirty minutes. We would be over our target for about twenty minutes every time we passed over the Colony City site. Our shuttles were loaded with colonists and as we approached our twenty-minute window we launched several shuttles. It took another twenty minutes for them to reach the landing zone near the apartment complexes. The shuttle passengers deplaned, gathered all their belongings and headed for their apartments. As soon as the shuttles were empty and the landing area cleared, the shuttles launched to rendezvous with *Faith* as soon as the starship approached on its next orbit.

To avoid possible problems (such as shuttles leaving a shuttle bay running into the returning shuttles), we used both the forward and aft shuttle bays. As an example, the first launch was through the forward shuttle bay. During the next orbit, a second group of shuttles launched though the aft shuttle bay. After they launched, the returning shuttles landed in the forward shuttle bay. That seemed to work well; at least we had no collisions.

We used the large transport shuttles which held a hundred people and all their personal goods, including their pets (they weren't thrilled about the G loads, neither were most of the passengers). We instructed our pilots to minimize their maneuvering and maintain 1-G loads as much as possible. Judging from the amount of vomit, some pilots were better than others at following that order.

We used ten shuttles to accomplish the transport. Five left one of the shuttle-bays every orbit which was about ninety minutes long. We transported all 2,500 colonists in five trips which took us roughly eight hours. All of our trips, as well as *Hope's,* were performed in daylight to provide optimum visibility, not only for the pilots but also to make it easier for the colonists to get their belongings put away in their new apartments.

I was very impressed at how smoothly this all went. From the time our two starships began orbiting Proxima-b until we had Colony City up and running went almost exactly as planned; there were very few obstacles. It must have taken millions of hours of planning, designing, fabricating, assembling, testing and another hundred things I know nothing about to make this happen. The cost of the program had to be in the trillions of dollars range. Just the computer time alone was at least a trillion.

I had heard a rumor that before we left on this magnificent adventure, the odds makers in Hong Kong gave us a billion-to-one odds we would even reach the Alpha Centauri cluster and a trillion-to-one we would be able to established a colony on Proxima-b. I wished I'd gotten a piece of that action. Unfortunately, The Plague made sure there were no winners.

Our work was almost done. We remained in orbit for another six months to ensure everything was going well. By the time we left, everyone aboard both starships had the opportunity to spend time on the surface. It gave them time to see a real sun and play in an actual river; most importantly to share with friends who would stay.

There were numerous parties and I had to hand it to Malcolm Cole, the first chairman of the Ruling Council, he brought it all together, especially the integration of colonists from both ships and inspiring them to great things. He was a true leader, one the colony needed in order to succeed.

Just before we were about to leave orbit and head for home, I selected *Faith's* new captain. I was stepping down to the role of mentor. The new captain had some interesting ideas about returning to Earth much faster than planned. This was going to prove interesting.

<u>Without Colonists—Governor Britt-Marie Sjöblom</u>

Once the colonists had been transported down to Colony City, *Hope* seemed like a ghost town. We'd lost over fifty percent of our people. We'd been insanely busy getting everything ready for the last few years. Now that they were gone, it seemed to those who remained on *Hope* they no longer had a purpose.

More tragic for many of us was to lose friends we had grown up with. It was as if we had experienced our own version of The Plague. More than half of us were lost in one day.

What eased the separation anxiety was we had the better part of a year to socialize with them in Colony City. We all enjoyed having the colonists showing us around their new surroundings. There was a big park by the river, perfect for picnics. The dogs liked it too, the cats, not so much.

Björn and I spent many hours reminiscing with old friends and taking in all of the sights the city offered and not just within the city. We went on excursions into the mountain ranges on both sides of the valley. The views were magnificent. The taller mountains even had snow on them. That was something we had only seen in vids. It's a lot colder than it looked on a screen.

Throughout the year, we made a point of visiting every restaurant in the city. The brew master from *Hope* was among the colonists and he had wasted no time setting up his microbrewery. Beale was available to the public within a month.

One thing that took getting use to was having a sky above us. Instead of looking up and following the curve of the habitat all around us, there was real sky with large white fluffy clouds of every size and shape. We spent several long afternoons laying on the park grass and looking up at the sky trying to decide what shapes the clouds looked like. Once, something totally unexpected happened. The clouds began to get darker and all of a sudden, water began falling out of the sky. Some people began panicking. I was one of them until my know-it-all husband (just ask him, he'll tell you) it was a natural phenomenon called rain. We were soaked to the skin by what Mr. Know-it-all said was a rain shower. He went on to explain to anyone who would listen this was a very beneficial natural event that occurred from time to time resulting in better crops and pasture land.

One thing I really enjoyed were the natural sunsets. It seemed every night was different, especially when there were clouds. As the sun set below the horizon the clouds looked like they were on fire. I think the pink tint from the planet's red dwarf star added to that. As the sun sank lower, the red color slowly became a deeper red, then purple until the night sky was dark however not empty.

Millions of stars could be seen at night and as night passed they seemed to move. Like the clouds, we tried to make out patterns or images from the stars' locations and traced them as they raced across the sky until they slipped over the horizon, only to be replaced with new stars rising from the east.

Whenever we were on the planet, Björn and I laid on the park grass or sat on a park bench and watched the sky and discussed our future. We had both decided to step down from our leadership positions and become mentors for the next generation. We discussed who we might recommend to replace us and I think I detected a hint of sadness in his voice or maybe it was my own sadness at no longer being in charge.

However, I think we both looked forward to begin our journey back to Earth. We speculated on what had become of Earth since we left. What would it be like after two centuries? Surely, we thought, The Plague would have run its course. Neither of us believed humanity had become extinct. Hopefully, enough people had survived to begin to rebuild civilization. If the worst had happened and mankind had disappeared from the Earth, perhaps the people returning from *Hope* and *Faith* and other starships could be the seed of a new humanity, a new civilization.

Of course, this was all just the musings of a couple of old folks. After all, it would take another hundred years for the starships to return. We would be long gone by then. I was sure we would be remembered, at least if the starships survived we would be remembered. As long as there was faith and hope.

Part 5

The Fourth Generation

Leaving Proxima-b—Captain David Davis

As the new captain of *Hope*, I feel I should share a little bit about myself. I was selected by Captain Björn Sjöblom who recently stepped down from being the commander of the ship, into the role of mentor. I'm sure I will be consulting with him in the near future to become more familiar with my duties as captain.

My previous assignment was as leader of the Flight Control group and I acted as the squadron commander for *Hope's* shuttle team which transported our colonists to Colony City. While that assignment gave me important experience overseeing the ten shuttles, it in no way prepared me for my new duties. Captain Sjöblom and I practically lived together for the first two weeks going over the most critical issues prior to leaving orbit.

My wife, Kathi, has been a huge supporter. She shared with me her experiences as a shuttle pilot in command. She not only flew a shuttle during the transporting of our colonists, she also flew survey teams and made scouting flights of the countryside surrounding Colony City.

Faith was the first starship to leave orbit. We followed a week later. All of the required upgrades had been completed almost a year before and we continued to run diagnostic tests right up to the time we left. The ship was working up to design standards then and I'm happy to say they continue to work that way.

Leaving orbit consisted of powering up our EM ion drives and running them at 0.1-G thrust. It took us a little over fifteen months to reach our cruise speed of five percent c, a little longer than when we left Earth's orbit. That was due to the slightly higher gravity of Proxima-b. I should add that we circled Proxima-b in an ever increasing spiral until we reached escape velocity. Astrogation played a critical part in when we turned on the drives. When we reached escape velocity we wanted to be pointing towards our sun. That minimized our transit time to Earth.

We all watched our vid screens as Proxima-b got smaller and smaller until it could no longer be seen. Proxima Centauri, the red dwarf star, was still visible, eventually even that disappeared. Alpha Centauri A/B would remain visible for most of the remainder of our journey; by then we were looking for Earth's sun.

With the reduced size of our population, we needed to use our remaining people in what Kathi called a multi-tasking mode. Everyone in our civilian population had to cover at least two jobs, a few even handled three. Our son John volunteered to maintain the ship's parkland, which included the lake and waterfall. He started off by adding to the tasks handled by the maintenance robots. When the pumps for the lake/waterfall began to fail, he took care of getting replacements for the bad parts and installing them himself. It only took him a day to fix the problem from start to finish. Most people didn't even realize we had the problem because he performed most of the work during the last two watches. For those of you who don't know, the last watches are 0000 hours to 0800 hours the next day.

Of course, things will get back to normal as our population continues to grow. It seems everything is going well in that department. The manager of Population Control informed me, "Those who remained on *Hope* are breeding like rabbits!" Her comments produced a visual I didn't need.

Many of the tasks performed by the third generation were aimed at providing food, clothing and material things for our colonists to take with them. Now that they are on Proxima-b, our priorities have changed.

Our new governor and I have discussed at length the goals for generations four through six. We agree we should consider preparing for a number of scenarios for our return to Earth. Since The Plague didn't occur for a decade after we left Earth, our planners assumed when *Hope* and our sister starship *Faith* returned, we would be greeted by a civilization two hundred years more advanced than when we left. Obviously, that wasn't going to happen. We decided there were four likely possibilities to consider:

1. A civilization still exists and has made a full recovery from The Plague.
2. The Plague decimated civilization but a substantial remnant remains with a technology level equivalent to when we left.
3. The Plague decimated civilization however a small remnant remains with very little knowledge of technology.
4. The Plague became an extinction event with no human survivors.

We needed to review all the information we possessed regarding The Plague to establish the probabilities of the four likely outcomes. Then we and the follow-on generation leaders needed to decide how to divide our resources to adequately prepare for our arrival at Earth.

We needed to make this a joint effort with *Faith*. I had our com officer contact them to inform them of our plans and invite them to join us in our planning. I was surprised when they didn't reply to our message. We were aware there would be a time delay due to our separation distance and relative speed however we were well past the anticipated delay time.

We sent another message asking if they needed a rescue; still no reply. We began considering shutting down our drives and using our shuttles to begin a search. A month after our first com attempt, we finally received a lengthy vid-com from *Faith's* captain. It was encrypted and for my eyes only. I watched it alone, then shared it with the governor, eventually we made it known to all of *Hope*.

I had the message decrypted and sent to my private bridge quarters com. When it started, I found myself looking at *Faith's* captain, a man I had met briefly in person on Proxima-b just before our ships left orbit. He was dressed in his dress uniform and looked directly into the vid com unit. He wasn't smiling.

"This message is intended for Captain David Davis, commander of the generation starship, *Hope*. I am Captain Gordon Fletcher, commander of the generation starship *Faith*. Please feel free to share it with whomever you want aboard your ship.

"We are presently in synchronous orbit over Proxima-b on the other side of the planet from Colony City. We aren't experiencing any difficulties with the ship. However, we are involved in a ship-wide discussion as to what our fate will be.

"There is a substantial part of *Faith's* population, perhaps even a majority of our people, who don't wish to return to Earth. They feel there is a high probability Earth could still be infected with The Plague which would result in our sudden death as soon as we entered the atmosphere there, well not us, our descendants. This latter group wants to return the ship to a lower orbit and eventually live in Colony City.

"Another group thinks we should return to Earth faster than originally planned. Both our Power Systems and Propulsion Systems group leaders ensure us we could safely increase our velocity to ten present c and cut our flight time in half. This group believes The Plague has run its course and the sooner we return the better we could help rebuild civilization.

"The last group, a very small group of which I am the leader, think we should follow the original plan because it has the least risk.

"We received your message and I apologize for not replying sooner. I will keep you informed of our decision, if and when we come to one.

"God's speed, Captain Davis. I wish you and your people a safe trip home."

Status of *Faith*–Captain Gordon Fletcher

To: Captain David Davis, commander of Generation Starship *Hope*

From: Captain Gordon Fletcher, commander of Generation Starship *Faith*

Subject: Problems Aboard *Faith*

It has been more than a year since I last comm'd you. I am sorry to report we still haven't decided regarding our return to Earth and remain in synchronous orbit around Proxima-b. The three factions vigorously refuse to compromise on their positions. Our discussions on this topic are evolving into heated arguments. I'm concerned no matter which position is selected, a mutiny will soon follow.

A recent suggestion was made by a member of the group favoring our return to Colony City. They suggested we contact the colony leader, Chairman Malcolm Cole, to see if he would welcome an additional large group of people.

An option to the suggestion was for only those who wish to return to the city would leave *Faith*; the rest would continue back to Earth. That sounded good on paper, however our starship was designed to operate with at least 2,000 crew members and civilians. We would be well below that number if all those who wanted to stay on Proxima-b left the ship.

It has become apparent, either we all stay or we all return to Earth. We are planning on contacting Chairman Cole within the next month to see if he will accept us. Before we do, I would welcome any suggestions you might have to mitigate my situation.

Best regards to all of you on *Hope*.

Captain Gordon Fletcher.

<u>Six Months Later</u>

To: Captain Gordon Fletcher
From: Captain David Davis
Subject: My Thoughts On Your Situation

You may not like what I'm going to say however I feel it must be said. Any ship, from the smallest shuttle to our monstrously large starships are commanded by their captains. They are the absolute authority on their ship. It has been that way ever since people began sailing the seas.

There is no democracy aboard ships. A wise captain will listen to suggestions but it is up to them to make the decisions. Once they are made, they must make sure commands are carried out. Anyone who doesn't follow a captain's orders will be punished as the captain sees fit.

I believe it is up to you to decide what you think is best to accomplish your mission and then implement the orders to make it happen.

Don't let a munity happen on your ship. If the leaders of these various factions don't follow your orders, place them in the brig. If that doesn't stop them, begin executing them. At all costs, you must remain in charge for the good of the ship, for the good of the mission. You cannot let others make these decisions for you, be decisive, speak with authority however don't become a tyrant.

I hope this helps. Good luck on the outcome. Please keep us informed.

Captain David Davis.

Two Years Later

To: Captain David Davis

From: Captain Gordon Fletcher

Subject: A Decision Has Been Made, Finally

This is an update on what has happened aboard Faith during the last two years. First, I want to thank you for your comments. It helped me personally a great deal. I had lost sight of my responsibilities and authority as captain.

Shortly after I received your vid-com, we left synchronous orbit and descended to LEO (actually LPO), contacted Chairman Cole and presented our case to him and the Ruling Council.

I was invited to shuttle down and to hear what I and our faction leaders had to say.

We were at Colony City for three days. At the end of that time, Chairman Cole told us they couldn't absorb another large group of people. They didn't have enough facilities or food to accommodate a huge percentage increase in population.

We thanked him and the Ruling Council for their consideration and returned to *Faith*.

As soon as we got to the ship, the leader of the contingency who favored abandoning our mission and staying on Proxima-b verbally attacked me for accepting the chairman's decision.

"I can't believe you accepted that...that idiot of a chairman's decision. We need to ignore him and take our people down to the surface anyway," said Dolf Johansen. "He shouldn't be allowed to deny us access to the planet's surface. If you weren't so weak we could..."

"Enough!" I shouted. "The decision has been made...Mr. Johansen."

"Why are you accepting that clown's decis..."

"It's not his decision I'm accepting. I'm making the decision. And my decision is that we will no longer debate this issue. We are returning to Earth; *all* of us are returning to Earth."

"How can you say that?!!" He screamed into my face, "How can you sign the death warrant for all of our descendants?"

"You have no proof The Plague is still active. All of the data on these types of diseases say this type of virus lives for only a brief time, especially when there are no potential victims."

"There has never been a virus of this type in the history of our planet. Listen captain, if you don't do what I tell you, there will be mutiny on this ship and it will all be your fault, you pompous idiot. My people will take over this ship and…"

I struck the man in the face, sending him backwards from me and causing him to lose his balance. He fell to the floor screaming in pain and rage. "Get him, attack him," he yelled at his two associates.

Before they could move, I said to my two security officers, "Arrest all three of them. I charge all three with treason."

The other two men offered no resistance. Mr. Johansen continued to resist and yell obscenities at me until one of my security men hit him with a stun gun shot. All three were placed in the brig.

The following day, I made an announcement to the ship.

"Ladies and gentlemen of *Faith,* based on information I received from Chairman Cole, we will no longer be considering a return to Proxima-b. That course of action will put too great a strain on our neighbors. Instead, we will be returning to Earth. We will be exploring a possible approach that will shorten our return to Earth by fifty percent.

"I know that some of you will be disappointed by my decision but let me be very clear. I will not tolerate any actions that countermand my direct orders. As I'm sure many of you know, a few people have been charged with treason for disregarding my orders. If convicted, these men will be executed. Please consider your next actions carefully. We must, and we will, act as a team to get our grandchildren to the end of this important mission."

<u>Update—Captain David Davis</u>

It's been ten years since we left Proxima-b and began our journey back to Earth. Since my last report, we have heard very little from the captain of *Faith*, other than the monthly status reports our two ships exchange.

Faith's last status report indicated they were beginning an upgrade to the ship to permit them to cruise at ten percent c, twice *Hope's* current velocity. They reported it may take a few years to complete the upgrade. The captain decided it was prudent to remain in synchronous orbit around Proxima-b until the upgrades were finished and tested.

Meanwhile, *Hope* continues to cruise at five percent, distancing ourselves from *Faith*. This results in our status reports taking longer to be received. Our com people inform me we are quickly approaching the range limit of our com system. At that point, we will not be able to exchange status reports or communications of any type. We will remain out of com range until they get their upgrades completed and close the distance between us.

Enough about *Faith*. I'm happy to report things are going very well on *Hope*. Our population is steadily growing and our Population Control department projects we'll be back to our maximum capacity of 5,000 around mid-generation five. They report our current population is now approaching 3,000.

With the new population growth, we have reopened several restaurants and shops. Attendance at the worship center has also increased, both in weekly services as well as mid-week Bible studies. With the jump in births during the last ten years, we have expanded our children's swim classes. Those are being held in our lake area with two classes each day, one in the morning and the other in the late afternoon. Attendance has grown steadily and a third class is being considered.

While I'm speaking of children, I want to explain why I'm reporting on civilian issues. Our governor, Loren Sheppard, is in the process of having a baby, actually two babies. A few days ago, she contacted me and asked if I could temporarily take charge of the civilian side of *Hope*. She stressed the word 'temporarily.' Normally her lieutenant governor would step in. With so many colonists leaving the ship, she decided to wait to select an assistant. As I record this message, I was just told she had gone into labor. So, for the next few weeks, I'm the king of the ship. I promise I won't let the power go to my head.

Let me get back on track. In addition to the above, more recreational activities are opening up. There are senior tai-chi classes being offered every morning in the park next to the lake. Many of our mentors, most of whom have been retired for a while, can be seen practicing this ancient Chinese art.

In addition to tai-chi, a karate club has been formed. They meet three times a week in the recreation center. This Japanese form of self-defense is being taught by Shojiro Koyama II, the great-grandchild of one of the ship's former Astrogation leaders. Sensei Koyama (The word 'sensei' means teacher in Japanese) follows the strict tradition of this art. Everyone must wear the proper uniform (called a gi) and learn the Japanese terms for all the techniques. The sensei informed me there has always been a Koyama on board *Hope* teaching this art, even when only family members were training; now even the gai-jin (non-Japanese) are coming to train.

There's one last recreation activity I want to mention, it's called rock climbing. I know what you're thinking; the rocks on *Hope* are a few boulders near the lake that the kids climb on. And you'd be right. I was told by the club leader, "A more accurate name for the sport would be wall climbing however it was named by people who would climb up the vertical rock walls in various mountain regions on Earth." He said it was very dangerous and many people died but they found a safe way to do it. They built their own 'rock walls' inside buildings and participants wore a safety harness connected to safety lines so if they fell they wouldn't die or even get a scrape or bruise. The sport part was to see who could climb the wall in the shortest time.

They got approval to build a climbing wall on the very large forward and aft circular plates of the habitat. The climbers would begin on the 'ground surface' of the habitat and climb to the central tube. One large difference between wall climbing on Earth and *Hope* was our artificial gravity. On *Hope*, the gravitational effect at the habitat surface would be 1-G however as the climbers ascended the wall, the gravity would decrease until they were at a zero-G condition at the central tube. That would make the climb less dangerous to my way of thinking, less challenging and probably less fun. *But what do I know?* It became the new rage almost immediately. Perhaps I should just focus on running the ship and let the civilians plan the recreational activities.

Speaking of running the ship, I am happy to report the ship is operating perfectly. During the last ten years we haven't had even one emergency declared. Essentially, with our refurbishments while orbiting Proxima-b, our propulsion system is practically brand new. Based on how well *Hope* performed leaving Earth, I'm not surprised.

In spite of the outstanding performance of the ship, I do have one concern. When the colonists were selected, almost 500 of the 2,500 were from the Navy. That cut our Navy personnel in half. It also limited the number of cadets in our academy. We lost half of our shuttle pilots along with half the shuttles. We also lost the technicians who supported and maintained the shuttles. That was the plan from the beginning. We also lost several of our beam operators and their technicians. The majority of the Navy troops who became colonists were skilled people, not easy to replace.

Some may ask, "Why do you need a thousand people to run the ship? Isn't it pretty much run by computers?"

Let me answer those two questions with an example: before the Alliance of World Nations was formed, the world powers built huge ships, war ships. The largest of these ships were called aircraft carriers. They were controlled, in part, by the most sophisticated computers ever made. They still needed 5,000 Navy personnel to operate the ship and carry out their missions. Compare that to *Hope*, a ship ten times larger than an aircraft carrier and much more sophisticated. The designers managed to cut the number of Navy personnel to 1,000 as the bare minimum needed to comfortably operate the ship. We're down to 500 now and I'm not comfortable.

We have had to recruit new Navy personnel from the civilian population and run them through accelerated training. We have to do this without minimizing the needs, the critical needs, of the civilian population.

My goal is to increase the active duty Navy to a roster of 750 before the end of this generation. In the meantime, I will call on the retired Navy people, many of whom are mentors, to fill the gap. I hope to be moderately comfortable by the time I retire.

Twins—Governor Loren Sheppard

I want to thank Captain Davis for reporting on the civilian side of the ship while I was busy giving birth to my two beautiful babies. Actually, I'm still not fully functional and asked my husband, Moses, to become my interim lieutenant governor. If he does a good job, I might promote him to permanent lieutenant governor, although I'm sure he has no political aspirations. He is very satisfied being *Hope's* full-time Christian minister. I must admit, my man knows his Bible and he leads the Wednesday night Bible study. The group is currently reading the book of Exodus in the Old Testament.

I'm not sure if he planned this or if it was just a coincidence but just before I went into labor, the Bible study group was reading about Moses sending out twelve spies to check out the promised land before the Israelites were going to invade. Only two of the twelve were positive the Israelites could defeat the current pagan inhabitants because God was on their side. The other ten said there was no way they could defeat their great walled cities and trained armies.

As a result, all of the Israelites said they should return to Egypt instead of fighting a war they couldn't possibly win. Well, this really made God angry. As a punishment for doubting His power, the Israelites had to wander in the wilderness for forty years, until that whole generation passed away…except for the two men who'd said all they needed to win was God. They got to enter into the promised land, flowing with milk and honey, along with the next generation of Israelites. The names of the two men were Joshua and Caleb. And that's the names Moses gave to our twin boys.

Twins Five Years Later—Governor Loren Sheppard

It's been five years since the boys were born. It took me almost two years to recover from their delivery. Both boys were close to ten pounds and I needed some reconstructive surgery. Fortunately, not all of *Hope's* surgeons left with the colonists and my doctors did a really great job putting me back together, although I have to admit the physical therapy was arduous. Once that was over, it was recommended I consider tai-chi as a follow-up activity.

During my recovery, Moses asked to be relived on his interim responsibilities and I agreed. I appointed Carla Blankenship to be my permanent lieutenant governor. Moses was anxious to return to his religious responsibilities and I really did need a full time assistant. Carla hit the ground running and we have gelled into an effective team.

I'm so glad I began tai-chi. It helped me physically and mentally as well. It had such a calming effect on me and an added plus was being able to spend time every morning with so many wonderful people.

I loved exercising outside in the park with the waterfall in the background. It has become part of my daily routine. I tried to get Moses to join me however he said he preferred a more vigorous form of exercise and joined the karate club and now trains three times a week. They have a day-care facility at the rec center and he takes the boys with him when he trains. He said Captain Davis invited him to attend one of the training sessions and he was hooked. When our boys turned five, he signed them both up for Kid's Karate.

I've rambled on about my family, sorry if you found it boring. It's time to share some information regarding what's happening aboard ship.

Population Control has reported the baby boom is officially over. We are well on our way to reach Captain Davis' goal of having 750 Navy personnel by the end of the fourth generation. They project the overall population of *Hope* will be 4,000 by that time as well. Therefore, they are cutting back on the number of approved pregnancies. Not all the way back but slowing the birthrate to bring us to 5,000 by the end of the fifth generation. At that point authorized births will be limited to the number of deaths during any given year.

To accommodate the increase in population, food production is also being stepped up. Fields that were fallow after the colonists left are now being prepared for planting again and the birthrate of livestock has also increased.

As the population increases, the need for multitasking is going down and there is more time for some of our old activities to get back on line. Next year, we will begin our week-long festivals, specifically Rodeo Days and Harvest Festival. A poll of our civilians indicated an overwhelming desire to start both of those events again.

Let me close this report with something near and dear to most of us. The old distillery is currently being renovated. The brew master who left us to become one of the colonists, was good enough to leave his recipe for Beale along with instructions on how to get the distillery up and running again. Two of our restaurateurs have joined in this project and estimated the microbrewery will be opened within the next few months, and a complete line of adult beverages will be available when the entire distillery is online. They project it will happen before our first festival.

Upgrades to Training—Captain David Davis

It's been twenty years since we left orbit around Proxima-b. We have had no contact with our sister starship *Faith* since we left them in synchronous orbit around the colony planet. We continue to monitor an agreed upon frequency in the hope they will eventually contact us.

Hope continues on course for Earth. The Navy ranks are growing and it looks like we will have 750 active duty personnel within the next ten years. I will focus on two items during this report. I feel they are the most critical to accomplish our mission.

The first is to prepare our young co-workers to assume the responsibilities of running the ship. The second is to reestablish flight training for our shuttles.

I have implemented a junior cadet program as an adjunct to our Naval Academy. Its function is to fast-track well qualified people into positions of authority. The program was integrated into the existing high school curriculum and available to candidates sixteen years and older. It is a two-year program that gives the junior cadets a taste of being in the Navy as well as giving us the opportunity to select the best and brightest for the Academy.

To date, we have had over a hundred young people apply for the program. It looks like perhaps fifty or more will qualify for entering the Academy.

The junior cadet curriculum calls for the student to attend three one-hour classes each week during high school. At the end of the first year, we offer a special summer training which involves shadowing a number of active duty Navy personnel. The summer training lasts two months with each week offering exposure to a different critical discipline. At the end of the summer, each junior cadet has to decide if they want to proceed to the next year's program.

If they chose to proceed, they are issued a junior cadet uniform which they are required to wear in class. There is a second summer training session in which they will be required to stand watch. At the end of the second summer they are evaluated by the Academy faculty. If chosen, they are invited to join the Academy. An added bonus for the cadets is they can skip the first year of Academy training and finish the program a year earlier. The two years as junior cadets would be equivalent to the first year at the Academy.

So far this has worked out very well, both for the Navy as well as for the cadets. One point I found interesting is both of the governor's sons signed up for the junior cadet program. Caleb finished his first year but decided not to continue. His brother, Joshua, continued on with the program and is currently in his first year at the Naval Academy. The faculty tells me he is an outstanding student.

We have restarted the flight training program using our simulators. During the last twenty years there really was no need for flight training. Once *Hope* left orbit and was at cruise speed, we couldn't launch any of the shuttles. A few of the pilots, my wife included when her duties permitted, visited the sims a few times a week. However, the centrifuge training was totally shut down due to lack of manpower to support it. None of the rated pilots complained. Like Kathi said, "Where's the fun in weighing a ton when you don't have to?"

One reason for including simulator training was a lot of cadets really enjoyed it. Once they got familiar with the basics, it served the same function as a very sophisticated, interactive computer game.

Our shuttles have very limited weapons capability, primarily for defense. However, the simulators can be programmed to carry all types of offensive weapons, from laser cannons to missiles with nuclear warheads. The simulator software permits upgrades of any number of weapons systems.

These upgraded sims can be programmed to battle against computer generated opponents with a wide range of difficulty. Most cadets begin with easy competition, then as their abilities develop, they move on to more challenging targets. Of course, everyone wants to go up against other pilots. That's the real challenge.

It has become so popular the pilots line up to fight against each other. A computer keeps track of the victories and losses and a list is available daily on who is the baddest, nastiest pilot on the ship.

In the beginning, the rated pilots were dominant however as the cadets gained more experience, they began moving up the chain. The last time I checked, cadet Death from Above was at the top of the list. I found out his real name was Joshua.

<u>This is Not a Drill—Captain David Davis</u>

I was in my last year as *Hope's* captain when the emergency occurred. During the last thirty years, the ship and its crew had performed flawlessly. Of course, we routinely continued our emergency drills to prepare for any contingency.

I was very impressed at how well the newly graduated academy cadets integrated into the crew and duty rotations. The new blood reenergized the older members of the crew and kept them on their toes, answering all sorts of questions thrown at them from the newbies.

Twenty-five years into my reign as 'King,' my executive office decided to retire due to some medical issues. King was the nickname the bridge officers tagged me with about ten years after I had been selected as Captain. I used the Officer Selection software to help me come up with a list of potential XO candidates. The software considered every imaginable criteria required of an executive officer and it looked at every Navy officer on active duty. I could have included the retired officers as well as the active duty group however thanks to the new influx of very energetic officers, I decided to let the retired Navy personnel enjoy their retired status and continue to act as mentors.

It took all of about thirty seconds for the computer to give me a list of the top five candidates. I was very surprised to see Lieutenant Joshua Sheppard at the top of the list. I read through the report that justified Josh's qualifications rating him number one of the candidates and I couldn't find a reason not to select him.

So, at the tender age of twenty-four, Lieutenant Joshua Sheppard became *Hope's* youngest XO. I'm happy to say, he never gave me any reason to regret my decision.

The emergency occurred during night watch at 0345 hours. The XO had the watch that night, once he confirmed the emergency, he woke me and my wife (who wasn't happy being roused from her slumber at such an ungodly hour). By 0410, I joined the XO on the bridge still in my pajamas.

"Tell me again, XO," I asked, "I was barely awake when you told me the first time."

He handed me a cup of coffee and waited until I had a few sips. "At 0345 hours, two of our maneuvering thrusters went offline which resulted in the flight control computer shutting down all of the remaining thrusters." Since I was still not fully awake, I must have looked like I didn't understand why all the thrusters were shut down.

I took another sip of the coffee as he added, "All the remaining thrusters were shut down to prevent asymmetrical loading on the habitat frame which could result in catastrophic failure of the entire habitat."

I nodded as I finished the last of my coffee. A yeoman appeared at my shoulder with a second cup and quickly disappeared. "How long before we lose gravity in the habitat?" I asked, beginning to realize the scale of the problem. Death by starvation being the worst.

"It depends on several factors. The best estimate would be a little over twenty-four hours, the worst, would give us only twelve."

I looked down at his feet and noticed he had put on his magnetic boots which would keep him in contact with the metallic deck plate. I was still in my slippers. He saw me look at his mag boots and said, "I didn't think we needed to call an all-hands-on-deck order yet. We'll do so at 0600 hours and have everyone put on their mag boots, unless you think we should scramble everyone now."

I shook my head, "No. 0600 hours is good enough. I'm going back to my quarters to get dressed. When I get back, I'd like to see what we can do to prevent us from going to a zero G condition in Habitat City."

It took me thirty minutes to shower and get dressed in my uniform, take down my mag boots from a shelf in the closet, put them on and return to the bridge. Josh was waiting with another cup of coffee and a plate of pastries.

I took a chocolate frosted, chocolate cake donut, my favorite, and gestured for him to begin. As I took my first bite, he said, "We might be able to get along by bringing the operative thrusters on-line in a pattern that provides almost symmetrical loading on the habitat structure. There are five rings spaced a half mile apart which support the habitat walls. Each ring has four maneuvering thrusters for a total of twenty thrusters. The two damaged…"

"Wait," I said around a mouthful of donut. "What damage? You didn't say anything about damage."

"Sorry, King," he said almost sheepishly. "We got a damage report after you left to get dressed. I should have opened with that. Apparently, we had a partial failure in our shields which permitted some very high velocity space junk to penetrate and destroy two of the thrusters. It also effected the forward magnetic bearings which support the habitat in the ship's external frame. We are currently investigating the degree of damage to the mag bearings, both front and rear. We should have more detailed information on the degree of damage shortly."

I put down my donut and took a sip of coffee, attempting to process this new information. "If the habitat support bearings are damaged, we may not be able to avoid stopping the rotation. The bearings are our first priority. It's time for all-hands-on-deck."

Magnetic bearings work by using a strong, in our case, extremely strong, magnetic field to keep the rotating central shaft of the habitat from ever touching the non-rotating frame. Very delicate sensors continuously measure the distance between the rotating and non-rotating parts and instantaneously adjust the magnetic field to maintain the correct spacing. If the rotating and non-rotating parts touch, it could result in what is known as a cascading failure which means things just keep getting worse and worse until the worst thing happens. The worst thing is a catastrophic failure. In our case, a catastrophic failure means everyone dies. We'd like to avoid that.

We got the good news a few minutes later. There wasn't any metal-to-metal touching. The bad news; the shaft is experiencing too much warble. I wasn't familiar with the term warble.

A tech informed me it what it meant. "The shaft is moving outside of the design tolerance. The rotating shaft in a magnetic bearing always has a slight amount of movement. It can't be helped however it has to be controlled within what is called the design tolerance. If the movement of the shaft is outside the design tolerance, it is on the edge of becoming unstable, which could lead to metal-to-metal contact, which in turn could result in the aforementioned catastrophic failure."

Very bad!

I asked the tech, "How do we get the bearings back within the design tolerance?"

"We have to slow down the rotational speed of the habitat," she answered.

"How do we do that?" I asked.

"With a magnetic brake," she replied.

Of course! Why didn't I think of that, I thought to myself, not having the foggiest idea how it would work. It turns out it is similar in principle to a brake on one of our mag lev cars. To slow down the car, brake pads make contact with the mag rail. The harder they grip, the quicker the car slows down. In our situation we use the magnetic field to reduce the rotational speed of the shaft. We would gradually slow the shaft until the movement of the shaft was within the design tolerance.

I knew this was what we needed, no, not needed, had to do. It was going to cause a mess. When *Hope* was built over a hundred years ago and once the habitat was completed, before anyone was allowed on board, they spun the habitat up to the rotational speed to produce a 1-G environment on the inside wall of the barrel. Only then was the inside finished and populated. We've been spinning non-stop ever since, always at the same speed. If we start braking too fast, people, buildings and everything else inside the habitat are going to experience the braking effect.

Think of driving along in a mag lev car. The car is moving at constant speed when unexpectedly debris falls out of the mag lev vehicle ahead of you. Your autopilot automatically slams on the brakes to avoid hitting the debris. During the braking maneuver all the passengers are thrown forward into their restraints, keeping them from being smashed into the windshield.

We have to be extremely careful how we slow the habitat's rotation to prevent any deceleration injuries. There aren't any safety restraints for the habitat

We began executing our deceleration plan before 0800 hours the same day. Four hours later, with all the maneuvering thrusters inoperative, the drag of the magnetic bearings slowed the rotational speed by three percent. That translated into our surface gravity being reduced to 0.97-G

I received and interesting com message from my wife. She wanted to announce she had lost three pounds overnight. I didn't have the heart to tell her she hadn't lost an ounce.

At 0800 hours an announcement was made to everyone aboard *Hope* as to what was happening and what we wanted them to do. We were going to gradually slow the ship's rotational speed until the central shaft was operating within the design tolerance. While rotation was slowing down we would feel lighter because our artificial gravity was being reduced.

We had to tether all of the livestock. They weren't going to be happy about it but we couldn't have cattle, sheep, pigs, horses and other four-legged creatures floating away. Chickens, ducks and rabbits were contained in roofed cages. We didn't think we needed to do anything with the crops. We shut off the fountain and stopped the waterfall. Even a slight amount of gravity should keep the crops and water in place. At least we hoped so.

Our repair crews would replace the two damaged maneuvering thrusters. Once those two items were restored, we would use the thrusters to bring the habitat up to speed and everything would return to normal. We gave them an emergency com code to use in case of accidents or injuries. A team of well-trained medics were on standby for anyone needing assistance.

Orders went out for everyone to wear their emergency mag boots and remain inside their residences. The floors of all our buildings were designed for this type of situation. Metal sheets were put in place and covered with flooring allowing people to safely move from room to room. If they went outside, the walkways weren't constructed with imbedded metal. It would have added too much weight to the ship. As the habitat rotation slows down, the gravity will get weaker. There may come a point where rotation stops completely. That means anybody outside a building could float away.

The XO volunteered to lead the team to replace the damaged thrusters. He had already generated a detailed plan for removing the damaged thrusters and replacing them with new equipment. Once the new parts were installed, they would run tests to ensure the whole system of twenty thrusters were performing correctly. He estimated the team would complete all the work within eighteen hours.

Once we had begun the braking process and I could see we were gradually slowing the rotation of the habitat, I checked to see what was happening to the shaft movements on both the forward and aft mag bearings. I was pleased to see they were trending towards the design tolerance level. I glanced at the readout of the surface gravity level and saw it had declined to 0.90-G. I told the watch officer that I was going to check on my wife and would return shortly.

"Hi, dear. How much weight have you lost now?" I asked as I walked into our quarters.

I heard the metallic lick of her mag boots as she came out of the bathroom with her hands on her hips and a frown on her face. "You could have told me about the reduction in gravity. You better not have told anybody what I said."

"I would never tell anyone anything you might be embarrassed about, my love," I replied. "Are you okay? I just wanted to make sure you got your mag boots on. I have to get back to the bridge pretty soon."

She stopped frowning and asked, "Are you really going to stop the habitat from spinning? I'm not a big fan of zero-G."

"Neither am I. I hope we don't have to go that far however we might have to. Just keep the vid com on. They will be updating the status every thirty minutes."

She clicked over to me and gave me a hug. "Be careful, Okay?"

I kissed her on the cheek. "Always," I answered.

On my way back to the bridge, it dawned on me there was one more thing to take care of.

When I arrived at the bridge, I contacted the leader of the Operations Group and asked, "The XO told me, the reason we are in this mess is because there was a gap in the shields which permitted some space debris to penetrate and take out the two maneuvering thrusters. Is that correct?"

"Not exactly, King," he replied. "It wasn't a gap in the shield, it was a weak point. There are numerous shield generators located on the habitat and support structures which generate a repulsive energy field. The strength of the shields at any given point around the ship depends on the distance from the generators. Ninety percent of *Hope's* exterior has overlapping shield coverage. Unfortunately, the debris penetrated a location that didn't have overlapping coverage and was at the extreme range of one of the generators."

"I wasn't aware of that. I want you to put together a plan to install additional shield generators to provide overlapping coverage of the entire ship. I want that upgrade done sometime today. We cannot allow this type of breach to happen again. Didn't the captain of the first-generation crew have a similar breach? I thought he had fixed that problem."

"You're correct, King," answered the Operations Group leader. "The upgrade was done under Captain Dagan's watch. The goal of that upgrade was to prevent any penetration of the habitat. Our current shields did deflect the debris from penetrating the habitat but the deflected debris still had enough energy to take out the two thrusters."

Before I could comment, he continued, "We have already installed the new shield generators and now have overlapping shield coverage of the entire ship. This won't happen again, sir."

I was mildly surprised at his initiative. "That's excellent, Lieutenant Grimes. Great anticipation. Carry on."

It turned out, we had to slow the habitat rotation down to only five percent G to get the shaft warble within design tolerances. If you weighed a hundred pounds at 1-G, you weighed only five pounds at five percent G. It took a couple of weeks to get there without causing any noticeable deceleration effects.

A few of our teenagers wondered how high they could jump in the low gravity. Most of them attached themselves to tethers before jumping, however a few who had forgotten to bring tethers, jumped anyway. A couple of the larger, stronger boys discovered they could achieve escape velocity and ended up floating for a couple of days before we could get them down.

Joshua was good to his word. He and his crew replaced the two damaged thrusters and tested all twenty within fifteen hours crawling around on the outside of the habitat in pressure suits.

It took another couple of weeks to get the habitat up to the rotational speed to produce 1-G again. My wife said we must be spinning at greater than 1-G because the scale said she had gained two pounds.

We were back at normal operating conditions just in time for me to retire from being the King and become a mentor. Not surprisingly, I selected Joshua Sheppard to become the captain for the fifth generation.

Part 6

The Fifth Generation

Parting Comments–King David Davis

As usual, there was a party to celebrate the change in authority from one generation to the next. It was also tradition that the senior officers' line up to have a still vid shot taken of them in dress uniforms. Those pictures were hung in the hallway that runs from the transport beam platform to the large conference room. Actually, still vid shots were taken every ten years and hung on the wall. The ones at the generation transition were a little bigger and the plaque on the frames were a little more special.

We had exceeded our Navy population goal of 750 active duty personnel by five and the entire ship's population was now 4,013.

The party lasted into the night with a special dinner, toasts and dancing. It was a special night for the governor as well. She was stepping down to become a mentor and both her sons were being promoted. Joshua was captain and his brother Caleb was now the new governor. At my recommendation, Joshua's replacement for XO was Lt. Commander Lawrence Grimes, the man who took it upon himself to upgrade our shields. He recognized the need and made it happen.

The ship was now back to normal and operating at peak efficiency. The best part of being a mentor wasn't having to stand watch or be on call twenty-four hours a day. I could sleep in if I wanted and some days I slept in just for the fun of it. It was good to be King however I was ready to move on.

One afternoon, about a week after I had retired from command, I was having brunch by myself at a restaurant next to the lake while my wife was attending her tai-chi class. I noticed the new captain walking towards me. "Mind if I join you, King?" he asked.

"Sure, Captain, have a seat. You don't have to call me King anymore," I said gesturing to one of the chairs next to me.

As he sat down, he said, "You'll always be King to me and just call me Josh when were together, 'Captain' seems too formal right now."

A server came out to our table and Josh ordered a sandwich and iced tea. When she left, I glanced at him. He usually had a smile on his face; this time I noticed he looked in a very serious mood for some reason.

"What's on your mind, Josh? Is this just lunch between friends or do you need a mentoring moment?" I joked.

"Neither King. I have a confession to make to you. It's been bothering me for a long time."

"Are you sure you don't need to speak with the chaplain?" I asked

"I already did. He suggested I speak with you." He paused for a moment then looked me in the eyes and asked, "Have you ever regretted choosing me as your XO?"

His question surprised me. "No Josh. I've never regretted selecting you as my XO. If I did, I would never have recommended you to be captain. What's this about?"

He looked away for a second then down at the table top, fidgeting with his silverware. "You used the XO Selection software to help you decide who to choose, didn't you?"

"Yes, most captains use the software to get a list of potential candidates, then make their selection based in part on the perceived strengths and weaknesses of each candidate."

"Do you know if they always select the top candidate or do they sometimes pick a candidate that was rated lower, say third or fourth?" he asked. His voice was flat, masking his emotions.

"I can't speak for other captains; I usually select either the first or second candidate recommended by the computer." There was silence for several seconds. When Josh didn't say anything, I asked, "What did you do, Josh?"

He waited for several seconds. He turned toward me and began to speak when the server showed up with his food. He turned away; when she left he turned back and said in a rush, "I hacked the software. It originally had me rated third. I reprogrammed it to emphasis my strong points and deemphasize my weak ones. I played with it until I was the top candidate."

I sat stunned. He started to stand up to leave but I said in a firm voice, "Sit down, Captain."

His knees seemed to buckle and he fell back into his chair. "Look at me!" I ordered. "Tell me why you would do such a thing?"

He looked up at me and answered, "Because I truly believed I was the best person for the job. The major factor which resulted in me being rated third was my age and the assumed lack of experience. I knew all of the other candidates and I believed…no, I *knew* I was the best choice."

We both sat in silence for a moment before I asked him, "Did you hack the Captain Selection software too?"

"No. Did you use it to select me for captain?"

"I didn't need to. Clearly, you were the best candidate," I answered.

"What are you going to do?" he asked.

"Do about what?" I replied. "Eat your lunch. This conversation never happened."

Movin' On Down the Road—Governor Caleb Sheppard

It's been five years since we had to stop the habitat from rotating. Attempting to live in zero G was interesting to say the least. Praise the Lord, it was only about a month until everything was back to normal. Kudos to my brother for helping us restore everything. He had some great stories about crawling along the outside of the barrel in his spacesuit. He even said he missed a handhold and he started drifting away from the ship. I think he was just making his story exciting. With those mag boots he wouldn't have fallen off anything metallic. Even if he had, everyone always wore tethers so he could have pulled himself back to the ship. However, it did make for an exciting story.

Our real world may not be that exciting but I prefer peace and quiet and that's exactly what we have now. Everybody's back to working an eight-hour shift instead of twelve. Crops are growing and the livestock is flourishing. The only hiccup was just after the barrel was back spinning to give us a 1-G gravity.

It affected the chickens the most, they just stopped laying eggs for a bit, well maybe two bits. After about two weeks they started laying eggs again like usual. During that two weeks the eggs weren't…weren't exactly egg shaped. They looked more like golf balls than eggs. Some people swore they tasted different, not nasty or anything like that, just different.

Some of the milk cows stopped making milk for a while. When they started up again, people said the cream tasted bad. I'm not a big milk drinker, so it didn't bother me. I do prefer a bit of cream in my coffee. To tell you the truth, I couldn't taste the difference.

Enough about the past. Everything is back to normal and has been for several years. Crops are growing right on schedule. We still have our Harvest Festival and Our Rodeo Days each year.

One interesting new thing is the style of clothes people are wearing now. A few people with a flair for fashion are designing apparel for men, women and even children and is referred to as Nuevo Chic. They have programmed the 3-D printers to fabricate everything from casual and work clothes to more daring and risqué evening wear. Don't like the color of your favorite dress? Change it with a push of a button or program the dress to not only change colors but also change the style of the dress as well. It's all smoke and mirrors.

Let's not forget footwear. There's no end to the options of shoe designs; from something called baked shoes to thigh-high boots with adjustable sole thicknesses which have become all the rage, especially among shorter people. I have to admit, some have gone to extremes and it was necessary to limit the thickness of the sole to twelve inches. Too many people were falling off their shoes, ending up with twisted ankles or the occasional broken leg.

To get around the twelve-inch limit, some of the designers are offering adjustable sole thickness versions that can go up to fifteen inches but can be quickly decreased to ten inches if an inspector walks by.

All of the above is captivating however none of it can hold a candle to holomasks. They are like a complete face makeover. If you want baby blue skin with royal blue eyes surrounded by inch long contrasting eye lashes, and full lush neon purple lips, you can have it all with a touch of a button or a simple voice command. If you get bored with what you look like, have your face continuingly morphing from a wide variety of jungle animals to the faces of mythical creatures. There is no limit to what you can look like.

Going right along with all of that are the new fads in music. I won't even attempt to describe the new sounds that are being produced blended together into a crescendo of vibrations. Not only do you hear the music, you feel the various organs of your body in sympathetic vibration to the beat of each song. You have to experience it to believe it.

It's not all fun and games. It's my pleasure to report our worship center is seeing a rise in attendance. As we approach Earth, many of our population has begun to consider what we and our descendants will find. Prayer groups have steadily grown in activities centered around requests that The Plague has run its course and there is at least a remnant of civilization still existing.

There is also a trend for people to take better care of themselves. Many are beginning exercising routines offered by our fitness centers. They offer a wide variety of programs to suit almost every person's needs and desires. To name a few: yoga, tai-chi, aerobics, jogging, walking, dance classes, wall climbing, weight training and karate.

I mentioned karate last because I signed up with Sensei Koyama and began training about a month ago so I wanted to talk a little about this sport over the others. I find it very stimulating, sometimes exhausting. The first few weeks it seemed every muscle in my body was screaming for me to quit however I persevered and now my muscles have stopped screaming.

Sensei is inspiring. He always demonstrates techniques himself, even though he is in his late sixties. His flexibility is amazing. He can do splits in several directions without even straining. Once he showed us how we could get that level of flexibility all his students began adding it to their training. His fighting moves are incredibly fast and powerful but he constantly reminds us karate is only for self-defense.

I invited brother Joshua to attend our class. He was so impressed, he joined that night and has been training with me three times a week. There will be a tournament a few weeks from now and we both plan to attend. We haven't learned enough to participate however we wanted to see how the advanced students perform.

Both of us have seen changes as a result of our training. We have both lost some weight and our flexibility has really increased. Neither of us can do the full splits yet; I think we're getting closer. Like Sensei says, "You need practice and dedication. It is only a matter of time."

<u>Coms from Faith—Lieutenant Deborah O'Riley</u>

We began receiving garbled coms from our sister starship, *Faith*, approximately twelve years into *Hope's* fifth generation. It was assumed they had made the proposed upgrades to their ship and were now traveling back to Earth at a much higher velocity than we were traveling.

We could only make out a few words of the initial com however we were able to determine they were, in fact, catching up to us and would attempt coms every month on the agreed upon frequency.

Each month, we received Faith's coms and sent replies back to them to confirm we had made contact. Unfortunately, it took several years before we were able to receive complete, coherent coms.

The following is a summary of those messages.

It took *Faith* over a decade to design, fabricate and test the upgrades to allow the starship to cruise at ten percent c, twice as fast as *Hope's* cruise speed. Due to some undisclosed difficulties, it took almost a year to accelerate from their synchronous orbit around Proxima-b to cruising speed, about twice as long as anticipated.

Much later, we discovered the delays were the result of an onboard mutiny. The mutineers took possession of two of the transport shuttles, each with a capacity of a hundred passengers and attempted to exit the aft shuttle bay while *Faith* was still in synchronous orbit. Three of the shuttle bay technicians were murdered in the attempt to breach the shuttle bay portals. Both of the shuttles were disabled and over a hundred of the mutineers were killed in the ensuing fire fight. Many of the remaining individuals were severely wounded in the battle and died of their wounds. Those who survived were charged with treason and later executed.

Faith lost a total of 347 people, including the mutineers and the those who fought against them. It reduced the total population of the ship to a little over two thousand people, which included roughly five hundred children under the age of eighteen.

Faith's captain said he felt the survivors included a substantial number of sympathizers and was "very concerned there would be other mutinies before the trip was over." He also was concerned that he didn't have a "critical mass of people to operate the ship successfully."

Later coms seemed to indicate things had gotten better aboard *Faith*. They had successfully accelerated to cruise speed and were now traveling at ten percent c and all systems were functioning at optimum. No indication of other mutinous attempts was reported while *Hope* was in its fifth generation.

Captain Joshua and Governor Caleb both agreed that this information should be shared with all of *Hope's* personnel which they did via vid-com. The general response was one of shocked disbelief. How could so many of *Faith's* people act so badly, killing each other? It was inconceivable something like that could occur on *Hope.* It prompted several of our chaplains to schedule prayer meetings to pray for the people on *Faith* and to pray that this behavior would never be considered acceptable on *Hope.*

During our twentieth year of generation five, *Faith* passed us and it looked as if they might reach Earth decades before we arrived. However, as we reached the end of our thirtieth year, the last com from *Faith* indicated they were having "a number of severe problems with many of our critical systems. Apparently, our experts were overly optimistic regarding long term operations at ten percent."

They indicated they weren't sure if they would be able to reach Earth. We didn't receive any further coms from *Faith* during the remainder of generation five. We continued to attempt contact but never received any replies.

<u>Changing of the Guard—Captain Joshua Sheppard</u>

I can't believe thirty years have gone by so quickly but here we are, ready to step down to become a mentor and selecting my replacement. I think I have the perfect man for the job of ship's captain. His name is David Lawrence and he has been my XO for the last five years. When I selected him for XO, I checked to make sure he hadn't done what I did, hacking the XO selection software to move me up from the third best candidate to number one. David did it the right way. He had been the top-rated cadet in his graduating class at the Naval Academy and quickly worked his way up from an ensign in Flight Operations to the rank of lieutenant commander and leader of the Propulsion System Group. I promoted him to commander when I selected him to XO at the tender age of twenty-five, the second youngest XO in the history of the ship. I was the youngest at twenty-four.

I helped him go through the selection process for choosing his new XO. He settled for a close Academy friend who was a few years older than him. His name was Henry White and he was somewhat of a monster of a man. He was well over six-foot tall and weighed at least two hundred fifty pounds. He wore his African heritage like a badge of honor. Besides his background in Flight Ops, he volunteered for security detail. His background in Judo came in handy and just his presence at potentially dicey situations usually was enough to defuse any thought of a fight. He had recently begun weight training and already held the ship's record for the bench press with a lift of four hundred fifty pounds.

Lawrence and White made a dynamic duo. Most of the time they were easy going however when it was time to get tough, there were none tougher. Within a month, they were well established as the leaders of the ship that would return *Hope* to Earth.

It was obvious I wasn't needed to mentor these two men, so I shifted my focus helping other Navy personnel who were moving up in the chain of command. It was a very rewarding experience for me and, I hope, enlightening to those I mentored. It was good to have the mantle of authority shift to the new leadership. The new XO picked a nickname for him and the captain. Unfortunately, the captain wasn't amused. I kind of liked the way it sounded: Blackman and Robin.

Part 7
The Sixth Generation

The Last Leg—Captain David Lawrence

We were thirty years from Earth when I took command of *Hope.* Our sun was the brightest star in our universe. It glowed almost twice as large as any other star we could see. The Alpha Centauri cluster was as small as it was distant from us. We could barely make out the two biggest planets in our solar system with our sensors at maximum magnification. Our Astrogation group has made a vid recording of what they said was Earth passing across the face of the sun. To me, it looked like a black fly speck crawling across a bright white disk.

I inherited command of a generation starship that was in perfect operating condition. My job was to not mess it up, to get us home into LEO and then figure out what Earth had to offer us. That was a huge question.

Based on the studies which began during the fourth generation and have continued until this day, the best we can hope for when we arrive back on Earth is that some semblance of civilization still exists. The worst-case scenario is that Earth would be completely devoid of human life. Between those two extremes was the possibility some human beings exist having devolved into a hunter-gatherer existence or possibly scavenger gangs who live off what they can loot from the old infrastructure.

An equally important question that needs to be determined as soon as possible, is the level of technology available to us once we arrive in LEO. The design-life of our ship was projected to be two centuries. I have no doubt we will be able to complete our mission and end up in LEO during the sixth generation. However, if we need to remain in orbit for an undetermined number of decades, we are going to need to upgrade the structure of the ship. We don't have the capability to make those upgrades on our own. We need access to a technology at least as advanced as when *Hope* began its mission two centuries ago.

We are working on putting together a plan, a very detailed plan, on how to evaluate the resources available to us as quickly as possible. I will publish more detailed information on these plans as soon as they become available.

<u>Enjoying the Trip Home—XO White</u>

I love sitting in the captain's chair when he's off duty. I like the evening watch and seeing our three artificial suns begin to dim and convert to become three moon beams. it's best when the twinkling stars come out. Some very talented person in our Operations Group has recently figured out how to simulate shooting stars. Every night we get a chance to see anywhere from ten to fifteen shooting stars on a random pattern. Once a week, we are treated to a meteor shower. I never get tired of watching the display.

Another thing I enjoy is weight training. Actually, not just training with weights it's also competing in power lifting events. During my first year as XO, I convinced the manager of our recreation center to hold power lifting tournaments. That first year, he agreed to promote one tournament with the understanding, if we got a good turnout he would hold more tournaments. I got together with the other muscle heads (an old nickname I found when I was researching weight lifting and power lifting tournaments) and formed three teams with six different weight classes. We had at least fifty people interested in competing.

In my spare time, I got together with the rec center manager and solicited volunteers to help fill the rolls of judges, spotters and loaders. Some of the maintenance people put together grandstands that would seat a couple of hundred people. The people who operated the 3-D printers fabricated the weights, bars and collars and also fabricated the trophies. Come on! A tournament has to have trophies!

The three teams chose their names and began a three-month training schedule prior to the meet. I was the captain of the Navy team, called, what else, Team Navy. The other two teams were called The Cowboys and Farmers and the last team chose Muscle Heads.

We had a great turnout for the first tournament, standing room only. Of course, Team Navy took the team title with four first place winners, including myself. I easily won the super heavy weight class, with a 700-pound squat, 475 bench and a 655 dead lift for a total of 1,830 pounds. The rec manager approved us for three tournaments the following years. The event became a fan favorite and more teams joined as time went on. I managed to dominate the super heavy weight class for a few more years however some of the bigger boys were catching up.

The martial arts courses are also filling up at a pretty good rate. Sensei Koyama says he has so many new students he is using some of his higher rated black belts to lead their classes. The lower rated black belts are now required to act as mentors to ensure the new students are learning correctly. In addition to their rank exams which occur every three months for colored belts (non-black belts) and twice a year for black belts, they will begin holding their own tournaments at the rec center soon.

I've heard they are considering starting up judo classes. Since I just happen to have a first-degree black belt in judo, I may join them for a few classes in between my weight training sessions.

It seemed as we got closer to Earth, many people started taking better care of themselves. All of the rec center classes were filling up at an unprecedented rate. The senior tai-chi class went from a few people to what looked like an entire company, around a hundred people. The grounds keeper was complaining all those people every day was killing the grass around the lake.

Similarly, the walking paths around the lake which usually had only a few people strolling along, began to resemble rush-hour traffic on a freeway.

Also seeing more action are the flight simulators. It's one thing to play vid games. The challenge of real flight has a different allure or so I'm told. I heard Flight Ops is planning introducing new candidates for flight training once we are ten years out from Earth. The centrifuge training won't begin until five years out.

That's all I have for now. Hope I didn't step on the new governor's toes by mentioning the rec center activities. I'm sure he'll have tons of stuff to share with you all.

The Ship's Population—Governor John Stewart

As the new governor of *Hope's* civilian population, I'm happy to announce we are at our optimum capacity. We now have a ship's population of five thousand men, women and children. That includes both Navy personnel and civilians. As the Navy captain said in his first report, "Our generation starship is functioning at perfect operating condition." That includes all aspects of the civilian side as well. As our Navy executive officer mentioned, all of our recreational activities are fully staffed and everyone seems to be taking advantage of the programs we offer.

I would like to add that all aspects of civilian operations are functioning at the highest levels, not just our recreational and worship centers. To cite a few examples, all of our crops have recently been harvested, producing a thirty percent excess above our needs. The excess is being stored for future use if the need becomes necessary. The same can be said for meat processing from our livestock. We are also meeting demands for clothing and footwear, however I have noticed the demand for high stacked sole shoes has diminished considerably over the last few decades. I believe that fad has run its course. In a related matter, there has been a noticeable reduction of patients at our medical center being treated for severe ankle sprains and fractures of the feet, ankle and lower legs.

I have also noticed an increased number of requests for vids on Earth's history, especially all things related to The Plague. Unfortunately, there is a limited amount of information on that topic available in our data bases. From the time it began until we lost contact with Earth was a little more than a year. I believe most of Earth's inhabitants were trying to survive, not document the development of The Plague.

We are one week away from the first generation six harvest festival. The harvest committee is busy setting up the pavilions and farmers market venues. One farmer told me, "We had a bumper crop this growing season," which I assume means we had a very bountiful harvest of fruits and vegetables. I wasn't aware farmers had their own technical vocabulary.

The dance floor has been reassembled near the lake and several musical groups have auditioned to provide something called hoedown music, another term I don't understand. When I asked what hoedown meant, a farmer on the music selection team told me, "it is like a shindig." I nodded as if that explained it all.

It occurs to me I have a lot of vocabulary I need to learn so as not to look foolish in front of the farmers. Six months from now, in our spring season, we will have Rodeo Week. I was wondering aloud to one of my friends if the farmers and the cowboys have the same vocabulary. He just smiled and said, "Good luck on that, buckaroo."

<u>Comms Between *Hope* & *Faith*–Ensign Jon Oak</u>

We have continued to exchange monthly updates between *Faith* and ourselves. Our last com exchange was when we were twenty years from Earth. It was estimated *Faith* was thirty-five years from Earth at that time and still cruising at ten percent c. They were quickly catching up with us. If we both continued to cruise at our present speeds, they would pass us when we were both about five years from Earth.

Hope would need to begin deceleration to orbital speed a little more than a year away from Earth. *Faith* would have to begin their deceleration two years before they entered orbit.

All that assumed we continued to cruise at our present speeds.

The monthly reports from *Faith* have been very short. They indicated they were still cruising at ten percent. There were no reports of any further rebellions. The latest report indicated all was well aboard and looked forward to beating us back to Earth.

<u>Training Commences—Commander Mike Archer</u>

At ten years from Earth we began serious flight training. Until that time, flight training was limited to what I would call video game training. It allowed pilots to hone their skills against one another however the likelihood of having to fly combat missions against other similarly armed opponents was nonexistent. Civilization had been destroyed by The Plague and it was inconceivable to me we would find any combat aircraft or well-trained pilots to fly them when we reached Earth.

Instead, we needed to focus on teaching our people to be transport pilots. I know how boring that sounds and I'm all for keeping the combat simulations going, just to hone pilot's reflexes in unforeseen situations, however transport pilots need their own special set of skills.

Flight training always begins with ground training, especially for new pilots also for qualified pilots who have been using the sims to play video games. I refer to this latter category as pretend pilots. They may not need as much ground training as the new students but they need to go through a refresher course.

Before we let anybody touch the controls of a shuttlecraft or even the shuttlecraft simulator, new students need to be completely familiar with all the systems they will have to deal with when in command of a shuttle. It's true, onboard computers can fly the shuttles from point A to point B and even launch the vehicle from the shuttle bay and retrieve it. I believe you need to have a human on board just in case those computer systems decide to do something wonky. Remember, our shuttles are almost two hundred years old. And even though they're serviced and upgraded as needed, we can't assume they will always work the way they're supposed to all the time. That's one reason every shuttle goes through a preflight walk-around inspection to ensure everything is correct with the shuttle before you kick the tires, start the fires and push on the go handles (an old, very old, saying by a man who lived to be a very old pilot).

It took a month to finish ground school, that was five eight-hour days of class and study along with a weekly test to see if they really understood what was required of them. Anyone who failed the weekly test, was sent back to repeat the training and the test. If they failed the test a second time, they were no longer considered a pilot candidate.

That may sound harsh but a transport pilot isn't only responsible for their shuttle, they're responsible for all their passengers as well.

Once the candidates successfully completed ground training, we took them out to the shuttle bays and showed them the real hardware. They got to sit in the pilot's seat and checked out the controls (under no circumstance were they allowed to touch any controls) and also met the launch and recovery crews and the maintenance people who maintain the shuttles in perfect working condition.

Then it was back to the simulators to begin the firsts step in flight training. This training consisted of two parts. A prep and debrief part, kind of like ground school except the prep part is determining what the mission requirements will be and how the student will execute the requirements. During the debrief the instructor evaluated how well those requirements were fulfilled. So, a typical training sequence was: prep for mission, fly the mission in the simulator, the next day debrief and prep for the next mission. The candidates flies the sim one day and worked with their instructor the next. A typical week entailed six days of training, three in the sim and three with planning and debriefing with the seventh day off. We liked to call it Flight Sabbath, where the student can rest from their work.

The Simulator Training Syllabus lasted almost a year. There was a lot to learn and not everyone made it through. A typical wash-out rate was around twenty percent. Once a student got their wings as a full-fledged simulator pilot they had to go through high G training followed by the real thing; flying a real shuttle out into real space. That began once we decelerated from cruise and were maneuvering for orbit insertion. All that will be covered later in a following report.

<u>Beam Training—Operations Leader, LCDR Lili Chen</u>

Our transport beam is a very important part of *Hope's* operational capabilities, even though it has been used on only two occasions during the last two hundred years. It was first used to transport equipment from Earth up to *Hope's* orbital construction site. It was invaluable in quickly and efficiently moving material and components weighing up to twenty-five tons. It worked twenty-four hours a day, transporting loads every ninety minutes when the construction hanger passed over the material prep location at Oak Ridge National Lab.

The next time it was used was a hundred years later when we downloaded equipment, materials and building modules on Proxima-b.

The third time will be when we finally return to Earth. We expect to transport supplies and materials to refurbish *Hope* at that time. Hopefully, there will be someone on the ground to assist us in those operations.

Training began by retrieving the components that make up the beam and assembling them for testing. The new beam operators assisted the maintenance crew during this process. While this was occurring, yards and yards of the powder blue cloth was being fabricated. The cloth is required to wrap or cover whatever is to be transmitted either from the ship to the ground or from the ground to the ship.

A side note regarding the cloth: One of our PhDs in material science believes we can eliminate the cloth requirement if we are lifting certain types of metallic objects. They are currently running tests on a small version of the beam to determine what type of metals need to be present and if they have any effect on how much weight the beam can lift without the cloth.

Once the transport beam had been assembled and installed it was attached to its control computer. The computer permits the operator to select specific coordinates for a pick up or delivery well in advance of our position with respect to the target area. As the ship moves into transport beam range, the computer automatically locks on to the target and initiates pick up or delivery.

The only drawback in using the transport beam is there must be a line of site between *Hope* and the target area. We can't move anything inside a structure, around a mountain or in a cave. However, with infrared sighting capabilities, clouds aren't a limiting factor for transporting.

Another feature of the transport beam is it's not limited to moving things from the ship to the ground or vice versa. The beam can pick up objects and move them to another location on the ground. That was routinely done on Proxima-b with relocating the rock crushers from one site to another.

Three crewmembers were selected to become transport beam operators. Not surprisingly, all three were chosen from our Information Systems Group. A high level of knowledge of computer hardware and software was considered a priority. Part of their training was to identify and classify a wide variety of potential objects to be transported. That knowledge was necessary to determine the amount of energy and frequency required for each transport.

Similar to the pilot training, the beam operators ran through several months of simulations. An extensive variety of scenarios was assigned to each operator who planned the transport and then carried out the simulated operation. Each simulation was evaluated and graded. The computer also provided suggestions to the operators on how to optimize each transport.

I am happy to announce that all three of our operators successfully completed their training and were certified to operate the transport beam.

Once we arrive at Earth, all three will be very busy.

<u>Disturbing News—Chaplain Byron George</u>

Our sister starship passed us when we were about five years from Earth. A few years later, I received a personal com from *Faith's* chaplain, Commander Frederick Dekker. I was very surprised that he comm'd me. Until I received his message, I had never heard of him or even knew his name. As far as I knew, all coms between the two starships were handled by our respective communication groups and were shared with the captains and XOs. The message which I received was sent to me directly.

As was normal for coms between our starships, messages were recorded and transmitted at light speed. When the two ships were a year apart, it took eighteen days for a message to be received. For a reply to reach the sender would take another eighteen days, over a month total time.

The content of the message was staggering, perhaps horrific would be a better description. The chaplain said they were about six months from Earth, braking to orbital speed. I thought they should have already been in orbit however he went on to say almost all of their critical operations were failing and that the ship might not survive to enter orbit. Mutinies had begun again as they began their sixth generation. Martial law had been put into effect by the captain however he had been assassinated by order of the governor. The XO had the governor murdered in retaliation, declared himself captain and reinstated martial law with a vengeance. Food crops were failing, people were starving and there were rumors of cannibalism.

The new captain barricaded all Navy personnel within their operational facilities and placed armed guards at every entrance and exit with orders to shoot to kill anyone who attempted to breach their facilities. According to Commander Dekker, the last couple of years was complete chaos and the ship's population rapidly declined below the self-sustaining requirements.

The propulsion drives began to malfunction about three years out from Earth and one of the drive reactors failed and radiation poisoning was suspected. Their plan was to use the maneuvering thrusters to get the ship into LEO and to shuttle the survivors to the surface to meet whatever fate had in store for them.

After watching the thirty-minute message, I comm'd the captain and shared the message with him. He in turn contacted the XO, the Navy group leaders, the governor and his staff to watch the message. After the shock had worn off, a reply was drafted and sent to *Faith* offering support. We never heard from them again.

We were able to track their progress as they managed to divert the ship into LEO. We watched it as it began its first orbit and disappeared behind Earth. It was never seen again. Once we established orbit, we made a valiant search for any of *Faith's* shuttles which might have delivered any survivors to the surface. We found nothing, nor did we ever locate any debris from potential crash sites.

The world is a big place. We continued to search for any remains once we transitioned to LEO but we had issues of our own. The best guess was that *Faith* hadn't maintained orbital speed and what wasn't burned up during reentry, crashed into what used to be called the Gobi desert.

May God have mercy on their departed souls.

<u>One Year to Go—Captain David Lawrence</u>

We are one year away from orbiting Earth. We have shut down our main drive and begun the deceleration to orbital velocity. The pilots have all gone through their centrifuge training and are just itching for the chance to fly a real shuttle. That won't come until we are established in orbit around our home world.

We have been attempting to contact somebody on the planet; so far, we've been unsuccessful. We have scanned every possible frequency, searching for any type of com signal or commercial vid channels and come up empty. It looks as if our worst-case scenario might be coming true, at least from a technological standpoint. We're still too far away to be able to see if there is any human life. That comes much later.

In the meantime, it's life as usual. We still plan on having Rodeo Week and Harvest Festival and all the recreational activities are going full speed.

Tournaments are being planned and held. The XO was ecstatic about making a 500- pound bench press for the first time and having a total for the three lifts of over a ton at the last power lifting tournament. He's looking forward for new personal bests in the next tournament.

I'm a great spectator, I like to support Team Navy in whatever tournament our men and women enter. About six month ago, I watched as Lieutenant Hiroshi Koyama was awarded his fifth-degree black belt from his grandfather Sensei Koyama. I recently promoted Hiroshi and selected him to be the head of our Navy security team. He became our youngest security team leader at the tender age of twenty-two. While his martial arts skills were a plus, I felt he was the perfect fit. His skills in dealing with people in difficult situations were unprecedented. There was some push back by a couple of the more senior security people but to my delight, Hiroshi met with them individually in private and they worked everything out. He certainly is a charmer.

I need to add my comments to those of Chaplain George regarding the outcome of *Faith*. I can't imagine how things deteriorated so badly. Even the *rumor* of cannibalism is too much to comprehend, as are assassinations and martial law resulting in the deaths of numerous civilians. In my wildest nightmares, I can't imagine those type of things happening on my ship. Ever since I watched Chaplain Dekker's com message, I have been haunted about what could've possibly occurred that drove them to such horribly tragic behavior. My wife Maurine could tell I was hiding something from her. There was no way I would let her watch that vid. It was bad enough my officers and I had to endure the story Dekker told. Sometimes not revealing a truth is a blessing. I know it took me and my officers several months to begin feeling normal again. I have to admit, I still have the occasional nightmare but not very often. Thank God for that.

We recently entered our solar system and Earth is beginning to look like a planet and not just a microscopic dot. It won't be long before our speed is slow enough to allow the pilots to begin really flying the shuttles.

Finally in Orbit—Captain David Lawrence

We are currently in a stable LEO about 250 miles above the surface of Earth. It takes us ninety-five minutes to complete each orbit. The path of our orbit changes slightly with every pass. Our path of flight looks like a sign wave crossing back and forth across the equator, almost reaching plus and minus 45 degrees latitude. This permits us to essentially map all of the major continents.

The view as we approached Earth was breathtaking. The bright blue of the ocean laced with brilliantly white clouds was incredible. The closer we got the more magnificent it looked.

Our path to our home brought us close to our moon. We were able to see the ruins of the abandoned Lunar Scientific Habitat. Some of it was still intact; the majority was in complete disarray, probably by meteor strikes during the two centuries *Hope* was away from home.

When we got close enough, we were able to determine human life had survived unfortunately only in limited cases. We were approaching from the dark side of Earth and as we began an inwardly spiraling path that would ultimately end in our stable orbit, we saw lights. Granted not many lights however definitely artificial lights. We also saw what appeared to be large bonfires but our real interest was in the location of the artificial lights. That meant some level of technology still existed.

Of course, we began broadcasting on every conceivable com frequency, in the hope that if there were lights there were also active com devices. Unfortunately, we weren't able to make contact.

Once we were in orbit, we began extensive mapping. We pinpointed the locations of all artificial lights during the night. During the day, we were able to take vids of the communities and make estimates of the population of each site.

One location stood out from all the others. It was easily the biggest community we discovered. It would probably be more accurate to call it a city, not a community. The average population estimated for the towns and villages were somewhere between a hundred to a maximum of a thousand people. The biggest city was estimated to have a population of at least one hundred fifty thousand, maybe as many as two hundred thousand. It had a large building at its center with five circular ring walls extending out several miles. Farmland and pastures were visible outside the last wall with a variety of crops and livestock. It was almost too good to be true.

However, one critically important feature was the icing on the cake. The location of the city was the same location as the Oak Ridge National Lab, the very place where all of the components used to construct *Hope* were either fabricated or stored. This was the very place we were supposed to return to. Perhaps, if we were very lucky or maybe blessed would be a better word, we would be able to find everything we needed to restore *Hope* to almost new condition.

What's the Next Step? —Captain David Lawrence

A meeting was called to make decisions on our next steps. In addition to my staff of people, the governor and his staff were invited. The governor and I had met previously to put together the meeting agenda and he asked me to be the keynote speaker.

"Ladies and Gentlemen, the object of the meeting is to define our next steps." I paused and a chart appeared on the vid screen behind me. "There are a few major questions we need to answer, such as," I gestured to the bullet chart and read through the bullets.

- How long can we remain in orbit and meet the needs of the ship's population?
- Do we want to continue to live on the ship or move to the surface?
- If we decide to go to the surface, how do we contact the inhabitants of the city?

"Let's begin with the first bullet. We're going to require input from both the Navy and Governor Stewart's people. Let's begin with Quartermaster Taylor."

Commander Geoffrey Taylor stood and presented the ship's status. "We have reached *Hope's* design life. Some of the major subsystems cannot be repaired. They need to be replaced and we no longer have spares available for a rebuild. We are completely out of the basic raw materials needed for our 3-D printers to fabricate replacement parts. Our air scrubbers are on their last leg and the list goes on and on. My best estimate, if we cannot resupply materials from Earth, we have between three to six months before we will have to abandon ship."

Commander Taylor sat down and I gestured to the governor. He turned to one of his staffers and said, "Your turn, Bob."

"I'm Bob Schwartz from Governor Stewart's planning department. I'm afraid I have equally dismal news regarding our food supply. We ran out of the nutrients needed to fertilize our crops. You may have noticed many of our farm fields weren't planted this last season, if we decide to stay aboard *Hope* we will need to resupply the nutrients. Many of our pastures have dried up and our livestock is at an all-time low. Additionally, we no longer have a surplus of stored foods of any type. Without resupply from Earth, I estimate we have three months of food at most." Mr. Schwartz sat down.

"Thank you, gentlemen. That seems to answer our first question. *Hope* has three months left to live without help from Earth. The second question is do we want to remain on *Hope* or live on Earth?"

Governor Stewart spoke up. "We took a poll of the civilian population and the vast majority said they would prefer to live on Earth as long as a few requirements were met."

"What are those requirements?" I asked.

"First," replied the governor, "they want to be sure The Plague has run its course and they won't die from the virus. Secondly, they want to make sure the existing Earth population will accept us."

"Reasonable questions which deserve answers," I replied. "It seems to me in order to answer those questions, we need to speak with the people on Earth. In fact, I think we have to communicate with leaders of the city in order to address all three of the bullets. Since they haven't responded to our hails, does anyone have any suggestions how that can be safely accomplished?"

"Send a team down in a shuttle and request a meeting with the leaders?" someone suggested.

"They might think of that as a threat," I answered. "Nobody on Earth has seen a flying machine for over two centuries. By the looks of the structure of their city with multiple ring walls, I'd say they may have been attacked before and don't take kindly to unannounced visitors swooping, down on them with flying machines. Any other suggestions?"

"Yes sir," responded my security chief, Lieutenant Koyama. "Send one person down by the beam and let them recon the area. When I looked at the daylight vids of the city, it seemed the outer rings had a lot of people. As they move closer to the large building in the center of the city, it appeared to have more security people in uniforms. To me, it looked like being just inside the third ring had only a few security people and enough civilians to provide cover for me."

"For you, Lieutenant?" I asked. "Are you volunteering for this mission?"

"Absolutely, Captain. I was custom made for this assignment," he answered with a slight smile.

I thought about it for a moment than turned to the others in the room and asked, "Any better ideas?"

Nobody offered any alternatives. The governor spoke up, "I think it's a great plan. Just be ready to beam him back up if things get dicey. What type of weapons will you be carrying?"

Hiroshi replied before I could say anything. "No weapons. I'm a living weapon." He changed his voice and continued with a Spanish accent, "I don't need no stinking weapons."

"Roger that, Governor." I replied.

Solo Mission to Earth—Captain David Lawrence

I had Hiroshi report to Doctor Soo Song in sick bay for a series of inoculations against viral and bacterial infections. The next day, after Doctor Song cleared Hiroshi for the mission, he reported to me for final instructions.

"We are going to beam you into the area between the third and second ring walls. It looks like our target drop will be about an hour from now. When we're done here, suit up and report to the beam room. Once you touch down, you will have fifteen minutes to decide if the threat level is too high. If you decide it is, just touch the stud on your collar and we will get you out of there. Once you are inside the beam, you will be safe from any form of attack they might try. If you think it's safe to remain, we will pick you up on the next orbit pass, about ninety minutes later. If everything is perfect and you want to remain longer, your suit has a built-in com, just let us know. We will be monitoring you as long as we are in range."

I met him in the beam room fifteen minutes before he was to be launched. His powder-blue jumpsuit had a close-fitting hood which completely enclosed his head. We waited quietly as the countdown clock continued. When it reached two minutes the operator said, "Stand on the platform, please and face forward."

When the clock reached thirty seconds, he turned to me, came to attention and saluted. I returned his salute. He turned back and I added, "Good hunting!"

Then he was gone. It took roughly fifteen minutes before I heard his voice, "On the ground, checking out the place. Captain you've got to see this."

Then we heard garbled voices in the background. A moment later there was a screeching sound and the line went dead. We attempted a recovery unfortunately the beam couldn't lock on to him. The operator tried continually until we were out of range.

Emergency Meeting—Captain David Lawrence

I called an emergency meeting to determine what happened to Lieutenant Koyama and what our next steps should be. I ordered the beam operator to continue attempts at contacting the lieutenant and if possible, extracting him every time our orbit brought us over to the target site.

Information systems had been visually monitoring his descent and landing inside the third ring of the city. They attempted to unscramble the dialog that had been recorded but were unsuccessful. The vid was a little grainy however we could still see most of the detail of what happened.

"Everyone, please take a seat," I ordered. "We are going to watch the vid and I want no interruptions until it is over. Our first priority is to determine what happened to Lieutenant Koyama; is he still alive, was he injured or was he taken prisoner?"

We knew he had been successfully beamed to the desired coordinates. That was where the vid began. He stepped out of the beam light and it immediately went out. We got an almost vertical look at him as the picture panned back to include other people on the plaza around him. Nobody seemed to notice his arrival at first and he began to check out his surroundings. We could see he was speaking, probably his report telling us he was down and looking around.

We noticed two men in similar uniforms get up from their seats at an outdoor café and began moving toward him. Both had what appeared to be some type of handheld weapon. One of the uniforms began speaking and Hiroshi turned to acknowledge him while the other uniform circled behind him. The crowd moved back from the three men. Some seemed to leave the area in a hurry, others formed a circle around the three men.

After a brief conversation, it looked as if Hiroshi was agitated. He didn't notice the uniform come up from behind him and lay the weapon on his shoulder.

For a moment, the vid screen was awash in bright white light. When we regained the picture, we could see two men lying on the ground at least ten yards apart. Neither man was moving and Hiroshi was on fire. A woman from the crowd grabbed a cape from a man in the crowd and tried to put out the fire. Then the vid stopped. We were out of range.

Everyone in the room sat stunned, including me. I had to clear my throat twice before I was able to speak. "Any comments?"

The XO was first to speak. "They attacked him without any noticeable provocation."

"Yes," replied Dr. Song, "but I think it was a mistake. The man with the weapon was injured too. It looked like he was unconscious as well."

An officer from our security team added, "I think the weapon was some type of stun gun or wand. Maybe there was something in Hiroshi's suite that caused a bigger discharge then planned."

We talked among ourselves as we waited for vids during the next pass over the target site. It seemed to take forever; when the vid began, it was a completely different scene.

Another man was talking to the two uniforms and he wasn't happy. The uniform who had attacked Hiroshi was in bad shape, the new man didn't seem to notice or care. All three men were standing next to a gurney that was brought out to Hiroshi's inert form. Medical people were checking on him. They gave him an injection and placed a mask over his face before lifting him onto the gurney. They began to move the gurney to a near-by surface vehicle. Before they could get him aboard, the man who had been talking to the two uniforms stopped the gurney and began checking out Hiroshi. He took special attention to Hiroshi's eyes, then stood and walked back to the two uniforms. The medical people loaded the gurney into the surface vehicle and quickly sped away. The video ended.

The next pass over the target area showed nothing new.

I looked around the room and noticed everyone seemed to be lost in thought, including myself. "Based on the vids we just watched, how would you describe what you saw?" I asked.

The XO was the first to respond. "I'd say something Hiroshi did or the way he looked, triggered the two uniforms to action. I think they were only planning to detain him and they were just going to stun him a little to soften him up. I believe the two uniforms were completely surprised by what happened. The one who stunned him was also hurt, obviously not as bad as Hiroshi however he was knocked unconscious for a bit. Did anyone notice during the second orbit the new guy talking to the two uniforms and the way they reacted? He was really chewing their butts for screwing up. They were in bad trouble. I think the good news is that Hiroshi is alive, at least for now. They were probably taking him to a hospital. I sincerely hope that man survives."

Dr Song went next. "I agree with the XO. It was an unfortunate accident but it troubles me they would stun him for no apparent offense. As far as the way he was treated afterwards was a little disturbing. At first, no one came to his aide until the woman grabbed a cape from a man in the crowd and put out the fire. If she hadn't acted when she did, he may have burned to death."

"Anything to add regarding the medical treatment Hiroshi received on site?" I asked Dr. Song.

"They acted very professionally," she answered. "They were well trained and went through the same trauma protocols we would've used. It looks to me like their medical technology level is similar to ours. I hope that applies to other areas of technology."

The XO raised the question we were all thinking, "So what do we do now?"

"I think we wait for a while and see what develops," I said. "I'm not willing to send anyone else into the city until I know more about how their government works. I want to use some of our stealth drones to gather more information. One question I have is, what happened to Oak Ridge National Labs? The city has the exact same coordinates as the lab, except I haven't seen anything that looks remotely like the lab facilities."

"How long do we wait?" asked the governor.

"Undetermined at this time," I answered. "Any last thoughts before we adjourn?"

Chaplain George replied, "Captain, if you don't mind, I'd like us to stand and say a prayer for Hiroshi."

I nodded my head and we all stood. "Our heavenly father," the chaplain began, "we come before you today to praise you for returning us to our home. You are the guiding force that has caused our return. We ask you to consider your servant Hiroshi. He has been injured and we pray you grant him your mercy. We ask for another miracle. Please restore him to health and may we join with the people of this city to move forward. We ask these things in the name of your son."

And we all said, "Amen and Amen."

That Concludes <u>The Generations of *Hope*</u> Story

If you are interested in finding out what happened to Lieutenant Koyama, please read the preview below:

What follows is a Preview of the first of the Generations Trilogy:

Generations (Preview)

A Science Fiction Novel
Written by Frank G Davis

Protector Kaplan

I was the first one to see him.

Protector Graves and I were having lunch at an outdoor café just inside Gate 3N. Graves was bored and I was scanning the passing crowd in the plaza as I ate.

"Come here little fly," said Graves. "Look what I have for you. It's your favorite food, all sweet and sugary, *yum yum*." A fly on the table was making a random walk pattern that took it close to Grave's wand. When it sensed the drop of syrup, the fly scurried quickly to the wand and began to feed. "Will you look at that!" exclaimed Graves. "I've got the wand set on three and it has no effect."

"Quit torturing the bugs, Graves," I said, as I pushed the last of my meat roll into my mouth while I continued to watch the crowd.

"That's just the point," he responded. "I'm not torturing them; they don't feel a thing. Let's see what level eight does."

I quickly glanced at Graves to be sure no one was standing close to him. "Be careful with the wand," I warned.

"Relax, Kaplan. You worry too much. And quit staring at the crowd, you're making people nervous. This is Ring 3, not the Outer Ring; nothing ever happens here."

Graves shook off the feeding fly and tapped the wand control to a level eight setting. The fly began circling, moving closer to the wand. My scanner went off.

"What've you got?" asked Graves.

"Citizen without his star," I answered, as I checked the scanner display. "I'll take it. You play with your bugs."

As I got up and started to move through the crowd, I heard a "zap" behind me followed by a giggle from Graves.

The lunch time crowd was pretty heavy but as usual, it parted as I moved in the direction of the sinner; no one wanted to get in the way of a protector. There was no mistaking him. I could tell by his clothes he wasn't one of the chosen; he was wearing a light blue, one-piece jumpsuit with a tight fitting hood covering most of his head and neck. Almost all of the chosen wear loose fitting white robes; none of them wear jumpsuits. My first reaction was to wonder how he had gotten into Ring 3. The protectors at Gate 3N were going to have to be disciplined.

He was standing by himself, looking up at the buildings on either side of the plaza, slowly turning to taking it all in, a look of curiosity on his face. His face…if I had any doubts before…one look at his face was all I needed to tell me he wasn't one of the chosen. His skin was dark with a yellow cast, wisps of short, jet black hair peaked out from under his hood but it was his eyes…it was his eyes that stopped me in my tracks. They were a dark walnut shade of brown.

I touched my communicator, "Graves, I need backup, now."

The sinner turned at the sound of my voice and smiled at me showing perfect white teeth. "Good day to you, citizen." I said in as calm a voice as I could manage. "You seem to have forgotten your star." He looked puzzled and started to speak just as Graves came up slightly behind him.

"Yes, citizen," said Graves, "the Star of David, your ID star. The one they gave you when you came in through the Outer Gate. From the looks of your clothes that couldn't have been too long ago."

He started to turn toward Graves but turned back as I asked, "What are you doing in Ring 3? Don't you remember what Orientation explained to you about staying in the Outer Ring until you are chosen?"

"I didn't come through the Outer Gate," he said in a heavily accented voice.

"Of course, you did. Every Gentile comes through the Outer Gate. You must have forgotten," said Graves sarcastically. He started to turn again but Graves had moved to the other side, still behind him, with his wand in his hand.

Like a yo-yo, he turned back as I said, "You have sinned, citizen, and as Protectors of the Law it is our job to punish sinners. Going without your star is a level one sin. After you are punished, we will find out how you got into Ring 3; there will probably be additional punishment required."

He took a step back and put out both hands in front of him to ward me off as I moved forward. "Now wait a minute. You can't punish me…I'm not one of you…I'm not from here…"

Graves stepped forward and laid the wand on his shoulder.

There should have been a slight zap, a simple shock, to serve as a reminder that everyone has to obey the law or suffer the consequences. Instead, there was a blinding flash and a clap of thunder as Graves and the stranger were ripped apart. Graves must have gone ten yards through the air before landing hard on a peddler's cart. His wand dropped straight down with a clattering sound practically at my feet. The stranger looked like a fireworks display. Blue-white sparks danced over his body as he laid jerking and twitching on the ground five yards away. Smoke was rising from the body as I stood there in shock.

A small crowd of curious citizens had gathered while Graves and I had started interrogating the stranger. There is always an element of the population who enjoys watching others get punished. But no one could have anticipated what just happened. Most scattered before the bodies had hit the plaza tile. Only a few remained to gawk. A young woman came running up. Her eyes grew wide at the sight of the smoldering stranger. "Someone help him!" she cried. And then, when no one moved, she snatched a cape off the man standing next to her and flung it over the stranger's body and began to pat out the sparks.

"Hey, you stole my cape! Stop that. You're going to ruin it. Protector, stop that woman! She stole my cape!" He grabbed my arm and tried to pull me toward the woman who was furiously trying to put out the fire. His touch startled me out of my shock. At the same moment, he realized his error; nobody ever touches a protector.

"Protector, please forgive me," he pleaded as he backed away. "But she stole my cape!" he ended in a fearful whimper.

I moved to the woman and grabbed her by the arms lifting her away from the stranger. I flung the cape in the direction of the still protesting man. "If you have a complaint, file it with the judge." I glared at him and he backed away inspecting his smoking cape.

"It's ruined," he whined, "That woman ruined my new cape. She's going to have to pay. And I want her punished too. She stole it."

I hardly heard him. I was looking at the stranger's body. The fire was out but there was a strong smell of burnt flesh. I rolled him over and checked for a pulse; it was weak but he was still alive. I touched my communicator. "This is Protector Kaplan. I have a medical emergency. I have a citizen and a protector down. Burns and electrical shock. Plaza near Gate 3N."

There was brief static in my left hear plug before the reply. "We copy, protector. Med team will be there in two minutes."

"Better send a security priest too," I added.

There was a pause. "Nature of the sin?"

"Citizen has no star and has…unusual physical appearance. Probable security violation."

"Copy. Security Priest Simon will arrive shortly. You aren't to leave the scene until dismissed by SP Simon."

"Understood. Out."

Graves was slowly walking toward me on shaky legs.

"You okay?"

He shook his head. "I don't think so…hurt all over. What happened?"

I walked back to what remained of his wand and picked it up. It was badly damaged; one end had partially melted and the black plastisteel was twisted out of shape. I looked at the control setting and shook my head. I handed the wand back to Graves and I heard the quick gasp as he saw the setting. It was still on level eight.

We stood silently waiting for the security priest to arrive.

Security Priest Simon

The med team was already treating the injured when I arrived on the scene. One man was lying on the ground and his clothes were smoking. The techs were placing him on a power gurney. There were two protectors standing nearby and a tech was checking one of them over. "Protector Kaplan?"

"I'm Kaplan," said the second protector. He was tall, good looking with wavy blond hair and blue eyes. He was also very young.

"I'm Security Priest Simon. You called in a probable security violation?"

He nodded and gestured towards the man on the ground. "The citizen didn't have his star and I don't think he is chosen."

"You mentioned something about his appearance being strange." The protector looked down at his feet and mumbled something I couldn't quite hear. "Speak up, man," I snapped.

His head came up quickly, "Sorry, SP. I said that his eyes had a funny shape and they. . .they were brown."

"Brown?" I snorted and shook my head. "How long have you been a protector?"

"Almost three years, SP," he answered quickly.

"And during those 'almost three years,' how many brown eyed people have you seen?"

"This was my first one."

"I don't believe it for a minute." The med techs had started driving the gurney towards the hospital. "Tech, please bring that citizen here. He hasn't been released," I said in an annoyed tone.

"SP, the man may die if he doesn't get immediate attention," answered one of the techs.

"The Law will be served," I said quietly. "Bring him here."

Without further argument, they drove the gurney next to Protector Kaplan and me. The man did have oddly shaped eyes but it was hard to tell if they were naturally that way or had been affected by the wand discharging. I placed my thumb on his right eyelid and peeled it back. The eye was brown. I looked closely; there was no colored contact over the iris, it was truly brown. Astonishing! "It looks like I owe you an apology, protector." I took my scanner out of its holder. "Computer, retina scan for ID."

The computer's electronic voice responded, "Proceed."

I waved the scanner over the stranger's eye until I heard the beep and then stepped back. Two seconds later the computer said, "Subject cannot be identified. Retina pattern isn't on file."

I stood there lost in thought until one of the techs coughed lightly to get my attention. "Oh, yes. I'm through with the citizen. Take him to the hospital." As they drove off, I added. "Keep him alive. He has lots of questions to answer." I turned back to the protectors. "Now, I want you to tell me exactly what happened."

Senior Healer Johnson

"We have a bad one, Madam Healer." The med tech was driving the gurney into the OR. I could see smoke rising from the patient's head and shoulders.

"What happened?" asked my apprentice.

"A protector hit him with a level eight."

"Level eight! Good Lord, what did he do, kill someone?"

The techs lifted the man from the gurney to the treatment table. "Naw, he just showed up in Ring 3 without his star." They laid him down and stretched him out. "I think it was an accident; it should have been only a level one sin. Well he's all yours now," said the tech as they started to leave. "Oh, by the way. A security priest said you need to keep him alive. He has to answer lots of questions."

"Wonderful," I said sarcastically. "Well, Junior, are you ready to go to work?"

"Thirty more seconds in the sterilization field, Senior Healer," he answered.

I pulled my hands out of the field and walked over to the table. "Computer, vital signs."

The electronic voice answered immediately, "Pulse weak and erratic, pressure sixty over thirty and falling, respiration…five to eight." There was barely a perceptible pause before it continued, "Unusual brain wave patterns, possible memory blank. Second and third degree burns over seventy five percent of his body. Prognosis is extremely poor."

"Says you," I said under my breath.

Junior hurried to the table giving the computer instructions as he and I looked at the patient. "Stabilize the vital signs and notify us if anything gets worse."

"Working," the computer answered.

"Let's get his clothes off of him and see how bad the burns really are."

Junior looked up at me in surprise, "Don't you believe the computer's appraisal?"

"I like to see things for myself."

I took the laser scalpel and sliced down the front of his jump suit, only it didn't slice. It didn't leave a mark or even seem to get hot, although it was hard to be certain. I tried again on a higher setting with the same results. "Strange, we know it burns. Why won't the laser cut it?"

"Try a blade," suggested Junior.

I did but the suit wouldn't cut. Junior was looking at the suit now, checking it over to see how we could get it off. In the process, he touched a stud on the collar and a seam that I would have sworn wasn't there a second ago, parted from the neck to the crotch and seemed to curl back. It revealed a dark-skinned torso, relatively free from body hair, covered with a fine square pattern of burn lines spaced about a centimeter apart. At the shoulder, apparently where the Protector's wand had touched him, there was a two inch hole in the suit. The ends of small diameter wires could be seen at the edge of the hole, apparently woven in the cloth. When the suit opened up it seemed to get loose all over and the hood fell back from his head. His hair was singed and it had the unmistakable odor of burnt hair but it was the color that caused me to do a double take. It was jet black, very unusual. And then I noticed the shape of his eyes and a chill ran up my spine. I recognized the epicanthic folds from some very old data banks I had scanned in medical history class. Somewhat hesitantly, I placed my thumb on the eye lid and pushed it open.

Junior gasped, "My God, his eyes are brown. How can that be?"

"I don't know but I bet we're going to have to find out, and soon too. No wonder the security priest wants to ask him some questions."

Junior and I quickly got him out of his jumpsuit and into the burn tank, hooked up IVs and monitor leads and set parameter flags for the computer.

"What now?" asked Junior.

"I want a data dump to my computer on his blood work as soon as possible," I said as I walked to my office. "And I want someone with him full time."

"You mean a nurse?"

"A nurse, an orderly, an aide, I don't care. I just don't want him alone for a minute. They are to call me the first time he shows any sign of life. You got that? I'll sleep in my office until this is over," I said as I rubbed my eyes. I could feel a tension headache coming on.

"Is he that important?"

"Son, this man is going to be the most important thing to happen in New Jerusalem since The Moses founded the city."

Junior blanched, turned, and hurried off to find someone to babysit the stranger. I walked into my office and poured a glass of water. I held the glass to my forehead and felt the coolness help ease the tension. I walked to the monitor and sat down with a thump and slowly sipped the water. I took a deep breath and let it out slowly.

"Well," I said to myself, "you'd better get to work. Computer, access all files on The Plague."

This concludes the preview of "Generations," a novel by Frank G. Davis. It is the first book in <u>The Generations Trilogy.</u> All books in the Trilogy are available online from Amazon.

Casts of Characters

Introduction

Samoa—Secretary General of the Alliance of World Nations (AWN)

Part 1—The Preliminaries

Samoa—Secretary General of AWN, wife of Tongo, former Chief of Staff to Tongo.

Tongo—AWN Chief of Staff to his wife, Samoa. Former Secretary General of AWN.

Judy Van Der Geist, PhD—Oakridge National Lab Program Manager for the generation starship *Hope*.

Vice Admiral Amanda Jackson—Head of Naval Selection Committee.

Commodore Gary Dagan—First commander of generation starship, *Hope*. Husband of his executive officer (XO), Captain Malinda Dagan.

Captain Malinda Dagan—First XO of Hope. Wife of Commodore Gary Dagan.

Governor Anita Ataksak—First Governor of the civilian population aboard *Hope*. Note: The Inuit name "Ataksak" translates to "Goddess of the Sky" in English.

Part 2—The First Generation

Commodore Gary Dagan—First commander of *Hope*.

Captain Malinda Dagan—First executive officer of *Hope*.

Marine Lt. Colonel Jason Kuhn—Flight Operations Leader.

Commander Priscilla Hoyt—Propulsion Systems Leader.

Dr. Cullum MacGregor, Contractor—Power Systems Leader.

Governor Anita Ataksak.

Arnold—Husband of the governor. Head of Planning Commission and Population Control

Commander Alicia Franklin—Communications Officer.

Dr. Judy Van Der Geist—Director of Civilian Contactors.

Lieutenant Greg Danielson—Head of Security.

Part 3–The Second Generation

Captain Jason Kuhn—Second commander of *Hope.*

Commander Priscilla Hoyt—Second executive officer of *Hope.*

Belinda Lopez—Second Governor of *Hope.* Wife of Josh White.

Anita Ataksak—Mentor to Belinda Lopez.

Josh White—Chief of Staff for Governor Belinda Lopez. Husband of the Governor

Commander Björn Sjöblom—Leader of Propulsion Systems Group.

Commander Britt-Marie Andersson—Leader Power Systems Group.

Commander Shojiro Koyama—Leader of the Astrogation Group.

Lt. Commander Stewart MacGregor—Interim Leader, Power Systems.

Lt. Commander Gloria Li—Interim Leader, Propulsion Systems.

Chief Warrant Officer Zipowicz—Security.

Part 4–The Third Generation

Captain Björn Sjöblom—Commander of *Hope.* Husband of Britt-MariSjöblomSjöblom.

Governor Britt-Marie Sjöblom—Wife of Björn Sjöblom.

Commander Alexander White—Executive Officer.

Major Thomas Bruce—Commander of Marine Light Brigade.

Commander Olga Stepvonovich—Flight Control Leader.

Lieutenant Chang Liu—Flight Control Officer.

Lieutenant Governor Malcom Cole—Leader of Proxima-b Team.

Lieutenant Marvin Eide—*Faith's* Communication Officer.

Captain Eric Jackson—Commander of *Faith*.

Part 5–The Fourth Generation

Captain David Davis—Commander of *Hope*. Husband of Kathi Davis.

Lt Commander Kathi Davis—Shuttle pilot, Squadron Leader, Wife of David Davis

John Davis—Maintains park area including the lake and water fall. Son of David and Kathi Davis.

Captain Gordon Fletcher—Commander of *Faith*.

Dolf Johannsen—Leader of Mutiny on *Faith*.

Loren Sheppard—Governor of *Hope*, Wife of Moses Sheppard, Mother of the twins Joshua and Caleb.

Sensei Shojiro Koyama—Astrogation Group Leader (Retired), Karate instructor.

Moses Sheppard—Christian Chaplain of Hope, Married to Governor Sheppard, Father of the twins, Joshua and Caleb.

Joshua and Caleb Sheppard—Twins of Loren and Moses Sheppard.

Part 6–The Fifth Generation

Captain Joshua Sheppard—Commander of *Hope*.

Governor Caleb Sheppard—Governor.

King David Davis—Mentor.

Lt. Commander Debra White—Communication Officer.

Part 7–The Sixth Generation

Captain David Lawrence—Commander of *Hope.*

Commander Henry White—Executive Officer of Hope.

Governor John Stewart—Governor of Hope.

Ensign Jon Oak—Hope's Communications Officer.

Commander Mike Archer—Flight Operations Leader.

Lt. Commander Lili Chen—Ships Operations Leader.

Chaplain Byron George—Hope's Senior Chaplain.

Chaplain Fredrick Dekker—Faith's Senior Chaplain.

Commander Geoffrey Taylor—Hope's Quartermaster.

Mr. Bob Schwartz—Hope's Planning Department Manager.

Dr. Soo Song—Hope's Medical Team Leader.

Lieutenant Hiroshi Koyama—Hope's Chief of Security.

About the Author

I've been a fan of science fiction ever since I was in grade school (a very long time ago). In those days there were three outstanding authors: Isaac Asimov, Arthur C. Clark, and Robert A. Heinlein.

My favorite author was Heinlein. He began writing his science fiction stories for young people. His first books were categorized as 'Boys Books.' Today, they're called 'Young Adults.' His stories were very believable to me and I couldn't wait to get to his latest books.

As I matured, so did his books. I have read every book Heinlein published and still have most of them in my personal library. I think my all-time favorite Heinlein story is *Stranger in a Strange Land.*

My current favorite author is Orson Scott Card. Again, like Heinlein's stories, I find myself 'living' the story as it unfolds. *Ender's Game* and *Prentice Alvin* are two of my favorite Card novels.

I've always had an interest in writing science fiction novels. I would read books by new authors and say to myself, "I could write a better story." However, when I tried, publishers didn't agree. When Covid-19 broke out, I had a lot of spare time on my hands and decided to give it another shot.

During the last two years, I have written seven novels with an eighth one in the works. And I'm just getting started. During the last two and a half years, I have written eight novels. I plan on publishing the ninth one in 2022.

www.ingramcontent.com/pod-product-compliance
Lightning Source LLC
Chambersburg PA
CBHW071229210726
48293CB00002B/640